INTERSTELLAR FLIGHT MAGAZINE BEST OF YEAR 4

INTERSTELLAR FLIGHT PRESS ANTHOLOGIES

EDITED BY

HOLLY LYN WALRATH

This is a work of fiction. All of the characters, organizations, and events portrayed are either products of the author's imagination or used fictitiously.

INTERSTELLAR FLIGHT MAGAZINE BEST OF YEAR 4

Cover Image by Man_Half-tube.

Edited by Holly Lyn Walrath.

Published by Interstellar Flight Press

Houston, Texas.

www.interstellarflightpress.com

ISBN (eBook): 978-1-953736-30-7

ISBN (Paperback): 978-1-953736-31-4

CONTENTS

ORIGINAL ARTICLES

REVIEWS

INTERVIEWS

ORIGINAL ARTICLES

I DON'T READ HORROR (& OTHER WEIRD TALES)

BY LEE MURRAY

At its simplest, horror serves to elicit fear, mankind's oldest and strongest emotion.

At a national book festival, a reader dashes from the bookstore, approaching me in a flail of pashmina. She's so sorry she won't make it to my panel, she tells me as she juggles a bag bulging with new books, but she's chosen instead to attend another session "because I don't read horror."

A cousin pops into my socials ahead of a prolonged hospital stay: "I need something to read," she writes. "Can you suggest a title by one of your friends? But NOT horror."

A local editor is surprised to discover my work. But then she makes a point to never read horror, so that would explain it. "Ha ha," she adds, as if merely writing the word horror might conjure a slick of grisly entrails.

No one *has* to read horror. People should read whatever they like. I read widely myself. But why this immediate dismissal of the genre, the look of shock tinged with distaste, the nervous giggle? The *denial.* "I don't read horror." It's as if horror is a Brussels sprout that must be pushed quickly to the side of one's plate.

As a writer of horror, I try not to take it personally. Sometimes, even writers sidle past the term, labeling their work suspense, dark fantasy, or realism. One colleague insists his brand is "literary" horror, not to be elitist—he isn't the sort—but with horror being literature's ugly stepsister, perhaps he hopes for a better reception if he squeezes his work into something daintier to appeal to the courtesans.

Yet horror doesn't lack for readers. A recent report cites it as literature's fifth bestselling genre, accounting for $79.6 million in US sales.

Perhaps the problem lies in the narrow definition of horror decided largely by industry professionals—publishers, booksellers, and librarians—those who select the titles to shelve under the horror rubric.

"Have you heard of Ebenezer Scrooge?" I ask the horror deniers. "What about the White Rabbit? Because who hasn't read Charles Dickens's gruesome cautionary tale, *A Christmas Carol*, or Lewis Carroll's weird classic *Alice in Wonderland*, much-loved titles first published in 1843 and 1865, respectively, and still in print today?

For centuries, we've been happily terrorizing our children with stories like "Little Red Riding Hood" and *Pinocchio*, telling our toddlers their bad behavior will get them eaten by wolves or skinned and turned into drums. And what is "Hansel and Gretel" if not a Grimm tale of child abandonment? Horror deniers have invariably read these books. "But those are classics," they argue. "Fairy tales and fables. They're not proper horror."

Only they *are* horror, because horror transcends genre.

A literary commentator once accused me of not writing proper horror. I ponder what he meant by that. Was he implying that horror must include gothic backdrops, haunted houses, or chainsaws dripping blood? It's true these elements don't feature much in my fiction. I usually set my stories in rugged Kiwi landscapes, wedging my characters between culture and myth.

At its simplest, horror serves to elicit fear, mankind's oldest and strongest emotion. H.P. Lovecraft, in his 1927 treatise *Supernatural Horror in Literature*, speaks of "a profound sense of dread, and of contact with unknown spheres and powers; a subtle attitude of awed listening, as if for the beating of black wings or the scratching of outside shapes and entities on the known universe's utmost rim."

Horror ranges in type—supernatural, cosmic, pulp, extreme, humorous, apocalyptic, folk, satanic, kaiju, and crime, to name just a few—and also in its intensity. In a well-cited 2014 social media post, Stephen King categorized fright levels from the gross-out of "a severed head tumbling down a flight of stairs" to the horror of the unnatural, such as "spiders the size of bears," and topping out at the terror of "when the lights go out and you feel something behind you, you hear it, you feel its breath against your ear, but when you turn around there is nothing there." While it's hard to argue with horror's most successful living author, the spectrum may be even wider and more nuanced, running from quiet through-a-glass-darkly unease at one end through to the blood-spattered scream-your-lungs-out terror that UK editor Stephen Jones described at the 2016 StokerCon convention as "eyeballs on a plate."

Horror is more than a hierarchy of scares; it's a grown-up genre addressing real-world issues, asking hard questions, and the growing focus of academic study. In a world that is increasingly confronting, confusing, and complex, reading and writing horror can help us find meaning and catharsis. In *Why Horror Seduces (Oxford University Press,* 2017), researcher Mathias Clasen explains: "We are born to be fearsome, but the things we fear are somewhat plastic and modulated by culture. That is why horror fiction changes over time and from culture to culture."

With horror being affective—related to moods and feelings—the things we fear are also inherently personal, based on our experiences and also the time and place in which we live. For example, as citizens of "the shaky isles," where Geonet registers around 20,000 earthquakes yearly, New Zealanders fear the big one, the quake that will trigger a volcanic event that might wipe us all out, whereas Australians might focus their anxieties on drought, forest fires, and venomous species residing in their letter boxes. For many women in the United States, Margaret Attwood's *The Handmaid's Tale* (*Mifflin Harcourt,* 1985) is starting to look like real-life horror, and at a time when attacks on people of Asian descent are escalating, readers have responded with fervor to the horror stories in my anthology *Black Cranes* (*Raw Dog Screaming Press,* 2023, co-edited with Geneve Flynn).

"What frightens you might not frighten me," writes *New York Times* bestseller Jonathan Maberry in Tim Waggoner's *Writing in the Dark (Guide Dog Books,* 2020). "What scares me might delight you. Horror fiction, therefore, is an exploration of those things that unnerve and disquiet us, written in a way that allows the reader to get into our heads and nerve endings, and to drive around in our phobias for a while." Horror creatives need to be aware of universal human triggers, but mostly they mine their own fears, bringing readers along for the ride, and "we don't just like the ride; we *need* the ride," says *Scare Me* filmmaker Josh Ruben in his introduction to Doug Murano's *Hideous Book of Hidden Horrors (Bad Hand Books,* 2022). "Horror serves as a "reminder to appreciate the air in your lungs and the feeling of planted feet." We need to "touch a little evil sometimes, only to close the book, shut the door, and survive." My *Path of Ra* (*Raw Dog Screaming Press,* 2017) co-author Dan Rabarts, agrees. "What is the point of facing down demons," he says in *Newsroom*, "if we can't hang their corpses from our battlements, so that others know they can be tamed?"

"Horror stories allow us to confront our deepest fears through the buffer of fiction," says three-time Bram Stoker Awards®-winner Waggoner, but he warns that "wrestling with the darkest questions of human existence—why is there violence, pain, cruelty, and death?—can be emotionally overwhelming."

Is that why people are so quick to declare they don't read horror? Because its themes are too emotionally overwhelming? Or is it they're ashamed of their secret fascination with nasty eyeballs? When we ask friends and family to list books they've read, they're proud to rattle off literary classics like

Tolstoy's *War and Peace* or Austen's *Pride and Prejudice*, but they're less inclined to mention a steamy urban romance or the book of Dad jokes stashed under the bed. Likewise, reading horror is a guilty pleasure we mustn't admit to.

Writing horror is an act of subversion. In the introduction to their Bram Stoker Award®-winning title *Monster, She Wrote,* Lisa Kröger and Melanie R. Anderson state: "Women are accustomed to entering unfamiliar spaces, including territory they have been told not to enter. When writing is an off-limits act, writing one's story becomes a form of rebellion and taking back power." Indeed, Mary Shelley's novel *Frankenstein*, published anonymously in 1818, wasn't just any monster story: the work foreshadowed the electric resurrection behind our modern-day defibrillators and purportedly spawned a genre.

Its transgressive underpinnings mean horror welcomes fresh approaches from new voices, including LGBTQ, disabled, indigenous, and diasporic narratives. Horror creatives are a diverse group with weird and innovative tastes—another reason people might distance themselves from horror, because if they embrace the macabre, it might imply they, too, are weird.

In a 1987 interview with Phil Konstantin, Stephen King said, "I have always felt a little bit uncomfortable with that question [why I write these stories] ...it is asked of the writer of horror stories because it seems that there is something nasty about our love for horror stories, or boogies, ghosts and goblins, demons and devils."

Not everyone likes Brussels sprouts, either. But horror can be an acquired taste, so don't dismiss it out of hand. You don't have to tell anyone you're reading it. Just watch how sprinkling horror into your reading diet can help you find meaning, embrace new communities, offer fresh perspectives, and nourish your soul. You might even slay some demons on the way.

HEROES AND VILLAINS IN THE LAND OF THE PANTHER: THE FUTURE OF BLACK FANTASTICAL NARRATIVES IN SUPERHERO FRANCHISES

BY TODD SULLIVAN

A woman cries, "Help me, someone stole my purse!" She's cornered in a dank alley blocks away from the Daily Planet, but with his super hearing, Clark Kent hears her desperate pleas anyway. He drops his pencil, pushes back his chair, and rushes out of his cubicle. He narrowly misses bumping into Lois Lane, who teasingly admonishes him for his bad sight and clumsiness. Clark gives a stuttering apology, steps into an empty elevator, and presses the button for the uppermost floor.

He rips open his shirt to reveal the bright yellow and red 'S' on his chest. He leaps through the trap door, and faster than a speeding bullet, he's through the elevator shaft, out of the building, and racing through the wide blue sky. His red cape flaps in the wind. The bright sun bathes his black skin and dreadlocks as he speeds to the rescue.

There is a growing trend in the entertainment world to replace fictional characters that are traditionally white with black characters. A black Superman, a black Spider-Man, a black James Bond. The idea behind this is understandable. The vast majority of money-making fictional narratives are populated by white characters. Many of these fictional franchises were created in the mid-1900s, when African Americans didn't have the opportunity or the means to have such material published. In the present day, re-envisioning already existing and recognizable storylines in order to diversify the mega-blockbuster movies being churned out today allows black actors to have a chance at wealth and superstardom.

Despite the fact this is a noble goal, is it really the best solution? When black people are portrayed in narratives written by white writers, or when they take up the mantle for characters intended for white people, plot holes are bound to manifest.

Take a black Superman. On the one hand, you can simply hire a black actor to play Clark Kent, and keep the story exactly the same otherwise. Writers can also create a whole new fictional character from Krypton who is, for some reason, on Earth. They already did something similar with a Supergirl, Krypto the Superdog, and Power Girl, all coming after the original Superman.

In a modern-day scenario, the new character is black, though the question of why a dark-skinned person was born on Krypton raises a few questions. Humans evolved from primates covered with fur and had light skin until we migrated out of the rainforest to the Savanna. Did Kryptonians on the planet Krypton, with its cooler-in-temperature red sun, have a similar evolutionary development? Since it's a fictional planet, any narrative background can be written, but trying to avoid contrivances becomes increasingly difficult in justifying the existence of black people, and potentially Asian, Mexican, etc. people on Krypton, if one day we wish to further diversity the Kryptonian race.

Similar narrative plot holes cropped up when white writers attempted to create black superheroes in the past, Black Panther being a prime example. Truthfully, Black Panther was a massive leap forward in the Marvel Cinematic Universe. Portraying its first black superhero in a motion picture featuring mainly black actors, the film went on to gross 1.3 billion dollars and is currently the 13th highest-grossing film of all time. The titular character, Black Panther, was specifically written in the 1960s to be a black superhero. The character was also created by two white writers: Stan Lee and Jack Kirby. This has, unfortunately, lead to one of the most unfortunate plot lines in superhero history.

As the story goes, 10,000 years ago, a substance called vibranium dropped from the sky as a meteorite. An African tribe in the fictional land of Wakanda found the vibranium, which granted them incredible powers and made them capable of fashioning advanced technologies. In order to conceal this valuable and limited resource, they kept vibranium a secret.

Only a white writer could have conceived of a narrative storyline where an African nation sits by idly during the brutal colonization of the continent in the 1800s, the slave trade which started two hundred years prior in the 1600s, the middle passage to America, which resulted in the estimated deaths of 2-4 million Africans, the subsequent slavery in the United States and its territories, apartheid in South and West Africa, the turmoil of the Jim Crow and Civil Rights era, and the current social and economic problems facing Africa in general today.

Only a white writer would have envisioned a technically superior African nation that would then sit by and do nothing while some of the worst atrocities in human history were taking place on the continent against Africans, all because Wakanda wanted to keep vibranium a secret from others.

Despite attempts to justify the Wakandan's decision, the fact that a black or African writer would surely not create such an absurd scenario is undeniable. Within the parameters of the storyline written by Stan Lee and Jack Kirby, is Black Panther really the hero?

If a black Superman was created, who would be the villain he would fight? Lex Luther is bad, but the systematic social injustices facing black people would seem like a better place to start, and those battles are probably better fought in local, state, and national government, not with street thugs in back alleys.

Instead of putting black people in narrative universes written by and for white people, a better long-term goal is to develop black fantastical narratives that make more logical sense in the storytelling. Not only would these narratives be more realistic in their approach, but they would also allow for spin-offs equivalent to popular franchises like Tolkein's Middle Earth, the MCU, George R.R. Martin's Game of Thrones, J.K. Rowling's Hogwarts, etc.

Fostering the talents of black writers who pen these fantastical stories is a better long-term strategy to develop authentic black narratives than simply sticking black actors in traditionally white narratives. As a short-term fix, a black Superman is fine, as there is a lot of money and international recognition behind these massive projects. But in conjunction with a black Superman, there should be narrative fantastical universes centered around a black perspective written by black writers.

TURNING RED AND NAVIGATING MESSY MOTHER-DAUGHTER RELATIONSHIPS: HOW PIXAR CENTERS ASIAN FAMILY DYNAMICS WHILE NEGOTIATING INTERGENERATIONAL TRAUMA

BY ARCHITA MITTRA

Like most teenagers, I went through a 'punk' phase where I rebelled against parental authority. However, I was no match for my American penfriend, who had already dyed her hair blue, gotten a tattoo, stolen money from her mother to pay for booze, snuck out of home to attend concerts, and became pregnant after hooking up with a stranger at a friend's party—all before she turned 13.

She couldn't believe me when I told her that I wasn't allowed to go to sleepovers, let alone attend the Poets of the Fall concert that one time an internationally famous rock band chose to come and perform in my hometown.

"I don't get it," she told me. "Why do you need your mum's permission and approval for everything, anyway?"

I sighed in exasperation, unable to explain *how* and *why* my family dynamics differed so vastly and culturally from hers.

Over a decade later, in a post-pandemic era where most of my friends and I still live with our parents with work-from-home jobs, Pixar released *Turning Red* (2022)—a light-hearted animated film about a young Asian girl defying her family's explicit wishes to attend a boyband concert. It raised questions about managing one's own independence and family expectations that brown girls have struggled with all our lives. I watched this film with my friends while connected over a Discord call; we laughed and cried in equal measure, as the familial circumstances that Mei had to navigate were all too real and relatable.

We felt *seen*.

Milien (or Mei), the 13-year-old protagonist, constantly struggles with living up to her mother's strict standards and pursuing her own desires. Although a straight-A student with a loving cohort of friends, she often has to skip after-school hang-outs to help with household chores. On the cusp of puberty, Mei naturally loves boys enough to draw mushy fanart in a school notebook which she has to keep a secret from her mother, who believes her to be "too innocent" for such things. Unable to have open and honest conversations about certain topics, she is forced to repress her emotions, lie whenever possible and live a double life when it comes to balancing school and parental pressures. Early on, she announces, "Honoring your parents sounds great, but if you take it too far, well, you might forget to honor yourself."

It's not very often that mainstream Western media breaks out of its comfort zone to make a film that centers Asian family dynamics at its helm in any meaningful way except perhaps as a tokenistic diversity nod (a reality that is changing, albeit very slowly). That *Turning Red* manages to talk about the complicated mother-daughter bond that is a lived reality for so many brown communities (diasporic or otherwise) without drawing unfair moralistic comparisons to traditional white family dynamics is nothing short of brilliant.

Each individual experiences the nebulous and fraught period of 'teenage' differently, although much of it depends on cultural upbringing. My white friend couldn't understand why my relationship with my mother had to be so different from hers. As we grew up on opposite sides of the planet, the insecurities and issues we battled with diverged.

Of course, this isn't to say that *Turning Red* speaks for *all* brown families (given that differences in class, socioeconomic privileges, and financial security play a huge role in determining parent-child power dynamics) but that it surely resonates with a fairly large middle-class majority, especially on three counts: how the children's own desires are often subsumed in a bid to adhere to the image that their parents have constructed for them; how this self-effacement is directly a result of a lack of boundaries; and how it ends up perpetuating the familiar cycle of inter-generational trauma.

When caught in a dilemma, Mei frequently thinks from her mother's perspective to the point where she neglects her own needs or becomes harshly critical of herself. Such is her desire to be in her mother's good books that she doesn't correct her when her mother falsely accuses her best friends of "corrupting" her or blames the boy (she secretly drew fanart of) for "taking advantage" of her. In her bid to be a perfectionist, Mielin has to carefully balance between being an overachiever and having an active social life. Thus, *Turning Red* highlights how daughters often end up internalizing their parent's voices to the point where their own selfhood becomes dormant, effaced, or subsumed into the mother's will.

Moreover, the film emphasizes how the teenager's self-effacement is a function of a lack of privacy and boundaries. While growing up, brown kids are not usually privileged enough to have their own rooms. Even though Meilin has her own room, she doesn't have *personal space*, since Ming, her mother, can barge in on her anytime or go through her things if suspicious. This predicament is made more acute when Mei (in her first transformation to her red panda form) seeks refuge in the bathroom. Ming, under the impression that her 13-year-old daughter has just started on her period, ignores Mei's protestations and pulls apart the curtains of the bathtub (behind which Meilin was hiding) with the noble intention to help. In another violation of privacy, Ming looks under Mei's bed, stumbles upon the paraphernalia, pointing to a plan to attend a pop concert by any means, and discovers that her daughter has been skillfully lying to her all this while.

Thirdly, Mielin's fraught relationship with her mother reveals the vicious cycle of inter-generational trauma they both are trapped in as a result of their repressed emotions. Meilin learns early on that it is virtually impossible to communicate with her mother as a friend or an equal. Unable to question Ming's authority, the only way Mei can *sometimes* get what she wants is by people-pleasing or crude manipulation. However, such negotiations aren't always successful, as exemplified by the fact that she creates a colorful flowchart to explain why she should be "allowed" to attend a pop concert and is promptly told off. Marvel's *Ms. Marvel* miniseries starring Iman Vellani's Kamala Khan as a brown Muslim superhero also has a very similar scene where the protagonist's ardent request to attend a comic convention is met with utter bewilderment and disapproval from her immigrant parents.

In *Turning Red*, Mei's entry into puberty is marked by her transformation into a red panda whenever she feels intense emotion. By controlling her emotions, she can exert some control over her transformations, although she isn't quite successful. Later on, Meilin learns that every woman in her family has a special "red panda" form that they must shut out in a special coming-of-age ceremony overseen only by close family members. Thus, the "red panda" form, passed down as an ancestral legacy, stands not just as a symbol to preserve family traditions but also as a metaphor for repressing one's authentic self.

When it is Meilin's turn, it is revealed that her mother's red panda form was an enormously vicious creature that had to be tamed and locked away. Ming also had an uneasy relationship with her own mother (Mei's grandmother) for choosing to marry a man she loved against her parent's wishes. This is a fate that is easily relatable to so many brown kids whose parents act as though they have a say in everything and their will is the law. Ming is strict because she herself had disappointed her mother; hence, she was treating Meilin as a vessel to fulfill her own desires instead of seeing her daughter as a separate person with needs often different and contradictory to her own.

Mothers often interpret this *difference* (in life goals, desires, or even something as trivial as musical preferences) as a form of animosity or a challenge—a questioning of their authority as they never learned to separate their needs from other people, not through any fault of their own but as a function of the patriarchal conditioning that teaches women to put the needs of the family over their own. As a result, their unpaid labor is taken for granted as a labor of love, their sacrifices are unacknowledged, and their needs are neglected. The inner world of the family becomes the *only* world they know, while external conflicts take a backseat, and they naturally expect those around them to do the same (Sons, to a certain extent, can escape this, while daughters bear the greater brunt of their mother's regrets and unfulfilled dreams).

As a family-friendly children's film from Pixar, Meilin is granted a happy ending. But the way *Turning Red* achieves this is worth noting and analyzing. When Mei finally speaks up, she is able to distinguish between her own needs and her mother's wishes and asserts herself accordingly. Yet, while a western feminist tale might equate "empowerment" with "successful rebellion," *Turning Red* showcases the importance of extending empathy, especially to those who were never given it.

Instead of just fighting for herself, Mei helps her mother resolve her own issues and even receives support and solidarity from her relatives. The family members acknowledge their flaws and blind spots and are ready to give Mielin the space she needs to be herself.

The very fact that Mei retains her animal form while the others do not shows her breaking a toxic cycle of trauma and making her own path without necessarily cutting ties with her family or cultural ancestry. Moreover, to take the shapeshifting metaphor further, it highlights Mei's role not as someone who appeases both sides (which is what she tried to do earlier and failed disastrously) but as a woman who makes both spaces (her Chinese family traditions as well as the dominant western world where she lives) her *home*. Instead of simply resisting and fighting parental authority, the film posits a process of mutual self-aware and empathetic collaboration as a means of healing and freedom.

Initially, Ming may come off as overbearing, but the film ensures that her humanity shines through in most scenes without her devolving into a "Tiger Mom" stereotype. As a deep and ever-widening rift opens up between Mei and her mother, *Turning Red* suggests that it is possible to bridge that gap instead of simply turning one's back on cultural traditions that no longer align with one's personal goals. The messy feelings that characterize so many mother-daughter relationships are often fraught with emotional violence and resentment that go both ways. To navigate the battleground of divisive opinions, both sides need to acknowledge how they are both capable of hurting the other for true healing and empowerment to commence.

Naturally, while watching the film, my friends and I had to pause at several moments to dry our tears or talk about how relatable a particular moment felt. A common thread that cropped up was our mixed feelings towards our mothers while accepting that they have always acted in our best interests. While writing this article, I realized that this was one of *those* conversations that I simply couldn't have with my white American penfriends.

At Mei's age, I was often candid about my heartbreaks with my mother. Yet, as I grew older, while I remained emotionally as close, there were times I often guarded my tone or worried about how her interpretation of an event might potentially affect our relationship.

My friend Subarna Banerjee who had a similarly emotional reaction to the film, said, "Even though it is based somewhere else, I constantly kept feeling, 'that is me.' My mother is my best friend, much like Mei was to her, and although she was not as overbearing, she was just as protective. I could relate to Mei when she was sobbing by the bed, apologizing to her mother's picture, after having fantasized about a boy and being caught, because that's what being best friends with your mom does to you—you want to be your own person, but you hate to disappoint her or let her down in any way. When Mei chose her mom over her friends, I felt for her because I understand not wanting to lose your mother's favor which you have always had, even if it means betraying your own self."

This sense of ambivalence that we first noticed as adolescents (when attending concerts and sleepovers was strictly off-limits) is something that we carried into our adult lives when we began to address the aspects of our personality (such as Mei's red panda) that we had shut out as they did not fit into our parents' narrative about us. It was this quality that Subarna identified with the most while discussing the film. She said, "I relate to Mei having a whole other side of her, her Panda, completely hidden from her mother (or she pretends she doesn't like her other side in front of her mom) because she thinks her mother won't approve. When she transforms, and her mother finds out, it broke my heart to see her curled up and crying because she heard her mother say, 'Did you SEE her? That was not Mei!' To her, it felt like her mother was disgusted by her when, in reality, she was probably just worried, and it came out wrong. And then, of course, I relate to Mei sneaking out to live her life. Like they say, overprotective parents make sneaky children."

This over-protectiveness can have various consequences. Sometimes, children do grow estranged from their parents and move out to build a life elsewhere. In other cases, they may reach a mutual understanding or a careful negotiation of boundaries. There are also families where having healthy disagreements is the norm, without either party feeling disrespected. Another friend, Alina, weighed her opinions after watching the film: "As an arty kid who drew a lot of, ermmm, questionable fanart, I related to Meilin a lot! That feeling of loving your mom but not really understanding her, resulting in an increasingly antagonistic relationship, hit HOME, man. It's hard to see your mom as a person outside of her role as a MOM, at least in my experience."

The finale of *Turning Red* suggests that with time, Mei and Ming evolve to have a relationship built on mutual understanding and maturity. With one of my college friends, that certainly was the case. When I asked her about her relationship with her mother, she said, "My mom is my best friend, and the older I have got, the closer I have become. Our relationship has improved because she has gotten increasingly liberal with the years, while I have questioned so much of the Western (and white) feminist ideals I once swore by. So it feels like we met each other halfway."

Of course, it is important to acknowledge that the cultural and generational gap that is bridged by the third-act climax of the film isn't always possible. For some viewers, the ending and final message that *Turning Red* leaves us with might seem like escapist wish fulfillment. I personally found it cathartic, as did Subarna, who said, "This is why the ending BROKE me. While it is unrealistic in an Asian household for a mother to be that understanding and even apologize, something in me needed that moment where Mei bursts out her truth, and in the end, her mother says, 'The farther away you grow from me, the prouder I will be.' I wish my mother had said that to me. Don't get me wrong, she's still my best friend and incredibly understanding, and she's a better parent every day. But I still wish she would say that and mean it, once."

Talking to her, I realized that even though it has been years, I'm still sad about the Poets of the Fall concert. While I understand why my parents wanted to shelter me (and also the fact that the tickets were very expensive) and I'm not angry with them, there is *still* that wistful longing to turn back time and do things differently.

Turning Red reminded me of my teenage years and the frequent disagreements I had with my mother that are often difficult to encapsulate with labels such as "toxic" or "dysfunctional," which, in turn, encourage a very one-dimensional view of things spurred by the capitalist pursuit of individualism.

This isn't to say that one should stay in abusive family situations or decry professional help, but rather realize that not all situations have black-and-white answers, and each family must come to a unique solution by having open conversations and being kind to each other.

In fact, the very conflict between Meilin and Ming acknowledges the complexity of Asian family relationships (which is rarely talked about without inviting Western judgment and censure) and celebrates it for what it is—a messy reality bound by both love and resentment that we must learn to navigate in our own ways. It reminds viewers that our notions of what constitutes "boundaries" and "privacy" are culturally constructed and often differ from one generation to the next. Meilin is able to successfully regain her autonomy without succumbing entirely to a violent retaliation against those she loves, and that is, indeed, a special kind of victory.

The happy-ever-after in *Turning Red* may not always be possible or feasible, but is certainly heartwarming and worth aspiring to.

CAT HORROR

BY CHRISTINA SNG

As a lifetime cat lover, it thrills me to no end when I see a cat in a movie. I tell my cat Kit, "Look, there's representation there!" She ignores me and later asks for a scritch. What I loved most about the movie *Alien* was the cat Jonesy doing cat things in the movie. Its sequel, *Aliens,* would have been a much better movie if Ripley just brought Jonesy along. Between you and me, I confess I only watched *Pet Sematary* for glimpses of Church, the cat who is probably the coolest cat villain on film. *Captain Marvel*, well... Goose wasn't really a cat. But we can pretend he is for most of the movie. In *Chilling Adventures of Sabrina*, Sabrina's cat Salem isn't even a real cat but a digitized version.

"There aren't enough cats in movies," I lament to Kit, who comes to sit on my lap, perhaps glad I'm fighting for her rights. No, she just wants to be petted with my eyes staring adoringly at her.

I'm too distracted, but I pet her anyway. It's hard to type when the cat is blocking the keyboard with her body.

Why are cats so awesome in horror?

Well, if you think about it, they're the perfect predator. They can eat everything smaller if given the chance. Their bodies are built for hunting. And they're absolutely fearless of everything except other cats and evil humans.

Zombies, vampires, werewolves? Pffftt... no challenge for a cat who can take on a Xenomorph.

The fact that they are utterly unafraid of this monster in front of them and will still attack them is why cats are awesome.

Have you seen videos of tiny cats intimidating the largest of dogs? Surely they know they could be killed by one swipe of that giant paw but they still try anyway. This courage has only been seen in final girls on film and television, who are usually as unequipped and small as a cat, but somehow manage to save themselves and, sometimes, the day.

We need more cats in film! Sure, cat actors are hard to find, but it is possible. If you want cat lovers—and you know we are rabid, lifelong fans—to watch your movie, put a cat in it.

Imagine cats in your favorite horror movies running circles around the monsters with enough time for a nap in a tree.

Imagine a cat nudging the front gate open in *28 Days Later*, letting the zombies in to eat the soldiers.

Imagine a cat biting off the xenomorph's head just as it emerges from its host in *Aliens*.

Imagine a cat yawning on the stairs and going back to sleep after Jack trips over her in *The Shining*, snapping his neck as he hits the bottom.

Imagine a cat hanging out with Hannibal Lecter and maybe sharing morsels in *The Silence of the Lambs*.

Imagine a cat slashing Freddy's ankles and darting away in *A Nightmare on Elm Street* before letting him pet it.

Consider the exciting possibilities of *Dawn of the Cats*, *Night of the Living Cats*, *An American Cat in London*, or *Cat vs Predator*—the Cat wins, of course! The Predator suit will be scratched to shreds by the time filming is over.

Filmmakers, I hope you hear us. Make a cat the hero of the story. They can outrun a zombie, outbite a vampire, howl fiercer than a werewolf, and outsmart any evil monster. What more could you want in a protagonist? They're cute as hell too. Look how well Netflix's *The Sandman* episode *Dream of a Thousand Cats* was received.

Add a cat, gain a following. Our cats will thank you for it! Actually, they won't. But their humans will, and you will have created a brand new genre right there: *Cat Horror*.

THE DARK FANTASIES OF SUSPIRIA AND THE BEYOND: COMPARING ITALIAN HORROR FILMMAKERS DARIO ARGENTO AND LUCIO FULCI

BY PATRICK BARB

The signature dark-fantasy-infused hits of Dario Argento (*Suspiria*, 1977) and Lucio Fulci (*The Beyond*, or *E tu vivrai nel terrore! L'aldilà*, 1981) play a not insignificant part in guaranteeing these filmmakers' seats in the Italian horror pantheon.

While both started their horror careers in the *Giallo* sub-genre (that sexy "whodunnit," black-gloved precursor to American slashers), *Suspiria* and *The Beyond* exist as waking nightmares, drawing from the traditions of the fairy tale, weird fiction, and dark fantasy.

From the witch's coven at an elite dance academy in the dark German woods (where one can imagine Hansel and Gretel losing their trail of breadcrumbs) to the New Orleans hotel as a stand-in for the cursed castle, Argento, Fulci, and their collaborators draw as much from the Brothers Grimm and other folklore traditions as they do from the gory horror tropes for which their films are also noted.

Once Upon a Time

Both *Suspiria* and *The Beyond* feature dream-like atmospheres. Argento has noted the application of fairy-tale motifs into the mise-en-scène of his tale of a witches' coven running a dance academy. While the Argento classic is more commonly noted for its connections to dark fantasy and folklore, Fulci's zombie-filled masterpiece shares many ties as well.

Suspiria begins, as any good horror film should, on a dark and stormy evening. As the film's protagonist, the American dance student Suzy (Jessica Harper), arrives in Germany and exits amid a downpour, she's transported to a land rich in vibrant colors and contrasting shadows—like the painted illustrations in a book of fairy stories. Her first exposure to the Tanz Akademie sees her witnessing a student fleeing from the building and running through the woods. There's a mysterious past here that Suzy's unaware of, stretching back further than she (or the audience) might expect.

Fulci's black-and-white opening to *The Beyond* employs a more direct approach to "once upon a time." The grim 1927 set sequence introduces two figures touched by magic in the painter Schwieck (Antoine Saint-John) and the soon-to-be-blind Emily (Cinzia Monreale). As Schwieck is murdered and Emily blinded, we see a curse placed on the hotel. This idea of a curse and transformation applied to people and places echoes the fate of the Beast and his castle in "Beauty and the Beast." Like Beauty, *Suspiria's* Suzy and *The Beyond's* Liza (Catriona MacColl) must unlock the mysteries of what befell their new dwellings.

Far, Far Away

While neither film is set in a castle or exotic fairy-tale kingdom, Argento and Fulci establish their central locations via tradition, gravitas, and mystery so that they serve similar functions. *Suspiria* takes place in Germany and *The Beyond* in New Orleans, Louisiana—a city steeped in French heritage. With Germany as the home of the Brothers Grimm and France, known for its fairy tale collectors like Charles Perrault, it's no surprise these two locations would serve their filmmakers' crafting of dark fantasy worlds.

Both *Suspiria*'s dance academy and *The Beyond*'s hotel play the castle. Argento and his crew purposefully raised the height of doorknobs to make his young female actors appear more childlike in comparison with the overwhelming set design, as though they're lost in a giant's castle.

In turn, Fulci subs America for a kingdom far, far away, and the choice is an inspired one. Not only do his Louisiana exteriors feature palm trees adding to the exotic milieu, but his early set piece featuring Emily and her dog Dicky on the Causeway evokes the dream-like image of a mist-shrouded bridge and its supernatural keeper.

Witches and a Warlock

Drawing from the deep bench of folklore and fairy-tale archetypes, Argento and Fulci both use witches, warlocks, and other dabblers in black magic as the prime antagonistic forces opposing their films' heroines. *Suspiria* marks the first film in Argento's "Three Mothers Trilogy," establishing a vast network of witches' covens as a formidable global threat. Argento's frequent collaborators, Goblin, provide a soundtrack filled with orgiastic howls, yelps, and shrieks, backed by pulsating drums, making viewers witnesses to dark rituals. Head witch Helena Markos, the "Black Queen" who has assumed the role of the Director of the dance academy, would likely find kinship with Snow White's wicked queen and her disguises.

Fulci's would-be warlock, the lynched painter Schieck, is not as directly antagonistic as Markos and her coven (at least not at first). But there is the sense that he, via his painting, and Emily, via her reading of the forbidden Book of Eibon, attempt to harness supernatural forces beyond their control, efforts which lead to devastating consequences.

Big, Bad...Dogs?

Additionally, both films share common secondary antagonists, spotlighted by jaw-dropping (and throat-ripping) scenes of violence that exist in conversation with each other. *Suspiria*, first out of the gate in 1977, features the disturbing scene of blind piano player Daniel's savage mauling by his seeing-eye dog, a wolfhound.

The Beyond re-runs this sequence but amplifies the gore, as is common when making the transition from Dario Argento's work to Lucio Fulci's. The blind woman's throat is ripped out like Daniel's, but her Dicky also severs her ear, covering his master in a hood of vibrant red serum.

In a further parallel to Red Riding Hood's plight, both films expose viewers to these doomed characters unaware of the dangers near to them in the forms of beings they've mistakenly trusted, all while ignoring "what big teeth they have."

The Undead and Ever After

For fans of Italian horror cinema, the "zombie" or *zombi* and Lucio Fulci are intrinsically linked. And yet, the undead of *The Beyond* aren't the flesh-eating ghouls popularized by Romero's *Dead* films. In Fulci's surreal classic, zombies are more of an ogre-, goblin-, or troll-like threat to Liza and would-be Prince Charming Dr. John McCabe (David Warbeck). These monsters are tools of a greater evil, originating from a dark fantasy world, or as the film's narrator explains, "And you will face the Sea of Darkness and all therein that may be explored."

While Argento isn't as tied to the zombie trope, Suspiria sees Suzy's friend Sara resurrected from the dead as Markos's final attack on the American girl. In the role of Sara, Stefania Cassini gives a fantastic physical performance that this writer suspects influenced some of the Deadite performances in Sam Raimi's *Evil Dead* films. Suzy, pure of heart and attentive to the clues around her, emerges triumphant at her film's end, stabbing Markos with a glass peacock feather. Here we find another murderous folklore villain undone—in part—by birds.

There's no such avian-based luck for Liza and McCabe, as the latter rejects the fairy-tale rules under which *The Beyond* exists. "I'm sick of hearing all these stories," he declares.

Pity.

Perhaps if they paid better attention to those stories, then these characters might've found a happy ending to go with their ever after—trapped in the surreal dark fantasy world from which the film's evil emanates.

Ultimately, audiences reap the most rewards after watching these Italian horror classics. These rich fantasy worlds, crafted by the two maestros and their casts and crews, provide a treasure trove of lush, dreamy cinematic moments. For those inclined toward fairy tales and folklore, these films open interesting doorways into the world of horror.

HOW TO READ A SPECULATIVE HAIKU

BY CHRISTINA SNG

The lines of a speculative haiku can appear to make no sense when you read it as it is. Once you unravel its form, you may find yourself spending much time contemplating and uncovering the nuances and layers of its words. Haiku is not meant to be read literally. It is meant to be sipped like a steaming cup of sakura tea, letting all its flavor slowly permeate your tastebuds. I liken haiku to a puzzle. Often, many layers of meaning are hidden within and it is up to the reader to unravel them. A typical one, two, or three-line haiku or five-line tanka contains a juxtaposition between two images or ideas that tell a story, and sometimes, with a surprise twist at the end.

The absence of capitalization and punctuation conveys timelessness and a sense of belonging nowhere and everywhere at the same time.

What I love most about haiku is the beauty in its brevity, how everything there is to tell is encapsulated in these short lines.

Speculative haiku is haiku steeped in science fiction, horror, and/or fantasy, giving it an added dimension. Consider my one-line haiku, "multiverse theory":

multiverse theory this feeling of déjà vu

In this haiku, sensations of déjà vu are contrasted with the idea that if we are living in a multiverse, these follow:

1. We may have knowledge of our other lives.
2. Events may seem discomfortingly familiar like we've experienced them before, and we have, in another existence—that sense of déjà vu that most people cannot explain.

In another haiku, "a world", the concept of parallel universes is brought to the forefront in the first two lines.

a world

of possibilities

my cat in a box

The final line alludes to Schrödinger's Cat, whom no one knows is dead or alive until one opens the box. When you read the haiku again, you'll see the juxtaposition of both images reinforce a third idea, that bookending a world of possibilities, life and death are everything.

This third example utilizes a 5-line form called a tanka. A tanka is an expansive version of short form poetry as haiku is, with the same format of a contrast between two images to tell a story.

seconds before

the asteroid hits

he finally tells me

he loves me

eye roll

Here, the narrator's annoyance at the irony that it takes an apocalypse for her partner to say he loves her is juxtaposed against the second image, her eye roll, which lends a sense of finality before the asteroid comes crashing down. There is dark humor in haiku and tanka, as there is in life. These are my interpretations of my work when I wrote and read them. Perhaps you can find more.

Returning to the question posed at the beginning of this essay. How does one read a speculative haiku? Read one poem at a time, close the book, and ponder. Speculative haiku is a truly unique poetic form, and uncovering its layered, hidden meanings is one of the highlights of reading it.

REVIEWS

THE GREATEST CONSPIRACY OF ALL TIME: ON TIMELESS, THE HISTORY OF RACISM IN AMERICA, AND HOW WE RECLAIM OUR TIMELINE

BY BRANDON J. O'BRIEN

In the fall of 2016, the show *Timeless* premiered on NBC, a science fiction procedural in the vein of *Timecop*, *Voyagers!*, or *Seven Days*. In the pilot episode, we first watch history professor Lucy Preston (Abigail Spencer) being passed up for tenure at Stanford and returning home to her supportive sister and ailing mother. We observe engineer Rufus Carlin (Malcolm Barrett) attempt to ask his office crush out on a date mere moments before shooters storm their secret warehouse/laboratory, kidnap an engineer, and vanish within what turns out to be a white, orb-shaped time machine. Back at Lucy's house, the doorbell rings. American Homeland Security personnel tersely explain everything we just saw: a terrorist named Garcia Flynn (Goran Višnjić) has escaped to some*when* unknown, and they need Lucy to help stop Flynn from doing too much damage to history. Also, they would like to get their very expensive, top-secret time machine back.

Only eleven and a half minutes into the first episode, Rufus utters the show's most iconic quote. He is the target of intense pressure from his boss, Connor Mason (Paterson Joseph), head of Mason Industries, to pilot a second time machine so that Lucy and he might pursue Flynn into the unknown past. Rufus immediately replies:

"I don't know how it works across the pond, but I am Black. There is literally no place in American history that'll be awesome for me."

Both Rufus and Mason are Black. Rufus is one of four people of colour we've seen on screen thus far, and all four of them are, in their own ways, complicated images of both progress and the consequences of power. Rufus and his love interest, Jiya Marri (Claudia Doumit), are both competent and thoughtful programmers and engineers. Mason is a brilliant though self-absorbed tech billionaire responsible for one of the world's most radical inventions. Denise Christopher (Sakina Jaffrey) is a deliberate, wise, but hardline Homeland Security agent who truly believes in her work (and is fortunate that the thornier politics of that work are not the topic of this series). The majority of the protagonist ensemble is people of colour. More regularly than any teaching of history I've witnessed, the show wrestles with the relationship between marginalisation and historical outcome, whether the challenge is Black emancipation, women's suffrage, or a person coming out as lesbian to one's immigrant family.

The show somewhat follows a mission-of-the-week format: Flynn goes back in time, they find out when and ask Lucy why, and then they go back to hopefully stop history from being rewritten, causing their own temporal messes in the process. In the midst of this are the characters' own mysteries and struggles as well. On their first trip back in time, Lucy and company witness Flynn prevent the Hindenburg from exploding, only to put a timed explosive on board as it heads back to Europe. As the team investigates, Lucy is accosted by Flynn in a nearby warehouse, and, unbelievably deferent, he confides in her: Flynn is just following instructions on how to unravel a long-established conspiracy in order to avenge his murdered family.

When she asks why he's telling her this, he seems more perplexed than upset. His answer? Those instructions were Lucy's, a handwritten journal she personally handed him, full of ways one would be able to dramatically alter the flow of history in America.

This mystery itself is significant to the story, but only insomuch as it fits into a much heavier challenge with which the viewer must wrestle. The character of Connor Mason seems brash and bitter but otherwise aligned with the overall mission to maintain the historical timeline. Yet, in several early episodes, we see Mason come to Rufus privately and ask him to... run ominous errands. To make phone calls to unknown numbers and reveal information about the team's efforts. To visit strange men in the dead of night. Rufus doesn't like it, and by the look in Mason's eyes, he doesn't like it either. The story later reveals that Mason paid for Rufus' college scholarship so he could be the first person in his family with a degree and immediately gave him a job upon graduation from MIT. Now, something dark has come between them.

The threat whose timeline Flynn is trying to eradicate, it seems, is closer than they realise.

On August 25th, 2020, Kyle Rittenhouse drove twenty miles north of his Antioch, Illinois home into Kenosha, Wisconsin, during the Jacob Blake protests. Social media posts would wrongly assert that his mother drove him, but he instead went with a friend, who also handed him a Smith & Wesson M&P15 semi-automatic rifle bought on Rittenhouse's behalf months prior. He was seventeen years old—too young by law to openly carry a gun in either Illinois or in Wisconsin, where he would later shoot and kill two people, wounding a third.

Kyle Rittenhouse is not the first of his element, a data point in the statistical study of ignobility and grotesque injustice in America. Rittenhouse is one of the most peculiar, however: A teenager who insisted upon traveling out-of-state late on a school night, unsupervised save for another teen in tow, with a bulletproof vest and a gun in the car, eager to perform some wild and unruly act.

Very few things in the real world may be as Kafkaesque as the Rittenhouse trial was. His defense successfully argued to dismiss the charge of illegal possession on the grounds that, even though it is generally illegal for a minor to own a gun, an obscure Wisconsin statute paradoxically holds that it is legal for a minor to own a rifle so long as it is not short-barreled.

Judge Bruce Schroeder insisted the prosecution was not permitted to refer to those who lost their lives as 'victims,' but was open to the defense calling them 'looters.' Judge Schroeder also declared that a video from Rittenhouse, literally stating his desire to patrol the streets with a gun and "start shooting rounds," was inadmissible on the grounds that it did not sufficiently prove premeditation.

To be sure, many legal commentators have insisted that Schroeder's decisions during the trial were common procedure—after all, one should be presumed innocent until proven guilty, and anything that threatens that presumption is disallowed—but then, one should ask how often other defendants are afforded the same procedural courtesy. If anything is revealed throughout this story, it is that American Justice, that immortal, alabaster-white woman holding the scales of right and wrong in her hands, is not blind. She could see. She could see all of it. She's blindfolded because she doesn't care to see.

Kyle Rittenhouse is the latest link in a long chain of undeniable legal injustice in the United States. The courts' assessment of Black lives as equal to their neighbours' is a "polite" fiction; the rare sentencing of a Derek Chauvin is more than counterbalanced by letting the Kyle Rittenhouses go free. The Rittenhouse acquittal also threatens to reinvigorate the white militia movement in America, an already powerful and unaccountable byproduct of the nation's relationship with firearms. This movement is itself inherently white supremacist, as these same gun enthusiasts have ensured movements like the Black Panthers could not have the same freedom.

Briefly, I would like you to imagine breaking that chain. Stepping back several links and severing it at some deeper root: What if gun control were stronger? What if Wisconsin laws were less peculiar? What if social media countered some of the hostile anti-BLM rhetoric? What if Rittenhouse simply had something more important to do, somewhere else, that night?

What if one could make it possible?

I, too, am Black. There are still very few safe spaces in time for bodies like mine, or like Tamir Rice's, or like Trayvon Martin's, or like Breonna Taylor's, or like Botham Jean's. Rufus was right that such spaces are particularly scarce in American history. It has been so since Sean Bell. It has been so since James Byrd, Jr. It has been so since Emmett Till. It has been so since fourteen-year-old Orion Anderson was lynched in Loudoun County, Virginia, for the crime of allegedly scaring a white girl. It has been so since the bombing of Black Wall Street in Tulsa, Oklahoma, and it has been so since the drowning of Oscarville, Georgia, to make room for a lake named after a beloved Confederate Army officer and poet.

I am not an American citizen, but that doesn't make history any safer or less harrowing. First of all, extrajudicial killings happen in Trinidad, too, and when they do, they can often come with the same racialised tint, even on an island nation where people of colour are the majority. Second, that doesn't mean that my body is immune to American violence; Botham Jean, after all, was Caribbean-born as well, from Castries, St. Lucia.

I remember hearing Rufus' words in the first episode of *Timeless* and being immediately struck silent. It's not every day a show (let alone a show written by a white man) just... says that part aloud. History is jagged. It is brutal. Surviving it in real time can often take all of our effort, and in some places, that effort is greater than in others. It can take the lives of Black people as it does of the white people who defend their dignity. It can take those lives under the pretense of safety or justice, or it can take them for petty slights and overtly wicked intentions. And in the same show that's trying to prime me for wild and thrilling romps through the backyard of America's past, one Black man told another Black man within earshot of dozens of white scientists and military personnel that he does not feel safe.

In its wider narrative, as well as the general protagonistic context of most action-adventure science fiction, it is also a brazen attempt to refuse a call to action. Rufus not only doesn't want to foil a time-terrorist plot even though he's their only pilot but doesn't want to suffer the marginalisations of the past because he knows well enough how much it stings.

There is little difference, after all, between the present and the past.

Rufus Carlin is a name that should rattle in your brain if you're a nerd, or stand out as an obvious reference if you're a *huge* nerd. The name is a reference to the time-traveling steward from the future who guides Bill S. Preston, Esq. and Ted 'Theodore' Logan through their eponymous *Excellent Adventure*. It's an undeniably deliberate throwback, publicly acknowledged by the cast: after all, our *Timeless* Rufus is similarly the pilot on a three-seater time machine, accompanied by his own (Lucy) Preston and (Wyatt) Logan.

For my money, these names are more important than a gag. In *Bill & Ted*, Rufus' duty was to ensure the timeline that gets their heroes to the promised future point where they bring peace to the universe—a timeline that they only learn about and can affect once given the ability to travel through time at all. Theirs is not an organic reality. It is gifted to them by temporal tampering. Without meddling, that future would die unrealised—without Rufus, there is no Rufus.

Timeless is a more complex assessment of history—one that refuses to make easy assertions about what the altered timeline would look like. Rufus Carlin serves the same role here—the pilot, the only person who knows how the damn machine works, without whom Lucy and Wyatt would simply be lost, left on the sidelines. Rufus is also, curiously, the person most willing to consider the past malleable and the least willing to do so for personal gain. Even when Lucy strives to regain her sister after meddling with the timeline has erased her, and Wyatt secretly longs to use the time machine to save his murdered wife, Rufus has no such self-serving desires. He is so very eager, however, to insist that people right in front of him should not suffer, consequences to history be damned.

In almost every episode of *Timeless*, Rufus is the only person with a truly harrowing moral conflict. Imagine being a Black man gifted with the power to travel to any timeline, accompanied by a peerless historian and an expert marksman. Further, imagine looking those timelines in the eye—meeting Wernher von Braun at the end of World War II, talking with coloured infantrymen the day before Lincoln would be assassinated—knowing what those timelines later become. Imagine watching some of the heights of injustice and turning to the (white) woman who knows how long it's going to remain terrible and the (white) man who can make it right with his fists. Wouldn't you also roar, "I want to do something about this!"

Now imagine being denied the chance to do so.

In the second episode, very obviously titled 'The Assassination of Abraham Lincoln,' Rufus is present on the day he knows Lincoln will die, murdered for the crime of promoting emancipation. Rufus beseeches Lucy to save Lincoln, but she adamantly refuses despite her fascination with Lincoln as a historical figure. "We would come back to an entirely different world," Lucy argues. "Who knows if it would be better, or if there would be anything left to come back to at all? The present isn't perfect, but it's ours. Awful as it is, what happens to Lincoln is meant to be."

... I dunno, friend. Is it? Is the present *ours*? Is it *wholly* ours? Is history, is time, so simple and predictable that the past suffering of our forebears—or, further, the forebears of the marginalised people you do not have kinship with—must go on for us to remain, their own lives be damned? If altruism is good done without hope of recompense, isn't there a purer altruism in sacrificing your present day (a present that barely leans toward justice) so that ancestors might experience some tempered hope? Isn't taking a chance on a better world the ultimate goal of all of our actions—present, future, or even past?

Later that episode, Garcia Flynn himself enters the Ford's Theatre box and puts two rounds from a 2016 semiautomatic pistol into Abraham Lincoln's head. In the moments before he fires, Lucy and Flynn share shocked glances, and she screams, too late to change the outcome. She confesses to Rufus later, "It's one thing to talk about history like this abstract thing, but when the man gets shot right in front of you..." She insists that she tried.

Is it allyship to make a paltry effort on the cusp of inevitability?

Very early in *Timeless*, we learn the name of the conspiracy that seeks to claim history for itself:

Its name is Rittenhouse.

Rittenhouse is responsible for bankrolling Mason's entire time travel project and does so entirely for their own ends. Even before we learn when and how it's accomplished, we learn that they have already placed sleeper agents throughout the timeline, awaiting activation in order to undo historical events, with the ultimate goal of accumulating power. The Watergate tapes? They contain a confession that Nixon was under Rittenhouse's thumb. Charles Lindbergh, the first to make a solo transatlantic flight? A Rittenhouse stooge. Joe McCarthy and the Red Scare? One delusional, self-aggrandising man working to consolidate political power for Rittenhouse.

It's worth noting that, whether this was purely purposeful or wholly an accident of dramatic writing, *Timeless* became the story of a conspiracy so deep and far-reaching that very few white people are not in on it. They meet a

Rittenhouse agent in every episode for a season and a half, just kicking it in the backwoods of time, waiting for activation orders so they can grab the past by the neck and wring a new future into existence.

A wealthy-looking, intimidating man confronts Rufus early in the first season, threatening his family's life if Rufus doesn't provide Rittenhouse with updates on the past. In the very next episode, Lucy tracks down that same man, unaware of his connection to the conspiracy, after learning that he is her father. At the end of that season, Lucy's mother reveals she was born into Rittenhouse and attempts an indoctrination of Lucy from which she must be rescued. After Wyatt discovers that his wife's murder has somehow been prevented due to time shenanigans, he considers leaving the team in order to save his marriage. This only twists the knife further when Wyatt's wife turns on him and refers to Rittenhouse as "the only family [she has] ever known."

In "The Watergate Tape," while handcuffed to a chair, Wyatt asks Flynn why he employs such scorched-earth tactics to undo Rittenhouse when the consequences may undo all of American history in the process. Flynn responds: "Rittenhouse and America are so intertwined, sometimes it's hard to tell one from the other."

In 2016, when *Timeless* was released, Rittenhouse was surely a reference to the astronomer, horologist, and public official named David Rittenhouse, a member of the American Philosophical Society in 1768 and the first director of the United States Mint from 1792 to 1795. By all accounts, this Rittenhouse was not a tyrant—not a man who murdered people, upheld an unjust legislature, or held to an immoral code.

One may ask why he would be a villain in this series, the progenitor of such a terrible organisation. What did he do to deserve being vilified by this show? This Rittenhouse merely built an orrery and minted some coins. Yet... isn't it uniquely telling that he had such power? To chart the transit of Venus for the American Astronomical Society with no other grace than wanting to do it? To have been home-schooled in the home his great-grandfather built, on Philadelphia land, literally bearing his name? To have the luxury of hand-pressing some of the first coins his countrymen would ever spend? Perhaps the lesson is that privilege itself is capable of rendering anyone into the trustee of a broken system, if there is perceived value in upholding brokenness rather than confronting it.

I don't make this comparison to imply that Kyle Rittenhouse is necessarily a deliberate villain, despite the harm he's done. I make it because *Timeless* makes the same case for almost all of history—that he is but one beneficiary of a longstanding conspiracy so large and so looming that it would seek to even defy description. Indeed, such a conspiracy literally does all that it can to avoid being observed. He is the child of many little steps to keep him on this path—

the cloying deference of a (white) judge, the trust and fearlessness of a (white) friend, the willful ignorance of a (white) neighbour, the unearned benefit of the doubt offered by just short of a dozen (white) people who did not care to know the victims.

Intriguingly, the Rittenhouse of *Timeless* is itself not so monochromatic. As a conspiracy, Rittenhouse is more than happy to make use of any and all bodies available. It has no problem turning Black women with photographic memories into living rosters of their membership, or single white women into dedicated assassins for the cause. Rather, Rittenhouse simply does not value any lives without the prestige of white masculinity. Once that Black woman needs help to defend her family, or that white woman insists that women's suffrage should not be undone, they stop being worthy of grace. They are, demonstrably and vividly, expendable.

Even the white men are merely tools in the service of hegemony. In 'The Day Reagan Was Shot', we meet Owen, a Rittenhouse sleeper sent back to March of 1981 not to shoot said president but to kill Christopher (the Homeland Security agent) while she's still a Washington, D.C. patrol cop. When they intercede, Owen gives up the game. He confesses that his father was tried for embezzlement, his family was ruined by the proceedings, and they would have hit bottom if it weren't for the alleged grace of Rittenhouse to bail them out. Their only price was loyalty. While his brother bought into the scheme, Owen was skeptical. They kept him in line the only way that remained: do as we ask, kill who we tell you, or your wife and children will disappear.

When Rufus hears the story, he offers to take Owen back as an asset once they've undone the mess he's made. Owen fearfully refuses. After the heroes rush off to save Christopher from another attempt on her life, they come back to the basement where they've tied him up... and he's wrapped his belt around his neck. Rufus is the first to respond, to even grieve. He confesses that once they learned he had told the truth, he wanted to let him go, and find a new life free from Rittenhouse if he dared. But he didn't dare. There is no walking away from that kind of superstructure. It is not afraid to destroy even its inheritors if they get in the way of its power.

Especially in a show about time travel, Rittenhouse serves as a very obvious metaphor for seeking control through history: not merely that it is written by the winners, but it is won by those who can rewrite it, by who can shape it to their will. Only a privileged few get to do that. And when they take control of that power specifically to deny others the opportunity to hold the pen, what results can only be described as conspiracy. America as an ideal has always had a very expensive upkeep cost, one paid with exceptionalisms and interventionisms that come cheaper the more you use them. The result is an envy for power whose fingers are long and whose grips are taut. With that kind of power over reality, no one can question you. No one can question the things you value.

With that kind of power, when you tell a young man that the scheme must be protected at all costs, he leaves home before anyone notices he is gone, gets dressed, gets in his truck, and goes where he thinks he is needed. He goes because he is afraid of what he thinks will disappear if he doesn't.

There is a point in the pilot where Rufus gives an absolutely galvanising speech, which showrunner Eric Kripke insisted was ad-libbed by Barrett. While locked up, Wyatt asks him to make a distraction while he tries to break them out, and he chooses to ask for a glass of water from a guard. When that officer speaks down to him in the way white men with batons spoke to unarmed Black men, Rufus hesitantly stands up for himself:

"I'm in the damn Stone Age, but, man, I hope you live a long, long life. Long enough to see Michael Jordan dunk, Michael Jackson dance, Mike Tyson punch, really, just, any black guy named Michael. O.J.? Yeah, he gets off. He did it, but we don't care. And Obama, he's the president. 2008. That's gonna suck for you! I hope you see it all. Because the future is not on your side, boy."

It is many fans' favourite moment in the entire show, for the obvious reason that it holds so much ferocity in it, uttered by a Black man to the past in a sci-fi series airing during the Black Lives Matter era. There is a kind of power in the promise that, for all the bullshit that those who hate you are willing to wield against you, there will come a time when the future will no longer condone them.

Like a lot of television moments, that ferocity that makes it special is difficult to transpose to our reality. In the real-world 2016 when the show was made, for all that the world has been better than the 1937 of that fictional timeline, the pendulum was working its damnedest to swing the other way. Donald Trump would be elected the following month, and with it would follow an ocean of disinformation, an uptick in racist violence, and a conspiratorial rhetoric that would culminate in thousands of Americans storming the United States Capitol at the end of the next election season in the hopes that they could prevent Trump from losing the Presidency.

In the years since the show has come off the air, not only has the movement for the safety of Black people continued against a countering tide of pro-police apologetics and racial division on social media, but it's been joined by so many other movements for justice clashing against similarly seemingly unending walls of suffering. *Timeless* came out months after the results of the first Brexit referendum, a year before the Harvey Weinstein allegations recatalysed the

#MeToo movement in public consciousness, years before multiple migrant crises and their resulting hypernationalist responses in multiple territories. The show about time is simultaneously too new and too old to have been able to reckon with some of the hostilities that persist anew in our present.

On the evening of the Rittenhouse verdict, Rabbi Danya Ruttenberg shared Aurora Levins Morales' 'V'ahavta' via a Twitter post. Published on Morales' website in July of 2016 (coincidentally, months before *Timeless'* first episode), its bombshell of a first stanza reads:

Say these words when you lie down and when you rise up,

when you go out and when you return. In times of mourning

and in times of joy. Inscribe them on your doorposts,

embroider them on your garments, tattoo them on your shoulders,

teach them to your children, your neighbors, your enemies,

recite them in your sleep, here in the cruel shadow of empire:

Another world is possible.

It is a radical thought in its poetic simplicity, as tempting as it is taunting as it is teaching. The world we live in is volatile, with every future struggling against each other to survive as a present. We can just... pick one. Barring the energy of a very powerful time machine, it requires the effort of countless people willing to hold the minute hand of time and wind it until it reads justice.

Perhaps that means something for men like Kyle Rittenhouse as well, simultaneously a beneficiary and a servant to the qualities of injustice that are part of the American institution. In an interview on Fox News' *Tucker Carlson Tonight*, Rittenhouse told the story of spending over eighty days in uncomfortable prison conditions while his legal counsel attempted to exploit the situation for his own gain, agreeing that "there needs to be change" in the system.

He isn't wrong. The structure as it stands exists in large part to propagate itself, ensure it keeps its tools and its capital, and prop up its agents and its heirs. Those who experience the same brokenness he did often suffer far worse fates, either languishing on death row for crimes they hadn't committed, or worse, being killed on the scene for the crime of being Black in the wrong place at the wrong time.

And we can do something about that. Imagine it.

'The Day Reagan Was Shot' is an episode intensely involved in the question of fighting death, more so than any other episode in *Timeless*. It is the premise of the series in microcosm—if Rittenhouse takes this life in the past, the future changes for the worse—but that future is whether this crew of time-travelers gathers at all to stop Rittenhouse in the first place.

When Garcia Flynn, a semi-good-guy at this point in the plot, hears Agent Christopher confess that she actually knows that *she's* the target and can't do anything about it, he gets livid. He fumes at her that on what may be her final moments before she—her marriage, her children, the mission to save time itself—may stop existing, she takes that time doing paperwork.

When she asks him why he's so upset about her decisions, he mentions his daughter. How, on the night that Rittenhouse agents came to kill her and his wife to send a message to him, she had asked to stay up and watch television. How he did what he thought a good father did at the time, tell her to go to bed, tell her that when she wakes up, he will still be there. And then he never saw her again. How every trip he took through time was in the hopes that he can come back home and learn it never happened. How he replays in his mind the desire to have given his daughter ten more minutes that night. He insists with all of his literal anger that Christopher go home, kiss her wife, play games with her children, like that night is not promised.

Earlier in that same episode, Rufus and Jiya fight over a vision she had episodes prior. (The visions are a long story; suffice it to say that time travel comes with shenanigans). In it, Rufus is going to die. And he is obviously freaking out about the idea that he knows it will happen and that when it does, he will die a stranger to the timeline he is buried in, alone, afraid. He wants to spend the last moments of his life embracing their love before it ends. But Jiya declares that isn't enough. "We're problem solvers," she says. "We don't just give up. We find a way. We make more time."

Of course, this is the luxury of time travel, but it's a lofty sentiment all the same: that with the effort of our minds and our spirits, we can fight death and win. We can challenge the conspiracy of a history which says that our bodies have no worth. We can make more time. We can save those we love before they are lost, or when we can't, at least linger within the moments between our love and our tragedy.

Rufus is the only member of the crew to die in the line of their work.

It appears very late in the show, as the emotional reckoning at the end of the second season. While trying to save the woman he loves, no less, a Rittenhouse agent shoots him outside a saloon.

When it aired, I'm sure there was a lot of concern about the scene: about the inherent irony of the man with the most trepidation about time travel—about history—being murdered in that history, but also being mourned in a past where he would struggle were he born there. Of course, that irony is even more bittersweet: there is little difference, after all, between the present and the past.

As the rest of the team return to their bunker hideout, lick their wounds, and mourn in silence or in rage, there is a rush of wind from beside their time machine, and to its left is... another one. The exact same one, but newer, matte and scratched, but faster and smoother in its motion. Out of it steps Lucy Preston and Wyatt Logan, emerging from what seems to have been a hell of a journey, rugged and sure-eyed and determined. That future's Lucy looks in the eye of her counterpart, who a season ago struggled with the very notion of troubling the past, and says, "You guys wanna get Rufus back, or what?"

We never get to see that alternate Lucy and Wyatt's journey, that intermingling of these heroes' future and the histories they've undone, or what is wrought from their effort. But we get to hear them say that part of that effort is the act of saving—restoring—a Black man's life. Of snatching it from the grave. Of rebelling against the structures that would take his life and forget about it, and taking the gun out of the minute hands of the clock.

Imagine the luxury of such power. Going back to the night that M&P15 fired and preventing a loss of life. Going back to the night that a teenager said he wished he could "start shooting rounds" at strangers in a time of turmoil and replacing the mood with compassion. Going back to the day an officer flinched in the presence of a Black man—pick any one of them—and defusing that situation before it draws blood.

We don't need metal and batteries bound together in machinery to bend time for it to happen. We only need the will of more people willing to stand up and confront Rittenhouse, be it a child or a conspiracy. Whether they be deliberate enemies or unwitting operatives. Whether the gun is a gift from a friend or handed to them by the state.

We find a way. We make more time. Another future is possible. I hope you see it all.

STRANGER THINGS 4 AND DISABILITY

BY CHLOE SMITH

THE LATEST IN THE POPULAR NETFLIX FRANCHISE DELIGHTS, BUT SOME FAN'S REACTIONS TO ONE CHARACTER'S FATE ARE ABLEIST, AND WE NEED TO TALK ABOUT IT

TW: ableist comments

Stranger Things Season 4 (Netflix, 2022) is a whirlwind of death, mystery, and music—and in Robin and Steve's case, talking about boobies. Just kidding, they get up to more than that, although that scene is everywhere online, so it's certainly a memorable part of the series for some.

Split into two parts, or volumes, and multiple plotlines, the series certainly packs a punch. And a couple of murders. And rescue from Russia—and of course, lots of D&D, thanks to the new outcast, fan favorite, and murder suspect, Eddie Munson.

To be honest, I think the series would have benefited by not being split into two parts and either dropping all at once or one episode landing on Netflix every week. It definitely lost its momentum with its fans and on social media in between the volumes.

And, while the series' predictability with what happens in terms of characters dying isn't terrible—it's understandable, given how strong the main cast is. Of anyone is going to die, we hope it's not them. It's also disappointing that so many great characters are bought in every season and become beloved fan favorites, only to then meet a grisly end, ultimately leaving the same fans who loved them heartbroken.

Eddie Munson is the most recent example, but there's also Alexei, Bob, and even Barb. But does that make those characters' sacrifices okay when the alternative is Hopper, Dustin, Lucas, Joyce, or Robin dying? I guess, but it's definitely a negative marker against the series when we know to try and not get attached to new characters (even if it's usually impossible).

However, this series' strong point definitely lies in the music—with Max's iconic escape from the clutches of Vecna set to Kate Bush's 'Running Up That Hill' being nothing short of amazing. Not only is it an incredibly emotional and tense scene that adds so much depth to Max's depression and grieving—it's also cinematically incredible and historically significant. Why the latter? Before this series of Stranger Things, Kate Bush only had one number one in the UK—'Wuthering Heights,' in 1978—but that scene alone earned Kate Bush her second UK number one ever, with 'Running Up That Hill.' It also got to number one in a couple of other countries, all thanks to Stranger Things.

Speaking of Vecna—it can definitely be said that not every character escaped 'Stranger Things' series four entirely unscathed.

One character in particular who faced the wrath of Vecna was Max (played by Sadie Sink). In Volume 2 of series 4, Max was even killed after Vecna broke her limbs and blinded her—until she was thankfully revived by El. The last we saw of Max, she was in a coma in a hospital bed. El then enters her mind and is then seen alone, in the dark, and screaming for Max.

It's not the most hopeful ending, given that it seems that Max is currently without her soul—but she's not dead, and there's a very real possibility that she could be back fighting amongst her friends in series 5—so while they might be concerned, fans shouldn't be too upset, right?

Unfortunately, I've only had to look at the comments on a few Tiktoks that have come up on my FYP to see horribly ableist comments about Max, and her fate. And I wasn't the only one to have to see them, either:

Some said that there was no point in Max even coming back in the next—and last, series since the possibility that she could return blind or visually impaired, or even physically disabled would 'ruin' the character. Others said that she would be better off dead than 'broken' and she should be killed off.

Even if they are upset about their favorite character being in peril, there's never any excuse for ableism. Some of the commenters didn't even seem to be upset —they just stated their ableism as if it was a fact.

This way of thinking is incredibly harmful and just incorrect. Any disability, but particularly the ones that Max might have in the next series, doesn't 'ruin' a person or a fictional character and certainly doesn't leave them 'broken.'

Disabled people are powerful and strong—especially given the discrimination and ableism they have to face daily, and it would be incredible for a show as popular as *Stranger Things* to have another disabled character in its main cast, kicking ass and saving the day with their friends—and just being strong and human and happy when the fight is over because Max deserves to be happy, too! I, for one, would love to see the incredibly powerful disabled duo that Max and Dustin would be!

Not that disabled characters should exist to educate others, but it might just help get rid of the disgusting ableist opinions that exist in the *Stranger Things* fan community if they see a strong and happy and openly disabled Max after the events of Season 4. Not that they would deserve her. (Just as they don't deserve Dustin if they hold these ableist opinions in the first place!)

At the end of the day, who knows what Max's fate will be? But until we do know, some fans of the show certainly need to tackle their ableism, and soon —after all, it's 2022, people, even if the show is set in the '80s.

LIGHTYEAR IS THE PRIDE MOVIE WE DIDN'T KNOW WE NEEDED: PIXAR'S LATEST TOY STORY SPINOFF CHANNELS PULP SCIFI WHILE TAKING DOWN TOXIC MASCULINITY

BY HOLLY LYN WALRATH

Toy Story (1995) is the queen piece in Pixar's long history of stellar animated films, as well as the first movie from the beloved animated studio. The original film was very meta—even down to having its spacesuit-wearing, laser-toting co-hero at one point discover that he is, indeed, just a toy.

Lightyear (2022) is no different. The opening lines read, "In 1995, a boy named Andy got a Buzz Lightyear toy for his birthday. It was from his favorite movie. This is that movie." Lightyear follows Buzz and his best friend, Alisha Hawthorne (new to this movie and voiced by Uzo Aduba), as they are marooned on a planet in uncharted space. As space rangers, their job is to protect the universe by traveling to investigate new life on planets.

Instead, they are trapped on a tentacle-vine-infested planet when their ship's hyperspeed crystallic fusion fuel cell is damaged. The group of intrepid space rangers plants roots and awakens their cryo-sleeping scientists to create a colony and try to re-engineer their fuel in just one year.

Buzz is the first test pilot, because of course he is. In this film, we get the full brunt of the negative side of Buzz's hyper-independent personality. He self-narrates everything, keeping meticulous logs that no one reads, but that seems to serve as a way of keeping himself company and focusing on how important he is. He hates rookies, doesn't work well with anyone other than his best friend Alisha, and is so hell-bent on telling himself "I can do it" that he never stops to think, "I need help." It is this toxic machismo personality that causes the ship's fuel to be damaged.

In order to test the hyperspeed fuel, they decide to slingshot Buzz's ship around the sun. The film plays off one of the most interesting tropes in science and in scifi—the slingshot maneuver. In space science, this is when the orbit of the sun is used to speed up a spacecraft. The slingshot also appears frequently as a method of time travel in scifi media—including in Star Trek. As McCoy says, "A slingshot around the sun, you pick up enough speed, you're in time warp. If you don't—you're fried."

The scene of Buzz's first test flight reminded me strongly of the fantastic and harrowing film *First Man* (2018), in which Ryan Gosling plays Neil Armstrong. The film chronicles not only Armstrong's missions to the moon but also the difficult realities of balancing being an astronaut with the grief of loss (Armstrong's daughter died at age two of a brain tumor). Both films portray space travel not as cool and exciting but terrifying. They also touch on the idea that astronauts have to be highly intelligent and accomplished and, as a result, end up lonely. They are the only people on this planet to have experienced being in space and the terror of not knowing if they will come back.

I was also getting a lot of pulp scifi vibes. The opening scene, where they are exploring the new planet, is very old-school. There is even something about the color palette of the animation in this scene that channels pulp mags with gold and green tones. The film places Buzz in the role most scifi media places men—as adventurers, explorers, and lone heroes who have to think fast against a hostile planet.

Buzz ends up time-traveling in his failed test spaceflight to return four years later. He finds that his friend Alisha is now engaged (to a woman) and the colony has moved on from the idea of escaping. They have put down roots, but Buzz is too focused on the mission to realize what that means

There's a fantastic moment of recognition on Buzz's face when he realizes that his best friend is not only queer, but she has also moved past their relationship. They are platonic friends—but there is still a loss of that closeness that naturally occurs when one friend finds true love. I also interpreted this moment as Buzz realizing that he needs to support his friend—even though he might be surprised by her queerness.

Buzz insists on more test flights. As he returns over and over again, his best friend marries, ages, and has a child, then a grandchild. Inevitably, she dies while Buzz is gone on one of his flights. It is this last flight that does the program in—without Alisha, there is no one to approve Buzz's obsessive need to prove himself. The program is scrapped, and they even try to take away Buzz's therapy cat Sox, a gift from Alisha.

But that's not going to stop Buzz Lightyear, right? So he pushes on, eventually returning over twenty years later this time, but successfully testing the fuel necessary for interplanetary travel.

Of course, it's too late. When he returns, he finds the colony en-bubbled in lasers, trapped by evil robots from the evil Emperor Zurg. He also meets Alisha's granddaughter, Izzy (Keke Palmer), and a rag-tag group of Junior rangers, who eventually help Buzz overthrow Zurg and save the colony.

Over and over again, Buzz makes decisions motivated by toxic masculinity. Instead of motivating the others, he ends up making them feel bad about their mistakes. Instead of taking the time to teach them, he pushes them into situations they aren't ready for, and it ends up a disaster. The film forces Buzz to come to terms with his own self-centered, hyper-focused mindset, a mindset all too common in the United States. Shoot first, ask questions later. Other people will only slow you down. *Feeeeelings, ewww.*

Very Spoiler-y Parts Ahead.

Queer Representation Saves the Universe

I was delighted with how Lightyear maneuvers Buzz into change. One aspect of this is Alisha and Izzy. Alisha is a black woman in a queer biracial relationship. Buzz Lightyear represents cis straight white male privilege, and thus, he should be outraged at his best friend coming out. But for years, she has been the only emotional point of contact for Buzz. She is his only friend. He has no choice but to accept and love her.

The second key point of Buzz's transformation is the reveal that the evil emperor Zurg is actually Buzz himself—from a different timeline. Buzz has literally been fighting himself the entire film, and even the Big Bad is actually himself, too.

There is a moment in the film where Izzy tells Buzz that he's thinking about it all wrong. He's convinced that Alisha's life is wasted because she never got to be a space ranger again. But Izzy tells him to stop thinking about it that way—her grandmother's life mattered. She had a full and happy life. Buzz realizes that although *he* wasn't the center of Alisha's life, she still mattered.

The realization that queer and black lives matter is what the entire film hinges on. When Zurg wants to go back and change the timeline, Buzz realizes this would erase Izzy from time. Given the importance the film places on insisting that even a life lead quietly matters, is it any surprise that this film has seen so much vitriol from the far-right?

How central the film made the queer romance to the plot surprised and delighted me. There have been thousands of people online claiming that "it's a two-second kiss" and implying it doesn't matter. But Alisha's queer love literally saves the day.

It even occurred to me that if Buzz had been around, he might've become a surrogate Granddad to Izzy (not to speculate too much on the technology of reproduction in a Pixar universe, but let's assume it works the same way it does here on Earth).

The third and cutest change-maker in Buzz's new life is Sox, his robot cat. Sox is meant to help him adjust to life back on the base. He ends up being pivotal to both the plot and Buzz's emotional growth. This is contrasted by Zurg's squashing of Nega-Sox and killing him. Zurg is so obsessed by his mission that he ends up becoming a villain. Buzz realizes that if he doesn't change, he'll become his worst nightmare. (And if killing a cat doesn't change you, what will?)

The Backlash to this Film Is Proof that Change Is Necessary

It was strange watching this film as a queer person who grew up in the 90s. When the opening lines ran across the screen, I couldn't help but feel uncomfortable. The truth is, a film like this would never have been made in the 90s. My discomfort came from knowing that I would be in a theatre full of people accustomed to mainstream media, but not accustomed to it having such a positive queer story.

That queer story almost didn't exist. In March of 2022, LGBTQIA+ employees of Pixar wrote an internal statement against Disney, stating that they had repeatedly censored queer stories. "We at Pixar have personally witnessed beautiful stories, full of diverse characters, come back from Disney corporate reviews shaved down to crumbs of what they once were. Even if creating LGBTQIA+ content was the answer to fixing the discriminatory legislation in the world, we are being barred from creating it" (Variety).

It was revealed that Disney had attempted to censor the "kiss scene" from Lightyear, a scene between two characters that is pivotal to the plot and to its hero's character development.

We are in a moment in time where corporations have more power than people in enacting anti-discriminatory change. Disney has been under fire on multiple fronts—for first donating to Republican sponsors of Florida's "Don't Say Gay" bill, then refusing to denounce the bill, and then flip-flopping under public pressure, not to mention refusing to pay writers who had their book rights acquired by them, and for censoring what character performers can and can't say.

The fervor over *Lightyear* is so heated that most on the far right won't bother to see the movie. My mom (who totally missed the kiss because she was so wrapped up in the movie) mentioned to me that her Baptist pastor was railing against the movie because it had a "boy-boy" kiss. This just further illustrated to me the homophobia of conservativism—that he had to change it to two men kissing because two women might be too tame. (I have repeatedly told my mother to change churches, but that's a whole other can of beans, y'all.)

Ultimately, I think Lightyear was made for people like myself, 90s kids who grew up aching for more representation, and that's why there is so much backlash. We are in a moment where the mainstream is colliding with queer culture in new ways. Whereas queer people have to sit with the discomfort that a larger acceptance of queerness means queer culture will be far more "out" than we may be used to, it also means straight people sitting with a narrative that may not fulfill their own representation.

Lightyear is a fun, action-packed, kid-friendly film with lots of heart and laughs. My two nieces loved it and were unfazed by the kiss scene. Through shifting Buzz Lightyear from a toxic, self-centered, overly independent dude bro to a kind, friend-focused, and team-working member of a diverse crew, *Lightyear* shows that change is possible. And although this ends up centering the emotional struggles of men, I think it is still a story we need.

Because change doesn't happen without help. And we need all the help we can get.

MOON KNIGHT AND THE IMPORTANCE OF BEING SEEN: MARVEL'S MOON KNIGHT DEPICTS CONTEMPORARY EGYPT IN A REAL, LIVING WAY

BY MAHMUD EL SAYED

The Arabic word for superhero is superhero. Actually, no, it's *suberhero*—because there are no p's in Arabic. Marvel's *Moon Knight* (*Disney+,* 2022) was not a show that was particularly on my radar. I didn't read the comics. I wasn't especially curious to see what a superhero with dissociative identity disorder would be like. I felt no particular affinity for Moon Knight (or Steven Grant or Marc Spector or Jake Lockley) even if I was curious to see Oscar Isaac's portrayal (Who doesn't love Oscar Isaac?). I didn't anxiously await the series premiere or worry about how they were going to portray Khonsu—a real actor or CGI?. However, and in a way that's hard to describe, *Moon Knight* is the show that I've been waiting for all my life.

Identity is a funny old thing. It's not static. It's an ever-changing constellation of shifting features, and each one can always be boiled down and reduced further and further. To borrow a line from Walt Whitman, we contain multitudes. So, I'm Arab, I'm Muslim, I'm Egyptian, I'm British, I'm Turkish Cypriot. Is that it? I'm a guy, I'm straight, I'm a Londoner, I'm confused as to whether I'm Working or Middle Class. No, wait, still not finished. I'm a reader, I'm a writer, I'm a Man Utd fan. Is there more? Should I talk about my family? My friends? My cats? Should I clarify exactly what kind of Muslim I am? Where in Egypt my family is from? Where in London do I live?

For most of my life, there were large parts of my identity that never saw a positive reflection in popular media. When I was growing up, the only Arabs and Muslims I saw in film or TV were ranting terrorists (*True Lies*) and that was before 9/11. Afterward, things only got much, much, worse (*24*, I'm looking at you). Arab and Muslim good guys were few and far between. The best we could hope for was to be the "good guy" Muslim who joins the hero to fight against all the 'bad guy" Muslims, which is to say, everyone else (*The Siege* and a slew of American procedurals from *NCIS* to *Homeland).*

Alternatively, we could aspire to "moral complexity." Sayyid from *Lost* is a good example of this. So, not the hero, but not the villain either. Yet still tainted with an underlying *otherness*—dangerous and with a propensity for violence ("I'm a torshurur." OK Sayyid, we get it!). Moreover, despite his complex portrayal of an ex-Iraqi Republican Guardsman, Naveen Andrews is neither Arab nor Muslim. So, even when we were portrayed somewhat positively, it was not by ourselves but by others.

The same thing happened a few years earlier in *The Mummy*, which features a heroic Bedouin character played by an Israeli actor (Oded Fehr). Even the native comedy sidekick part was played by a non-Arab, Iranian-British actor and comedian Omid Djalili who made a Hollywood career out of playing Arab scumbags (*Gladiator*, *Spy Games*).

Skip forward more than twenty years and not much had changed. A large portion of *Wonder Woman 1984* was set in Egypt, except this was an Egypt that only ever existed in media—not a simulation, a simulacra. One of the minor antagonists in the film is Emir Said Bin Abydos, dubbed the "new king of crude." He dresses like Peter O'Toole in *Lawrence of Arabia* and his major aim is to restore his "ancestral homeland" in Cairo. Needless to say, none of this is authentic. In case you were wondering, no, it's not likely that an Egyptian "Sheikh" would be selling oil to the Saudis or that a Bedouin tribal leader would or could have any claim on Cairo, whose settlement can be traced back more than 3,000 years to the Early Dynastic Period. The only positive, if you can even call it that, is that this character is played by Amr Waked, an actual Egyptian actor.

And then comes *Moon Knight* to save the day. It eschews problematic Orientalist tropes and depicts the real living and breathing contemporary Egypt. I admit, at first I was worried. Episode Two ends with Steven Grant (or should that be Marc Spector?) waking up in a strange apartment. The camera swoops past billowing curtains while Orientalist music swells—The Pyramids of Giza are framed against the horizon. Cut to black. Ugh, I thought to myself, not all this again. And then the intro to Ahmed Saad's *El Melouk* (The Kings) drops, modern beats replacing that orientalist swill, and the distinctive timbre of Egyptian rapper 3enba (pronounced Aenaba) hits you like a gut punch.

Ana mish shayef fiykum had / Into ayal aisheen aal hak.

Y'all are nothing special/ You're just some kids living on the chase.

Now, this is the real Egypt, I thought. Finally, an authentic depiction and one that almost never sees the light of day in western media. The above is not a perfect translation by the way. Arabic is a diglossia which means there is a formal written form of the language and an informal spoken one. *El Melouk* is the sound of the Egyptian street. As it played out over the credits of Episode Two, I dared to hope.

Moon Knight's third episode made a believer out of me. The first scene depicts Layla El-Faouly (played wonderfully by Palestinian-Egyptian actress May Calamawy) holding the distinctive green Egyptian passport in her hand. I have a passport like that, I thought to myself. Cut to the Marvel logo, but instead of that familiar sweeping orchestral theme, it's a remix of Warda's *Betwanes Beek* ("You're Always With Me"). This is the Egypt of *Mahragannat*. The Egypt of protest songs and Arab Springs.

Moon Knight director Mohamed Diab (yes, an actual real Egyptian) is even confident enough to play with the stereotypes. So, yes, we get the Arab street toughs twirling their knives theatrically, only these ones are dressed in knock-off Versace. Later on, Oscar Isaac dramatically jumps out of a taxi to chase after said youths. He is inevitably pursued by the Egyptian taxi driver who understandably demands, "*Ya amm, feen floosi*?" ("Mate, what about my money?"). Running through a market, he knocks over a cyclist carrying a pallet of *baladi* bread and dodges around a three-wheeler *toktok*. I know what that bread tastes like. I've ridden in a rickshaw like that.

There's something special about seeing yourself in the media you consume. For many people, this is normal. It's every day. But if you are Arab or Muslim, you're more used to scanning the craggy faces of bearded terrorists (or rapists or comic-relief scum bags) and wondering, "Is that supposed to be me? Is this how other people see us?" That is why *Moon Knight* with its authentic portrayal by authentic actors was such a departure and such a treat.

For me, this feeling culminated in the season finale when Layla dons the mantle of the Scarlet Scarab. In the final battle, she saves a group of civilians fleeing in a microbus (a particularly Egyptian mode of public transport). A young girl she has just saved breathlessly asks, "*Enti suberhero Masriya*?" Are you an Egyptian superhero?

"I am," she confidently answers.

That's a scene I've been waiting to see my entire life. It's a scene that also completely erased many of the other criticisms I had of *Moon Knight* in general and its finale in particular. That is another vital aspect of representation. When you are represented, you are likely to feel a greater sense of ownership and empathy. So, will this change the way Arabs and Muslims are portrayed by the rest of the industry? Not likely. But it does give us a standard-bearer. An example to point to and say, "There. That is how good things can be. That is what we should be aiming for."

Now, how about that Scarlet Scarab spin-off?

INDIE QUEER COMEDY UNIDENTIFIED OBJECTS UNDERSTANDS INTERSECTIONALITY

BY HOLLY LYN WALRATH

HOW A FILM ABOUT A SEX WORKER AND A LITTLE PERSON ON A ROAD TRIP TO FIND ALIENS STOLE MY HEART

> "Only the language of dreams and fantasies can capture how I (and so many others in this melting pot world) feel. Immigrants and other outsiders share a liminal space together. Neither here nor there." —Juan Felipe Zuleta

Every once and a while, you come across a film that breaks you open in the best of ways, and for my trip to Fantastic Fest in Austin, that film was *Unidentified Objects* (Juan Felipe Zuleta, 2022).

The film follows the story of Peter (Matthew August Jeffers), a gay little person dealing with chronic pain and illness, as well as depression after the loss of a friend. When the not-your-average-girl-next-door Winona J, J for Jordan (Sarah Hay) convinces Peter to drive her to Canada, he knows her reasons are disingenuous but agrees to go out of economic necessity since he's struggled to find work lately.

Peter loves Anton Chekhov, which I'll forgive (I'm only kidding), and thinks of himself as intelligent, perhaps too intelligent for the world he's forced to be a part of. He's also cranky, unsentimental, realistic, and a delightful character to watch the talented Matthew August Jeffers bring to life on screen. This plays well against the starry-eyed, hopeful, and somewhat trashy-yet-loveable Winona, a sex worker who is convinced she has been abducted by aliens.

What follows is an unexpectedly heartbreaking road trip through the strange and magical.

As Peter encounters more and more bizarre phenomena, including manipulations of reality (or fantasies, depending on your interpretation), his character begins to open up both in mindset and emotion. Peter's daydreams become vivid magical realism sequences where he acts out his desires.

Colombian filmmaker & commercial director Juan Felipe Zuleta does a fantastic job managing the speculative elements of Unidentified Objects—which could be interpreted as metaphor (two outcasts find acceptance by identifying with non-human entities)—but the filmmaker chose to respect the genre and avoid the kind of bait and switch common in low-budget scifi films.

The result is a heartfelt, hilarious, and arresting exploration of intersecting identities in the face of a harsh world. Oh, and lots of beautiful shots with magical bisexual lighting and Rocky-Horror-esque costumes.

The film was created by a first-generation American immigrant and is one of the few films in history to feature a little person in the lead. It was also made by a diverse crew in the height of the pandemic.

The soundtrack perfectly mixes punk and space music and was created in collaboration with lead actress Sarah Hay. Queer musical icon Perfume Genious contributed songs to the film, as well as an analog synthesizer by Sebastian Zuleta. Indeed, every aspect of this indie film was a collaboration, from the writing to sound to cinematography.

In the screening I watched, the director emphasized the importance of highlighting diverse characters. "We were asking ourselves: What characters have we never seen as the lead in a movie? Whose lives need to be lived on the silver screen?"

Matthew August Jeffers, who says that he draws inspiration from actors like Peter Dinklage of Game of Thrones fame, gives absolutely bar-none one of the most nuanced and delightful performances of the year. One of my favorite scenes is when Peter explains himself to Winona as "a circle within a circle within a circle." It's a poignant way of describing intersectionality: As a gay man, and a little person, and a person with a disability, Peter's identity is a constant struggle to him. As the circles get closer and closer, it's easier to feel more and more removed.

Intersectionality asks us to look at multiple aspects of marginalization. Usually, it's described as a pyramid—the least marginalized people are at the top. But this image has always struck me as less fluid. Both Peter and Winona are characters struggling to come to grips with different levels of being an outcast. They are trapped in these circles of identity. As Juan Felipe Zuleta says, "Only the language of dreams and fantasies can capture how I (and so many others in this melting pot world) feel. Immigrants and other outsiders share a liminal space together. Neither here nor there."

Matthew August Jeffers was born with a form of dwarfism so rare that it was initially only referred to as “Matthew’s Disease.” Jeffers does not approach the character with kid gloves, and he was responsible for convincing the director to go the full distance with one of the key scenes in the movie, which I won’t spoil, but I will say it is an extremely vulnerable moment on screen.

“Aside from *Unidentified Objects*, every part I have played on stage and screen was written for a person of average height,” says Jeffers. “I’ve always had to go into the audition room and change a director’s mind about how they see a role. But this project marks a change for me and for all of us in the LP community. So I’m here with my shovel to try and pave the way for others as much as I can.”

I can say, Matthew, you succeeded.

This one made me smile to watch, and I hope it gets bigger distribution.

After world premiering at 2022 Inside Out, the film won awards this summer at Frameline and Outfest LBGTQ+ film festivals. Fantastic Fest 2022 marked its Texas premiere.

JOHN CARPENTER'S HALLOWEEN (1978): WATCHING HORROR UNFOLD

BY GRETCHEN ROCKWELL

HOW THE CLASSIC SLASHER USES POINT OF VIEW TO ENGAGE THE VIEWER

For a long time, I thought I was unable to watch horror movies—or at least, I could only bring myself to watch science fiction horror movies. This changed when, in the interest of seeing more of John Carpenter's filmography (after enjoying *The Thing* and *They Live*), I sat down to watch his 1978 horror classic *Halloween*.

I was apprehensive about watching it, knowing this film had spawned the "slasher" genre. The film establishes many elements that would become traditional in slashers: the first-person point of view shot, violence against irresponsible teenagers (particularly teen girls*), a mentally disturbed killer, a distinctive weapon, and a "Final Girl" who survives the film and defeats the killer.

Slashers get their name from their excessive and bloody violence. Blood and gore is difficult for me to see as it sticks with me, which is one of the reasons I avoided the genre and this film in particular for a very long time. *Halloween (1978)* was a pleasant surprise in this respect—nearly bloodless and full of dramatic tension rather than jump scares and gratuitous violence.

This is not to say that *Halloween* is non-violent—in fact, it is deliberately and precisely violent. *Halloween*'s central villain, The Shape (later more often associated with his name, Michael Myers), is "pure evil," according to Dr. Loomis. In the film, the kids watch Howard Hawks' *The Thing From Another World*, and it seems that is what The Shape is: a monster from its own dark and alien world, here to hunt and destroy us because of its own terrible reasons. His violence is established from the opening scenes where he murders his sister and is emphasized as he begins to stalk and murder Haddonfield's teenagers on "the night he came back," to quote the film's tagline.

Carpenter never shies away from showing us the violence on screen; victims are strangled, stabbed, and hunted, while Carpenter refuses to cut away from it. The scenes, particularly Annie's death where she is strangled in her car, are almost uncomfortably long. The camera lingers—pointedly—on these violent scenes, forcing the viewer to confront them as we encounter them. We are not allowed to look away.

Roger Ebert wrote that *Halloween (1978)* is terrifying because it "is a visceral experience—we aren't seeing the movie, we're having it happen to us." And yet, Carpenter uses the medium of film to emphasize sight and watching.

In a way, *Halloween (1978)* is all about the act of seeing. Loomis draws attention to this theme textually when he describes staring into a young Michael's dark "Devil's eyes," but the film also does this apart from the script. What we see, when we see it—all of this is tightly controlled and staged.

The film begins with a first-person point-of-view shot, making the viewer see through young Michael's eyes (a point of view only emphasized by the eyeholes once he puts on the clown mask). As the film continues, The Shape watches Tommy, Laurie, or another person as they go about their lives. To intensify the horror, Carpenter manipulates the fore- and backgrounds to carefully create a game of now-you-see-him, now-you-don't with The Shape—some examples being the hedge, the clothesline, outside Annie's house, and in the shadows through a door. The film's final shots are a series of empty places, showing where The Shape is unseen—though possibly present.

However, going beyond this focus on what the characters in the film seem, which the camera narrates for us, the film is also about what *we* see. The camera, which is not always a neutral observer, paints us as voyeuristic watchers no different than the film's villain. The Shape watches Laurie walk down the street; simultaneously, in this long, static shot, we watch him watching her. As much as The Shape peers into other people's lives, thoughts focused on the violence to come, we do the same by virtue of occasionally following his perspective, watching both him and the subjects of his gaze. The film uses the nature of film as a visual medium to question what it means to bear witness to something, as well as whose eyes we are really seeing through when we watch something.

By emphasizing the act of watching and seeing in the film, Carpenter adds a layer to it that implicates—perhaps even condemns—the viewer in the act of witnessing and being entertained by the violent and disturbing acts of the film. *Didn't you come to see people die in terrible ways, to watch The Shape commit horrible violence?* Carpenter asks. *Isn't that what you wanted to see?* And if we are being honest with ourselves, the answer is probably yes.

**In subsequent slasher films, this was tied to sexuality, with a virgin "Final Girl" outliving the other "promiscuous" (i.e., sexually active) teen girls; however, "punishing" the sexually active teenage girl does not seem to be a focus in Carpenter's Halloween (1978), at least to this viewer. The focus seems to be responsibility, instead, and paying the proper attention to the children in one's care.*

DREAM OF A THOUSAND CATS: THE POWER OF DREAMS CAN CHANGE THE WORLD

BY CHRISTINA SNG

A surprise entry as the opening half of Episode 11 in Netflix's TV adaptation of *The Sandman*, the wonderful animation *Dream of a Thousand Cats,* directed by Hisko Hulsing, thrilled viewers after an expected year-long wait for Season 2.

If *24/7* is the darkest story in *The Sandman*, certainly, *A Dream of a Thousand Cats* is the brightest. It isn't without sadness and suffering, but its ending, unlike *24/7*, is filled with hope.

A Dream of a Thousand Cats is my favorite *The Sandman* story from the graphic novels, beautifully illustrated in the book and perfectly animated in the TV series, retitled *Dream of a Thousand Cats.*

It is the story of a kitten who slips out of her home to join a secret gathering where a cat of renown, a purebred Blue-Point Siamese, tells a powerful tale with an important message.

It was past midnight. The house was locked up tight, but the kitten found a gap to escape through. She joined her friend, who waited for her, and together, they traveled to the place where a crowd gathered.

A Siamese cat stood on a pedestal, regarding the cats below, who watched her intently as she began her tale.

She once lived with a man and woman as their beloved pet, and believed she was free, safe, and loved by her human companions. But when she got pregnant by a tomcat and birthed a litter of kittens that were not purebred, her owners showed their true faces.

While the woman protested, the man forcibly took her kittens from her as she watched on helplessly. He put them in a sack and drove away in his car. When he arrived at the nearby river, he tied bricks to the sack and threw the sack in the water.

All this time, the Siamese cat felt what her kittens were going through. She felt their fear as the cold water surrounded them, felt them slipping away into the darkness until they were gone.

Grief-stricken by her loss and devastated by the betrayal of the humans she trusted, she slipped into dreams.

There, she found herself on a journey to find the Cat of Dreams. She asked him why the humans took her kittens from her. In response, the Cat of Dreams showed her a world where cats once ruled over humans.

In this world, cats towered over humans, hunted, and ate them for sport. Humans served them out of fear. Then one day, they rebelled and dreamed together of a better world. So many of them dreamed that they changed reality itself.

Overnight, cats became small and humans large, ruling over the felines as they do now. It was as if it had always been. Humans changed their entire history through their collective dream.

This meant, said the Siamese cat, that if enough cats dreamed, reality would reassert itself and return to how things were when cats ruled over humans. Perhaps, reality would change enough to bring her kittens back to her.

After her visit with the Cat of Dreams, she made it her mission to travel the world and convince cats to join in the dreaming.

Many of the cats at the gathering looked skeptical. But the kitten believed her.

In the morning, her humans found her sleeping soundly, certain she was dreaming. What was she dreaming about, they wondered?

The story ends there. It is unknown if the cats achieved their dream and the Siamese cat got her kittens back.

Regardless, the message is clear. If enough of us dream the same dream, we can turn it into reality. What a beautiful dream it would be.

MASCULINITY IN HORROR COMEDY: REVISITING VAMPIRE MOCKUMENTARY WHAT WE DO IN THE SHADOWS (2014)

BY GRACE KAMEYO GRIEGO

I have always loved horror movies. I find them to be incredibly entertaining and comforting in their formulaic design. When it comes down to its most basic rules, horror is all about building and releasing tension. This is also true of comedy. To best understand horror comedies and how they work, we must look to incongruity theory in comedy.

Incongruity theory suggests that "The basis of comic amusement is incongruity-the bringing together of disparate or contrasting ideas or concepts" (Carrol, 153). Interestingly, horror comedies also take monstrous forms of masculinity and transform them into sources of amusement for the audience. This is, after all, where the joy of horror comedies comes from: taking what is supposed to be scary and turning it into something humorous. Masculinity, being a societal concept that plays an important role in a significant number of popular media, is not exempt from being subverted for the purpose of humorous catharsis.

To see how both incongruity and masculinity at work, we can turn to the 2014 vampire mockumentary *What We Do in the Shadows.* This film follows four vampires who all share an apartment in New Zealand; Viago, Deacon, Vladislav, and Petyr. The audience watches as these vampires struggle to adjust to modern life. The typical horror genre vampire is a monster that is to be feared. Limpár says,

"Understanding that the monster signifies culture-related anxieties, and that the historical vampire monster relates to fears of colonization—a topic that fits into the discourse of power relations between the dominant and the suppressed—as well as to fears of female empowerment, it is easy to see the points of connection" (Limpár, 268).

As stated earlier, the typical vampire is a manifestation of cultural anxieties and depicts masculinity in crisis. The vampire exerts his power over his usually female victim by biting her and sucking her blood. The horror-comedy vampires, on the other hand, also represent masculinity in crisis, but instead, they do this by trying to live up to the horror vampires who were able to assert their masculinity over their victims. *What We Do in the Shadows,* vampires struggle to find their place in the modern world and often present as defanged vampires who lack the ability to inspire real fear, which causes the audience to laugh at them instead of scream.

Each of the vampires in *What We Do in the Shadows* is modeled after a popular vampire based in horror fiction or film. Vladislav was modeled after Dracula, who was "capable of transforming himself into a wolf, a bat or fog; he is scary, and although he comes from the backward East, he is intelligent, and is thus able to adapt to the challenges of the modern, Western world; he attacks mostly women, who find it impossible to resist him, as he can hypnotize his prey; he is able to turn his victim into a vampire, which in the context of Dracula, points to the aggressive process of colonization."

While Dracula was immensely powerful and able to be a source of terror, "all these fearsome manifestations of power are limited to the realm of nostalgic reminiscence, while the remnants of that power generate laughter instead of terror." (Limpár, 269). For example, while Dracula was able to transform himself into other creatures at will, Vladislav can only transform into a cat, but not fully, so his human face remains on a cat's body which is such an incongruous image that it inspires laughter from the audience, not fear.

Deacon is also based on Dracula, but specifically in his eroticism. The joke, of course, here is that Deacon is unable actually to impress or court any women throughout the film. An important aspect of this film is how it feminizes the vampires. Deacon, for example, "has not done the washing up for the past five years, as he does not think vampires do such things. Yet, the scene concludes with showing him wearing pink plastic gloves at the sink, washing up the dirty, blood-stained glasses, suggesting that even the rebellious ones become tamed." (Limpár, 272).

Viago resembles the high-society Lord Ruthven, the vampire figure at the center of John Polidori's 1819 short fiction work *The Vampyre,* and is also introduced early on as taking on a feminine role, which will get more into later, and in the first scene of the film is introduced, "as a neat-freak who is worried about the negligence of his flatmates." (Limpár, 272). We also see his status as effeminate and defanged when we see his attempt to bite his victim.

He hits the main artery in her neck, and her blood sprays out onto him and the couch. He worries about the mess he's made of the apartment and apologizes profusely to his roommates.

Lastly, we have Petyr, who "Obviously alludes to Count Orlok's character from the 1922 film Nosferatu—the count whose character is based on Dracula, but could not have his name for copyright reasons" (Limpár, 269), and is the oldest vampire in the household. Throughout the film, Petyr does not talk and does not abide by any of the rules of the house because of his respected age. He remains in his coffin in the basement, and Viago tends to his needs, like brushing his fangs. Interactions between Viago and Petyr like this, "Disclose that the more modern monsters find the ancient one scary, monstrous, that is, 'Other'—an idea that inherently carries the claim that the younger the vampire, the less monstrous he is." (Limpár, 270). We can see how this statement rings true as we look at the youngest vampire, Nick, who was turned into a vampire against Deacon, Viago, and Vladislav's wishes.

To better understand the masculinity of the recently turned character Nick, we must look at the young adult vampire series that had a chokehold on the monster romance genre for years; *Twilight.* Edward Cullen is a vampire who is portrayed as "Angelic and the semidivine as opposed to the traditional demonic" (Limpár, 272) in the movie series, despite his own insistence that he is a monster that the love interest, Bella, should stay away from. *Twilight* is unintentionally comedic in this aspect; whenever Edward is trying to convince Bella that he is a horrific monster who could kill her at any moment, he is also shown to be as ethereal and beautiful. For example, in the famous scene where Edward reveals why vampires don't go out in the light and shows Bella that his skin sparkles when hit by sunlight, she tells him that he is beautiful, and he scoffs and responds, "This is the skin of a killer, Bella" (Catherine Hardwicke, *Twilight*).

Limpár points out that the character and fantasy that Edward provides is most criticized through the newly turned vampire joining the gang, Nick. Basically, "Nick desperately wants to become a vampire because he is aware of the Twilight saga's gender-skewed popularity, and therefore he is convinced that becoming a vampire will make him irresistible to women who have fallen in love with Twilight's fictional sparkling undead" (Limpár, 273).

On a night out, Nick drunkenly insists to everyone around him that he's like Edward from *Twilight* but is met with blank stares and no flocking women. This is because in the vampire rules of *What We Do in the Shadows,* being a vampire is a lot less glamorous than in *Twilight.* Nick becomes extremely pale, but if he goes into the sun, he would burst into flames. He discovers, much to his dismay, that he cannot eat any human food like his beloved chips, or else he will get violently ill and throw up blood in a projectile manner. He realizes that it's hard to hold down a job and a social life when you can only go out when it is night. Ultimately, Nick does not end up with anyone and does not fulfill his *Twilight* fantasies.

There is a comedic yet heartwarming jab at Edward and Bella's relationship from *Twilight* that can be seen through the characters of Viago and the love of his life, Katherine. Viago is a very sweet vampire who likes to make sure everyone keeps the house clean and is doing their part to assimilate into human life and takes on a very domestic role in the household. Viago longs to be with his lover, Katherine, who moved on after he died. Instead of killing this new love interest and exerting possessiveness over her, unlike how Edward is extremely possessive of Bella, Viago steps aside and watches as Katherine lives happily with her husband. Now in the present of the mockumentary though, Katherine is a ninety-six-year-old woman and her husband has long since passed away.

At the end of the film, Viago does go to her and they rekindle their love. Viago turns her into a vampire and tells the audience that he does not care if people think he is a cradle robber, they are in love. Limpár points out that this visual image is not only comedic but "the visibly old image of the lady reminds an audience that extreme age difference is an extreme age difference even if its signs are concealed by magical rejuvenation, thus the ideal image of the Edward-Bella romance becomes damaged, too" (Limpár, 275).

This also subverts expectations of masculinity because no one calls Viago "gay" for longing after Katherine. The human-vampire romance has always had a level of predatoriness to it since the vampire is an ancient being who feasts on human blood, but since vampires are always portrayed as being young and beautiful in these romances, the age difference is something that is forgotten or excused. Showing this incompatibility in *What We Do in the Shadows* both points out the creepiness of the idealized Bella-Edward romance, but also puts "the beauty-fascination that defines Bella's view of the world," to shame. (Limpár, 275). Because while Bella is drawn to Edward's outward beauty, Viago loves Katherine despite her withered looks and instead loves her for who she is.

Works Cited

1. Carrol, Noél. "Horror and Humor ." *The Journal of Aesthetics and Art Criticism , Spring, 1999, Vol. 57, №2, Aesthetics and Popular Culture (Spring, 1999), Pp. 145–160*, 1999, https://www.jstor.org/stable/432309.
2. Limpár, Ildikó. "Masculinity, Visibility, and the Vampire Literary Tradition in What We Do in the Shadows." *Journal of the Fantastic in the Arts , 2018, Vol. 29, №2 (102) (2018), Pp. 266–288 Published by: International Association for the Fantastic in the Arts,*

2018, https://www.thefreelibrary.com/Masculinity%2c+Visibility%2c+and+the+Vampire+Literary+Tradition+in+What...-a0581865722.

3. Hardwicke, Catherine, director. *Twilight,* Summit Entertainment, 21 Nov. 2008.

FATHERHOOD, A PANDEMIC, RACISM, AND THE SILENT HERO: REVIEW OF ANIME THE DEER KING

BY HOLLY LYN WALRATH

> "Humans cannot see within their bodies…Bodies and souls are separate things."

The Deer King (鹿の王, Shika no Ou, from studio Production I.G) is directed by Masashi Ando (of *Princess Mononoke & Spirited Away) and Masayuki Miyaji (Fusé: Memoirs of the Hunter Girl).* The screenplay was adapted by Taku Kishimoto from a Japanese novel series by Nahoko Uehashi. *The Deer King* is a faithful adaptation of the novel series, despite being shorter and flourished with the usual anime conventions of heightened emotion and the occasional amusing insert character.

The lusciously animated film, which calls to mind some of the best Studio Ghibli films, follows Van (Shinichi Tsutsumi), a man who is in prison in the midst of a pandemic. When his jailers are killed by a mysterious magical pandemic that infects wild wolves (the Mittsual—Black Wolf Fever), he escapes only to discover a lone girl-child (Yuna, played by Hisui Kimura) left in a stove who has survived. Of course, in the process of escape, he himself is bitten but somehow is immune to the disease.

As a "medical fantasy," the film explores a pandemic that might feel all-too-familiar for US viewers. Given that the film is based on a 2014 book, the prescience is both fascinating and disturbing. The film itself was made during the COVID-19 outbreak and explores what a medical disaster would look like in a pre-technology fantasy world—complete with anti-vax propaganda, the importance of herd immunity, and a young doctor dedicated to spreading truth-based awareness.

The complex difference in this pandemic is that it seems to infect only the Zol people, while the Aquafese are safe. In an interesting exploration of power dynamics, the Aquafese were invaded by the Zol empire some decades before. This means that the Aquafese are marginalized by the Zols, who believe the Aquafese are responsible for the disease because of a curse.

Viewers might not be used to seeing racism depicted in an anime—let alone an anime set in a fantasy setting. These layers give real depth to *The Deer King,* challenging how we view anime as a genre.

The US has had a hard time accepting that pandemics are intersectional. They impact the young and the old, different races, different communities, health care professionals, and governing bodies in varying ways. By exploring these different topics, *The Deer King* promotes empathy for marginalized voices.

Nahoko Uehashi was an assistant professor at Kawamura Gakuen Women's University, where she specialized in studying Australian aborigines. Her novels incorporate cultural anthropology and, in the case of *The Deer King,* unique attention to medical details. Uehashi's work with aborigine cultures directly influences *The Deer King*'s central plot points.

In an acceptance speech for the Americal Library Association's 2020 Michael L Printz award, she explains, "...I'm very aware of the differences that occur when we come from different cultures."

"I want to write stories not just about people but about people who live within the vastness of nature. My work as a cultural anthropologist, the trips I took with my mother, and all the people, cultures and lifestyles I have encountered in the process have greatly influenced the stories I create." — Nahoko Uehashi

The novel contains a lot of exposition that would have been helpful to have in the film. While it's gorgeous and heart-rending, it's also confusing and difficult to follow at times. It feels like this film is just a drop in a bucket of world-building that has yet to be explored.

The film is full of dark, all-too-real depictions of the pandemic, but these are juxtaposed with lighter scenes of Van bonding with the Aquafese. Van is a silent hero without much dialogue, and it's interesting to see the "cranky muscles dude" trope explored in this setting. If this film were set in the US, Van would for sure be an anti-vaxxer. Instead, he is portrayed as heroic because he helps those on his route.

Van is a stoic man with a heart of gold, and like most depictions of this trope, it's hard not to love his interactions with little Yuna. Van's identity is central to the film as a former member of the Lone Horn—a kind of samurai group of warriors called "death soldiers" in the novel. The Lone horn are a metaphor for the samurai practice of seppuku or ritual suicide meant to preserve honor in the case of capture. They also ride the signature "deer" in the movie.

The most compelling character by far is the young doctor Hohsalle (Ryoma Takeuchi), who believes that "saving the body saves the soul." It's a heartfelt representation of doctors who underwent significant psychological stress and burnout during the pandemic in Japan.

The film shows the difference in how the Japanese government viewed pandemics: logically, calmly, and with care for those infected. Yet Japan was not without its anti-vax rhetoric and hesitancy—As the Japan Times notes, Japan has a history of unease with vaccines that dates back to the 1990s.

Across the globe, the pandemic may be on the way out, but its impacts will be felt for years to come. *The Deer King* is worth a watch for its beautiful management of the complexities we have all been dealing with for the last two years. It provides a global perspective on what often feels like a US-centric problem.

JESSICA JEMALEM GINTING'S POETIC VOYAGES: REVIEW OF VOYAGES BY JESSICA JEMALEM GINTING

BY JAMILEH ALEXANDRA

GRANNY'S DELICACIES

By Jessica Gemalem Ginting

A wolf could never eat my grandmother.

Granny pardons evil eyes with a smile

skins off bad meats with a tender grip

a knife that makes one sound, sluch

Granny invites miscreants over for tea

mushroom leaves to absorb the poison

honeys over the bitterness, yum

A wolf would turn into a pup in front of her.

Granny makes infants out of rowdy uncles

stubborn grandfathers, impish grandchildren

demons turn to cherubims, dinner time!

I wonder if she has a wolfish side to her.

Granny has little-known tastes,

never passes down any recipes only lessons

via spoon and fork and full bellies, ah

there is perhaps even a lesson, now

here, in this delicious stew we're all wolfing down.

This summer, Brandon O'Brien (*Can You Sign My Tentacle,* IFP 2021) waxed, well, poetic about the joys of devouring poetry; reading multiple collections in a day served in bite-size pamphlets, snackable chapbooks, a tapas feast of poems and poets. I've typically consumed poetry in family-size variety packs, anthologies that double as doorstops which drop a giant's ladle into the universe of poets and serve up disparate schools, styles, tones, and decades cheek by jowl, loosely linked by geography or theme. A giant Whitman's Sampler of poetry. All poems, for sure, but the coconut bites don't necessarily complement the molasses chews even though they are nestled side by side.

Voyages by Jessica Jemalem Ginting (*Bottlecap Press,* 2021) was my first taste of gulpable, single-voice poetry. Not only was it delicious, the title and concept evoked some of my favorite flavors, comforting notes of works I already know, but recombined by a new chef into a light intriguing meal.

Described as a collection that 'follows the earth and its inhabitants through various stages of transformation, where science turns into dreams, then into a themed party at the apocalypse,' *Voyages* takes you on a wondering, wandering journey via 22 poems grouped in three itineraries. When Ginting picks you up, you're carrying your shoes, gawping at a melon sherbet sunrise over an undisclosed fantasia; And she leaves you off with some skeptical angels broken down on a desert roadside. You all have stories to tell. The stops in between are sexy, poignant, fabulous (as in fables), and piquant as you jet-set from a Xanadu sister city, to a shore of the cosmos, to a nameless fabulist's messy, weeknight kitchen.

A PASTOR DRIVES THRU A MCDONALDS

By Jessica Gemalem Ginting

Whenever my grandfather donned that sharp pastor uniform

I knew that I was going to get McDonalds after school.

He did several sermons a month, though never in my church,

and did them during the weekdays, curiously.

The two of us sat in his grey Suzuki, long gone,

ordering from the McDonalds drive-thru.
It was at a rest stop with a cluster of other, exported
food joints, like Pizza Hut and Dunkin Donuts.
The cluster was responsible for the traffic, still nothing
compared to the mall that popped up a decade after.
Eventually, my grandfather stopped driving home.
Another McDonalds popped up behind my school.
Students got discounts if they showed up in uniform,
but really, I preferred the sate padang stalls outside.
My grandfather's been having trouble eating lately and
it's been a long time since he's donned his pastor uniform.
I've graduated from three schools and I still can't drive.
I'd really like to take him into a drive-thru one day.

It's when Ginting's texts intertwine the personal with an embodied fantastic that the flint sparks for me. "A Pastor Drives Thru A McDonalds" is my favorite poem in the collection—nostalgic, familiar, present, and a little embarrassed—but I've kept revisiting more than a third of them. "My Summer Barbie" is a fast-flaring, torch song, of a sonnet. I can feel the reluctant British sun on my skin in "London Summer II." "Eve," "Warm Blooded," and "Granny's Delicacies" round out my top tier, but the runner's up change position with each re-read.

Several of the poems tickle at big thoughts: gods, holiness, forgiveness, climate change. I am interested to see her develop, both on these themes and in her explorations of form. But don't think you'll be away from the "End Of The World Party At The Barbican" for long. Philosophical themes and imagined worlds included, this collection is wearing a party dress with graffitied Chuck Taylors and waving to you with a cocktail glass in each hand.

When you sit down to *Voyages*' three courses, wear what you like. My suggested pairings are a sunny window, a samba soundtrack, and a Bellini. *Voyages* by Jessica Jemalem Ginting is available now from *Bottlecap Press*.

(Poems reprinted with permission)

Jessica Jemalem Ginting is a poet, translator, editor and comic writer from Jakarta, currently residing in London, England. Her poetry has been published in Toho Journal, Chogwa Zine, The New Verse News, Bristol Poetry Anthology and Anak Sastra. She was the editor of the poetry and art zine, UTOPIA in 2020. Her debut poetry collection, Moon Petals, was published in 2017 at the Ubud Writer's and Reader's Festival. She is also the writer and creator of the original Indonesian superhero comic, ROSANA!

BELLE AND THE NATURE OF THE BEAST: REVIEW OF BELLE, AN ANIME BY MAMORU HOSODA

BY MAR VINCENT

As a girl, Suzu shares her love for music with her mother. After her mother dies rescuing another child from a flash flood, Suzu abandons music and becomes withdrawn. Now a high schooler, Suzu still struggles with the loss of her mother and the attendant loss of her ability to sing. In the virtual world of U, she takes on the persona of Bell (the meaning of Suzu in English) and, embracing the platform's offer of "another world, another life," finds her love of singing once again. She soon gains popularity among the other users, who begin calling her Belle (beautiful, in French). During a performance, she encounters the Beast (Ryu, or Dragon, in Japanese), an individual who uses virtual anonymity in order to sow chaos and destruction among other users. Bell is fascinated by the Beast and his cloak of bruises and sets out in U to understand him and, in the real world, to discover who he is.

The most recent film from acclaimed Studio Chizu and writer-director Mamoru Hosoda (*The Boy and the Beast*, *Mirai*), *Belle* (2021) uses the classic tale of Beauty and the Beast to reflect on the nuanced ways that real and virtual lives intersect, create, and define one another. In the virtual world of U, Suzu is able to escape the enduring pain of her mother's loss and feel free enough to sing; to embody the avatar of Bell thanks to the anonymity it offers. Meanwhile, the Beast's destructive actions call the attention of a virtual police force who are intent on unmasking him so that he can be held accountable for his actions. Suzu and her friends hunt for the Beast's real-world identity themselves, curious what makes him so aggressive in the virtual world. What dark secrets is he channeling into U, or hiding in reality?

Gorgeous animation showcases the best that both traditional and computer-generated anime has to offer in *Belle*, logically dividing the use of these different modes between the real and digital worlds our characters inhabit. Rural Japan is illustrated with lush, almost photorealistic backgrounds that evoke the *wabi-sabi* aesthetic of beauty in natural forms and imperfection, while U is a glossy, slick realm of recursive skyscrapers and fantastical avatars. Although our current types of social media aren't the fully interactive experience U is shown to be, this virtual world nonetheless serves as a visual metaphor for how we can immerse ourselves in our online lives to the point that we begin to perceive ourselves as entirely different people. And yet, despite the escapism this virtual world offers, it can't prevent the bleed-through of our real selves, and the real world we're trying to leave behind.

A notable aspect of U is that it takes characteristics of the individual user to create their virtual self—thus why the movie's Japanese title translates to *The Dragon and the Freckled Princess*: Suzu's natural freckles become part of her avatar's unique appearance. It's safe for our main characters to deduce that the Beast bears some mark in real life, physical or otherwise, that reflects the bruises so distinctively displayed on his cloak.

As Suzu and her friends delve into the mystery of the Beast's identity, the story veers away from the fairytale's explanation of the Beast's origins and motivations, and from the implication that Suzu's potential love interest, Shinobu, may be the Beast. These expectations are subverted for a more nuanced and pragmatic exploration of the pain of being unheard, unseen, and misunderstood. While the Beast of the fairytale is a beastly person before ever being transformed, *Belle* argues that behavior in U doesn't make the user a villain in real life; in fact, the Beast is lashing out in this virtual world against a different, and far more sinister, monster, because he has no recourse in reality.

The intended escapism of U helps Suzu to do much more than escape; with it, she is able to come to terms with the selfless act that cost her mother's life, to work past her grief and back into her love for music, and to find within herself the selflessness to reach out to the Beast. The emotionally affecting ending suggests that healing one's own wounds provides the strength to help others who may be hurting just as deeply. While it seems that Suzu has done more than enough by baring her soul to the Beast in a climactic performance as Bell, she knows that she needs to act in the real world, to help the real person behind the virtual identity, if the words she sings for him are to mean anything at all.

A fairytale that transposes fantasy into the realm of virtual reality, *Belle* offers a beautifully animated story full of heart and sincerity. Besides this, it offers its characters one thing that fantasy can't: the chance to make lasting change and human connections in the real world.

STARVED FOR MEANING: A REVIEW OF A BANQUET

BY LAURA DÍAZ DE ARCE

ART-HOUSE HORROR FILM "A BANQUET" BITES INTO RELIGION, GENERATIONAL TRAUMA, MATERNITY, AND EATING DISORDERS

A Spoiler-Free Appetizer

Directed by Ruth Paxton and written by Justin Bull, *A Banquet* (Hulu, 2022) is centered on the fraught relationship between Holly (Sienna Guillory) and her daughter Betsy (Jessica Alexander) after Betsy stops eating. Betsy is mute about her reasons at first until she begins to reveal that there is a spiritual purpose to her starvation, which seems only reinforced by the fact that she appears to maintain her weight. This strains Betsy's relationship with her sister, Isabelle (Ruby Stokes), her grandmother, June (Lindsay Duncan), and her boyfriend, Dominic (Kaine Zajaz).

The family grapples with their anger, discomfort, and disbelief at Betsy's actions and situation, but the film is primarily focused on the fraying maternal bond between Holly and Betsy.

There are some very good horror moments in the film as well as some wonderful cinematography, but the overuse of horror-themed music and uneven dialog undercut the potential of this film. Guillory and Alexander do a lot with what little they were given as far as scripting goes, but there are structural issues with *A Banquet* that even very good acting has difficulty disguising. A lot of the story is also overshadowed by heavy use of over edited-cuts and framing that those elements distract from the story and make it difficult to immerse oneself.

It's a good film for psychological, art-house horror film lovers or for people who might gravitate towards the subtle camp elements, but overall, *A*

Banquet has the potential for substance and some very delicious bits but is full of empty calories.

****Potential Spoilers Ahead****

To Say Grace

The religious iconography and framing in *A Banquet* is fitting when it comes to starvation because of its historical use. In Rudolph M. Bell's *Holy Anorexia*, he details how spirituality and anorexia are interconnected among medieval, Italian saints. In his examination of religious anorexia, he asserts their psychology to mean that "the suppression of physical urges and basic feelings —fatigue, sexual drive, hunger, pain—frees the body to achieve heroic feats and the soul to commune with God." (1)

In my experience, as an anorexic in recovery, I have sometimes commented on the way that past a certain point, starvation starts to feel meditative. Past the aching hunger, the headaches, the exhaustion, it narrows down to the person, their body, their emptiness. No wonder many religions have fasting as part of their rituals, or why starvation is iconographic of many saints and heroes. The interconnectedness between hunger, starvation, and spiritual connection is palpable.

We see Betsy go through that subtle change in the film. She goes from despondent teen to rebellious, to finally a sleeping, but mostly calm recluse. She appears more and more determined in her course and purpose up until the climax. Its that heightened spirituality innate in her mission for starvation that sets it apart from other depictions of the illness.

While food features prominently, we never see Betsy craving it or focusing on it with anything but disgust, which (refreshingly) feels closer to an honest depiction of the disorder than we've really seen before. It is blatantly read and understood to be unnatural, and utilizing this understanding adds to both ground the film in its premise and raise the horror element. This internal surrender to what she believes aligns her behavior in this historical context. As Bell quotes Pierre Janet:

"'[Euphoria] as it is known in the ecstatic saints, for instance, does away with the need of eating. Our hysterical anorexy is to be traced to much deeper sources than was supposed.'"(1)

That "euphoric" feeling, or a feeling of "zen" as I have described it isn't uncommon to those of us with eating disorders. And thus Betsy's starvation, even outside of the supernatural tones of the film which outwardly links her starvation to some otherworldly phenomenon, could just as easily feel spiritual. It is the fact that Betsy's starvation takes on a religious tonality, with her talking about an impending apocalypse, is ironically, the most grounded portion of the film.

It is striking how this modern retelling of sainthood follows the blueprints of Bell's own documented saints. Saints, who were often fairly middle-class young women whose starvation is met with anger, disbelief, and forced feedings, but (for most) ultimately died in their religious conviction.

The Meat and Gristle

One of the other (blessedly) well-done things about this film is that although it is preoccupied with Betsy's lack of eating, the film never peruses her body, or makes excuses to mark her thinness. It never makes her body as it is, the center of the conversation. Part of the tension is more that Betsy does not eat, but her continued state of weight stasis is a source of frustration and comfort for Holly. Her frustration that her daughter is seemingly killing herself in front of her, and the comfort that, for whatever reason, she is not losing weight.

That tension between mother and daughter, spiritual and profane, leaves a lot of room for interesting exploration. Unfortunately, this is undercut by what feels like a lack of character development all around, but Betsy in particular. Her starvation is the source of the conflict, but we don't see much of her personality before the ensuing events. We are co-witnesses to some early trauma, and we get a minor sense of her as a sad and pliable teenager, but little else.

It could be argued that this distance is meant to reinforce her ambiguity as either an antagonist or spiritual figure. Ultimately Betsy becomes a type of object of incongruity—a sleeping figure whose actions are at the whims of narratives ascribed to her character either as a teen who demands attention or who may be an ascetic.

The only real preceding scenes between Holly and Betsy have to do with trauma or the aftermath, by which point they are distanced. Having that lack of a firm, loving connection ahead of the ensuing events makes it difficult to be invested in their struggle, precisely because they have always been struggling. Instead, we can only grasp onto Holly as this neurotic, always-suffering mother and Betsy as a pastiche saint. It lacks emotional stakes as a consequence.

To add onto that critique, women suffering through mental health issues, especially things like anorexia, are already typically depicted as two-dimensional tragic figures. While both Holly and Betsy have clearly revealed mental issues, (as Holly angrily recounts her own institutionalization), they are so far into their roles as the suffering mother or saint, that whatever individual characterization exists is an incongruous distraction.

That's the risk with doing a film that relies this much on allegory, wherein the characters are less characters and more symbols engaging in dramatic pantomime. As an audience, it leaves us little to sink our teeth into, because they are no longer people we can empathize with, they are shallowed caricatures.

The Bitter and the Sweet

I wanted to like this film. It had a lot of the hallmarks of something that would draw my interest. The idea of a mother-daughter relationship being the center of a drama that involved body modification and horror was deeply intriguing. As a recovered anorexic, I wanted to see how they would measure the strain of it, how it would intertwine with the themes they wanted to play with. I was also concerned with how it might portray a young woman not-eating, imagery that has terribly valorized, and perhaps, hopefully critique it.

In a lot of ways, the film does rise and exceed those challenges. Its use of starvation as the central conflict is novel in its execution, and Holly, while not given the structure she deserves from the script, has hinted layers. Her evolution through the film is still fascinating to watch as she unravels.

Ultimately, the film is frustrating in its lack of investment with its own characters, becoming a starved parody of itself. It's uneven dialog that turns people into talking metaphors becomes frustrating, even more so in the heavy-handed editing. But it is still worth the watch for all of you who don't mind devouring something a little undercooked.

References

(1) Bell's work is still pretty relevant although it is a bit outdated*. Bell, R. M. (1987). *Holy Anorexia*. University of Chicago Press, 13.

(2) Bell, R. M. (1987). *Holy Anorexia*. University of Chicago Press, 12.

**You have no idea how much it pains me to call a work that is my age "outdated."*

THE MENU IS A HILARIOUS SATIRICAL TAKEDOWN OF RESTAURANT CULTURE

BY HOLLY LYN WALRATH

If you've never eaten at an avant-garde restaurant run by a Michelin quality chef, let me tell you the story of one I visited recently. Nestled in between a small winery and the local biker bar T-Bone Tom's in Kemah, Texas, is Eculent: An "experience" restaurant run by David Skinner that features upwards of 20+ courses over three hours.

There are certain weird hallmarks of such dining experiences. Diners are expecting to pay upwards of $400 or more per person, and if you have to ask how much it costs, you probably can't afford it. The restaurant I visited featured all kinds of obsessive gastronomic fare—from edible air to flavored cotton candy to soup balls that melt in your mouth. The interiors of such restaurants are often intimate, with maybe 5-7 tables maximum. A different wine is served with every course, and the bottles are as expensive as they are outrageous. And the chefs who run such establishments are often a bit deranged themselves. It's almost a badge of honor.

Now, there's nothing wrong with enjoying such a restaurant. But I thought it was a pleasurable, albeit absurd evening. Did I enjoy every precocious minute? You bet your shaved ice and caviar I did. Would I go back? Probably not for a long while, and especially not after seeing the dark comedy *The Menu* (2022), director Mark Mylod's latest film.

Ralph Fiennes plays Chef Slowik, a man who worked his way up in the restaurant industry to become one of the most elite chefs who lives and works on a private island serving up dinners at $1200 a head (ba-dum-cha).

When Margot (Anya Taylor-Joy) and Tyler (Nicholas Hoult) head to the island, the audience can assume they are a normal couple simply out on a very fancy date. But as we learn, for every diner on the island, everything is not as it seems. It quickly becomes clear that this experience is going to be one they won't live through. In short, it's as bloody as it is rare.

What follows is an absolute feast of satire. As the diners (and staff) are slowly picked off in a series of twists and turns, the filmmakers craft a satire that's as sharp as a knife, honing in on exquisitely bizarre details that only those familiar with restaurant culture will notice (or, you know, if you watch a lot of Iron Chef.)

Ralph Fiennes delivers a poignant performance as Chef Slowik, embuing what could be a pat villain character with subtlety and intensity that shines through as he delivers lines that take down the restaurant industry and its problematic culture. In one example, one of the cooks on his team admits that he came on to her and that when she refused, he didn't speak to her for months, forcing her to work in humiliation. In another example, the sous chef admits to hating his job (and his life) because he will never be as good as Chef Slowik.

Psychological warfare in the form of toasted tortillas and a breadless bread course makes this film tense and yet watchable—for every uncomfortable moment of terror is a moment of pure joy at the ridiculous machinations of Chef Slowik's terrible last meal.

At the screening I watched, the filmmakers were present for Q&A and remarked on Fiennes' intensity. "He wasn't only looking into my soul, he was looking into my unborn child's soul," one filmmaker remembers one of the actors saying.

The film is perfectly shot, perhaps because a three-star Michelin chef was consulted (Dominque Crenn, the only woman chef to earn such accolades), as well as food photographer David Gelb of the Netflix documentary *Chef's Table.*

As per usual, Anya Taylor-Joy is delightful as a young woman who catches the chef's eye because she "doesn't belong." She's not above all this; she's below it as someone from an average background who isn't wealthy. Our final girl delivers street smarts and the ability to truly understand the megalomaniac's mind. It's clear that the improvisation the actors put into the film makes this culinary gem far more appetizing.

I won't get into the plot too much, as it's better to come into this film without spoilers. But I will say that *The Menu* nails how over-the-top such restaurants can be and the people who frequent them. From the "regular" with a hidden past to the over-obsessed foodie fanboy, this movie understands the subject it destroys.

If you're looking for a horrifically tasty movie that will make you rethink how you look at smores and change the phrase "Taco Tuesday" forever, this is the film for you. Or you know, if you just want to watch a movie that's basically Voldemort running a restaurant from hell.

DO YOU KNOW WHAT IT MEANS TO MULTIVERSE NEW ORLEANS? REVIEW OF THE BALLAD OF PERILOUS GRAVES BY ALEX JENNINGS

BY JAMILEH ALEXANDRA

The Ballad of Perilous Graves by Alex Jennings (*Redhook*, June 2022) is a sprawling urban fantasy set in contemporary New Orleans. Eight characters intersect throughout the city, time, and other versions of NOLA in the haphazard style of a D&D campaign. They hunt and fight a tremendous magical power that is wreaking havoc on the New Orleans this troupe knows as their home reality. It is a highly imaginative, music-infested Mardi Gras parade of story tropes that constantly surprises and, unexpectedly, all work together. Like an over-decorated living room with wallpaper, sofas, chairs, and throws all in different animal prints that somehow whisks you away on a make-believe safari instead of inducing a headache.

I've never read anything like this. I've read all of the ingredients before but this is a new recipe. The story is a super cut of mashed-up themes and genres. The first protagonists we meet are a middle grades boy, his younger sister, and their neighborhood friend, so I buckled in for a YA adventure. Then some magic was introduced, and Perilous Graves' uncomfortable relationship with it pointed toward a chosen-one self-realization journey. Then, an important letter, a couple of missing relatives, and a fiend named Yakumo entered the chat, adding a mystery and a villain to the tab, while the children ran around the city on sky trolleys for a soupcon of Steam Punk. That's when the next chapters introduced a brand new protagonist, his sidekick, a different type of magic, and the diegetic songs. Like when half of Middle Earth rocks up at Bilbo's for dinner, and the dwarves kick off the singalong.

The spiraling plot continues to unfurl zombies, seers, a city of the dead, and specific transit to get there. Graffiti comes to life, the protagonist's quest for magical objects, or the magic in themselves, and then they must learn to use it. The 'veils' are thinning between all these versions of New Orleans, and it is causing an existential threat. Hmmm. Anyone seen Dr. Strange nearby? This list of themes and elements could have come from randomly pulling eight books off my fantasy shelf and reading the jackets. That it has all come from one brain into one cogent tale is the alchemy of great cooking, the making of terrific jambalaya. It is an impressive feat of literary genetic recombination, but is the result an evolution of form or a Franken-plot?

This book is worth any fantasy lover's time. It has vast scope and efficient world building. It is important to the canon for being set in a 'majority minority' city and community being the foundation of the protagonists' successes and strength. The leading characters are people of color, many speak African American Vernacular English (AAVE). One of the protagonists is trans, and his journey is not centered on his identity or transition. And it's a fantasy set in New Orleans without a single vampire! These choices feel deliberate but not forced; a reflection of contemporary reality, not a diversity exercise. And the book becomes subversive by its grace and comfort, reflecting America's current reality when race, gender, identity, and community values are so politicized and polarized.

I deeply admire the achievement of this novel but found it to be a challenging read. It landed at a difficult period when I only had snippets of time on any given day and limited mental bandwidth. It's no *The Fifth Season* (NK Jemisin), but at over 400 pages, it wasn't something I could knock out in a weekend. And with the multitude of characters and novel ideas (alongside the old tropes), when I couldn't read it for a few days, it wasn't easy to slip back into the world. If a chapter started in some new fragment of the multiverse or with yet another new character, I usually couldn't remember all the 'previously on *Perilous Graves*' details I might need to get my feet under me and run along with the narrative. Finally, what got sacrificed to character and plot complexity is the extra nerdy stuff that I really like to read in a fantasy story: What is the unifying system of magic? What are its rules and history? What is the taxonomy of magic users? Etc.

Read this book. It's important and fun. If you're a moderate-paced reader like me, maybe pick it up for a longer break—4 days to a week—and try to devour it all at once so the multiple threads stay vibrant between reading sessions. Take note of the theme of community that rumbles through the book as an unfailing bass line. I've never experienced that in any fantasy novel I've read before. You can feel it in your chest. My favorite detail in the book is the villains; they were a wild new concept to me, and I loved the commitment. Reading 'Yakumo' on the page made me grin every time. It felt like a loving inside joke. Specifically, a riff on the lyrics from the Dixie Cup's 'Iko Iko,' which is itself a combination of inventiveness and history, the twin fuels of this book. And, honestly, I have to stan any tale in which the heroes fortify themselves for a showdown with home-cooked chicken and waffles. Delicious!

The Ballad of Perilous Graves by Alex Jennings was released by Hachette in June 2022. It is available at your favorite bookseller or request it as a purchase for your library. Jock-a-mo fee na-né!

RESIDENT EVIL FALLS FLAT AND IS CANCELED ON NETFLIX

BY EMILY WAGNER

THE HIGHEST-GROSSING HORROR FRANCHISE ADAPTATION STRUGGLES TO ADAPT

The highest-grossing horror franchise, Resident Evil, has been around for nearly two decades and has dozens of adaptations, so it comes as little surprise that Netflix decided to cash in on the fandom. It recently released an eight-episode live-action series by the same name, and while some aspects hit the mark, others fall flat.

The series operates between two timelines, 2022 and a post-apocalyptic 2036. The main premise is the same as the game—the evil corporation, Umbrella, has manufactured the T-virus to manipulate the population. Umbrella knows it turns people into murderous zombies called Zeros, but so what—power is more important.

The show opens in the earlier timeline with twin sisters, Jade and Billie, arriving at their new home New Racoon City in South Africa, with their dad, Albert Wexler, who is in charge of manufacturing the T-virus. Wexler is the only character in the series that also appears in the games. The Netflix version deviates in that he is portrayed as a loving father. All the houses in New Racoon City look the same, plain white with garages and few trees or greenery to be seen. Jade lives up to her name and seems thoroughly jaded as she enters the home. She proceeds to criticize everything, despite the pretty posh modern interior. The complaining really takes the viewer out of the storyline. For instance, soon after Jade enters her new home, she declares that she'd rather be watching Zootopia porn. What?

The series takes on a high school soap opera vibe as Jade and Billie attend New Racoon high. Billie, once again, becomes the target of bullying, which seems like a really convenient plot device. Billie is a vegan and her bully, whom she met just minutes ago, brags about killing animals and eating them. Before you know it, the two girls are on the floor fighting while others cheer them on. Jade and Billie seem to have a decent relationship, with Jade wanting to help Billie stand up for herself, however, Jade's over-the-top behavior only leads to more trouble.

The 2036 plotline focuses on Jade trying to find a cure for the T-virus. She's on the run from Umbrella and is away from her young daughter and partner. It opens with her in a gritty, bombed-out city where she sends a rabbit outside her tent to find the zombies. Then there's a big earthquake, and a massive caterpillar comes out of the ground and throws Jade into a windshield. Remarkably, she doesn't suffer too many injuries, and even more remarkable, the caterpillar doesn't kill her. A group of "good Samaritans" rescues Jade, but turns out they really want to turn her in to Umbrella because she is on their most wanted list.

The plot then goes back and forth between time periods which makes it hard to follow and even harder to believe. For example, when the girls become increasingly suspicious of their father's behavior, they break in to Umbrella by conveniently disabling the facial recognition security by shining a bright light in the camera and using their father's recorded voice to gain entrance, where, conveniently again, there are no security guards. In the lab, the girls find their blood, which their dad takes from them regularly, and a rabid zombie dog, who escapes his pen and ultimately bites Billie. The girls learn there is a 48-hour timeline for the virus to kick in and make people turn into murderous zombies. Billie shows signs of turning but never does.

Billie and Jade are separated when the world goes to shit, and while Jade becomes an outlaw looking for a cure. When we meet Billie again, she's turned into a rage-filled villain who's heading Umbrella, a major plot hole. Why did Billie become so evil? Is it because she got bit? Also, the clones of Albert Wexler seemed to serve little purpose other than a lazy plot device.

In the end, the creators tried to cram way too much content into an eight-episode series. The time jumps are too jarring, and the plot holes left this viewer more confused than intrigued. If you're into gruesome zombie scenes, chainsaw men who dismember people for zombie food, and a genuinely terrifying mega gator, go for it. Otherwise, you'll have to suspend disbelief completely to go for this version of Resident Evil.

Plus, the show is not being renewed, so all the plot holes will remain empty.

Lance Reddick, who received accolades for his acting on the show, posted this on social media about the cancelation:

"As all of you are well aware by now, our show *Resident Evil* on Netflix has been canceled. And the haters and the trolls notwithstanding, I want to give a special thank you to all the fans who watched the show, got what we were doing, and really loved it because there are a hell of a lot of you."

Worry not, though, there's plenty of quality zombie, post-apocalypse fare still out there.

INDIE FILM THE ANTARES PARADOX IS A LOVE LETTER TO WOMEN IN STEM

BY HOLLY LYN WALRATH

A SCI-FI MOVIE THAT EXPLORES GRIEF, OBSESSION, AND EXTRATERRESTRIAL LIFE

Lately, I've been thinking about how much we lost during the pandemic. I feel that my emotional capacity to manage trauma has severely diminished. And there's really no looking back—we are at a moment where we can't change what has happened to the world. Most of us will never be the same, and that can be said of our advances in science, too.

A few years before the pandemic, I lost my father to Parkinson's disease. I had a very clinical view of it that upset my family. In his last months and years, my father lost his ability to speak. His cognitive function was severely impacted. To me, the father I had known was already gone. It seems very cold—but I felt like the only person who had accepted the reality of the situation. Being a logical person is often difficult because to those who live with their hearts on their sleeves, those of us who manage emotions in different ways seem like automatons.

We all manage grief differently, and there is no wrong way to deal with this emotion. I'm not even sure I would call it an emotion—more of a series of emotions strung together to form the phenomenon of grief.

During the pandemic, grief was multiplied by the fact that most people couldn't visit their sick or dying loved ones. Deathbed calls became the norm. An elderly neighbor of mine was unable to hold a funeral for her husband and fell into depression after losing her volunteer job, the only thing that got her out of the house. When my spouse's father died in 2021, we hadn't seen him in two years.

In this context of a world dealing with the grief of a two-year pandemic we're told is over comes the heartwrenching indie film *The Antares Paradox* (Onirikal Studio, 2022).

The film follows Alexandra (Andrea Trepat), a researcher at the made-up observatory of the Spanish arm of SETI (The Search for Extraterrestrial Intelligence). Alexandra is dedicated in her job as a scientist to discovering whether there is life beyond Earth, but the world is against her. Her fellow researchers mock the work she does. Her workplace is slowly losing funding. And even her coworkers are quitting. Not to mention that her family doesn't understand why she's so obsessed.

When Alexandra discovers a signal from space, she begins the involved multi-step process of verifying its origin and authenticity. This is the breakthrough she's been waiting for her entire professional life, and it becomes threatened over and over again by an incoming storm, her irate boss, and technical malfunctions.

The film does a fantastic job of maintaining tension throughout, with more and more escalating problems and conflicting choices Alexandra has to make. The audience is trapped with her, forced to think through her decision-making, and thus it creates an empathetic experience.

Alexandra learns that her father, sick in the hospital, is dying. She has to choose between going to see her father in his dying hour and finding out whether there is life on other planets.

It's summed up by a question Alexandra gets asked in an interview: If you could choose to either cure cancer or prove that there is extraterrestrial life, which would you choose?

This is a choice Alexandra is forced to make over and over again as the film progresses. Over and over again, we watch her choose science—and not just science, but the acceptance that there is a bigger world out there. That we are not alone.

Of course, when it comes to grief, there are no binary choices.

The Antares Paradox was filmed entirely in one room, the SETI observatory that the director created himself. It is an entirely self-funded film, produced, written, and directed by (Name), who works in special effects.

This one-room aspect of the film adds complex dimensionality to how it feels as a viewer. Despite being shot in closeup in a tiny space, the film never feels claustrophobic. In the screening I attended, the director Luis Tinoco explained that he shot the film himself. The director put his life savings into the film, which was shot entirely in one location for three weeks on a GH5 $300 camera. The casting was done in the director's hometown and was limited by cost. Despite these aspects of the film's creation, it absolutely does not feel like a low-budget film.

Luis Tinoco explains that he spent over ten hours of video calls with some of the best astronomers in Spain to ask them questions about their work. This research makes the film feel authentic and believable, even though there isn't truly a set protocol for Outerspace transmissions. The filmmaker had these astronomers send him screenshots of the software they use so it would feel real.

Everything in this movie is authentic—from the faux software that is based on real-life software to even the phone and video calls Alexandra receives. Actors in sound studios made these actual calls in real-time, which gives the leading actress the opportunity to truly embody this character. The director also explained that he had Andrea Trepat learn what every switch and button did on set so it would feel more authentic.

This is also a "real-time" movie. As the clock counts down for Alexandra to authenticate the signal coming from Outerspace, the clock in the SETI observatory literally counts down to the second. Most of this was special effects—the film contains 535 visual effects shots.

The Antares Paradox is a movie for creatives and obsessives, those of us who love our jobs but can't explain that love to our families. The director spoke about how, when it came to casting, he didn't care if the lead role went to a woman or a man. But to me, the fact that Alexandra is a woman adds another dimension to the character.

Women are often overlooked in STEM. Even beyond careers in science, women are told they are too dedicated to their professions—whether it be as lawyers, doctors, or creatives. It Is far less likely for a woman to be accepted for choosing work over family. This judgment comes from all sides—and Alexandra's struggle with it feels particularly fitting.

For me, the film was an emotional roller coaster. The night my father died, I was in Houston and couldn't make it to see him. We were in the middle of moving, and the moving van was coming in hours. I never felt guilt for this because I knew my father was already gone. The amount of judgment and criticism women get for how they react to grief is far too common. We are taught to be caretakers but never carers of our own grief and personal agency.

The Antares Paradox is a gut punch of a movie. I can only hope it gets brought to the big screen or streaming soon because it's one of the best movies I've seen in a really long time.

LADIES AND GENTLEMEN, THE ICE PIRATES: THE WHACKY STAR WARS KNOCK-OFF FROM THE 80S THIS AUTHOR HATE-WATCHED FOR FUN

BY ROBERT DEAN

Back in the day, *Star Wars* (1977) dropped like a cinematic nuke onto the public consciousness. People from the south side of Chicago to Shanghai wanted to be a Jedi. But, before *Star Wars*, anything space-related was seen as box office poison. Every space movie was corny, and they bombed. Who could blame any studio head for being like, "fuck that," when it came time to part with millions to make a movie about shooting lasers at aliens?

George Lucas strolls in and makes a masterpiece with glowing swords, Japanese cinema references, a space pirate, and his best friend, this man-dog thing. Throw in a couple of Jawas and a spunky princess who doesn't wear a bra, and the world loses its collective shit.

In its wake, every studio made a Dollar General knock-off flick. From *Dune* to *Masters of the Universe*, everyone wanted a space opera. And they're all terrible. There's an entire genre dedicated to bad space movies. They had racks of these things in the local video store, and they became late-night movies that Joe Bob Briggs would put on his show for stoned teenagers to laugh at while munching on Cool Ranch Doritos.

One of them was 1984's *Ice Pirates*, featuring Robert Urich, who you may know from *The Love Boat*. Angelica Houston is in a throwaway role as a side-kick, and Ron Pearlman is also here, looking like a young Tom Waits. Michael D. Roberts plays Roscoe, the second in command, who's a whiz with robots.

The movie opens up with a scroller from the Book of Lucas. Only this one is in Old English, complete with an English dude giving us the breakdown on how water is the most prized commodity in the galaxy, but you know, without any analysis of why it became that way. But there is jazzy 70's porn flick music.

We open up to the Ice Pirates, who look like "Yo Ho Long John Silver!" pirates with boots, swords, and shit. These costumes aren't practical. They've got poor Angelica Houston in what looks like a converted birdcage, while Jason, played by Urich, has his chest hair on full display. The pirates address their new crop of robots to serve as part of the crew. The robots look like they were built out of the aisles of Ace Hardware. It's critical to acknowledge how talented the minds from Industrial Light and Magic were because, dawg, these robots ain't it. One looks like a garbage can spray-painted gunmetal, and they were all sitting around looking at a tub of random shit, being like, "yeah, glue the phone to his neck," as they take a rip off some cheap weed.

They break into the ship they've been trailing. This ship has water. They cut the door open and get all pirate-like to a muppet-looking alien pinching a loaf. When the defenders of the ship get wind, they attack. These dudes are in chainmail with mustaches, *WTF? Like, what?* They're called the Templars of Mithra, and I guess they have a monopoly of all the water in the universe.

They're running around, looking for water, which we still don't know why it's so precious, to find a princess sleeping in some hyperbaric chamber. Jason rolls over, immediately gets creepy, and wants to wreck shop on a sleeping chick. The crew is like, "naw, dawg, we're here for water," and Jason makes a whole "rape and pillage" joke, which was not fucking weird.

An alarm goes off; a big space fight occurs, but everyone uses swords. And somehow, Ron Pearlman gets a hand chopped off and is all, "no biggie." My man grabs it off the floor like it's a souvenir. What kind of person doesn't freak out about losing a hand? We kind of need them.

So, the pirates break through to steal water. They're holding the crew at gunpoint, and what does Roscoe, the only black guy in the pirate club, do? He eats fried chicken—not a stereotype or anything. They're about to bust out of this weird shit, but then Jason is all, "Me want princess," and straight-up steals her.

We zap into space on what looks like an 8th-grade science project. The pirates get busted, and the princess is returned (there's no mention of the stolen water), and in the process, the princess nearly gets smoked. But she's got the sads that her handsome kidnapper is getting locked up. They just met. He STOLE HER. This is real Tinder date nonsense.

The pirates wind up in a weird space prison where albinos in white space leotards act super gay. If you get locked up in this prison, you become an albino gay dude by cutting your ding dong off. (Don't @ me, this movie came out when I was three.) An excessive castration machine looks completely out of the funny papers with spinning blades and choppy chop monster mouth action whenever testicles come near their gaping maw.

Our prisoners are taken into this big industrial hanger, but it's not a Hollywood set, it's a real 1984 shipping yard. They seriously just slapped some space-looking mumbo-jumbo over a brand name like Honda to make it feel like it was "otherworldly." If you looked hard enough, you'd probably see a teamster taking a smoke break in a hard hat. Meanwhile, the pirates are about to get their dicks chopped off. The guys are on a factory conveyor belt while random workers with torture devices rev them over their bodies but never actually cut anyone. The devices these stooges are holding aren't something rad like a lightsaber, or like a space castrator—they're black and decker hedge clippers. They're even the signature orange and everything. I'm gonna go out on a whim here and say the props department did not get the Oscar call.

The princess appears out of nowhere. She saves Jason and Roscoe from getting their nuts snipped. She tells them they must play along and follow her lead. We're led to a weird slave auction where she buys humans, and her picks are Jason and Roscoe, dressed up as albinos but with plenty of sexual winks and nods. The two wind up at this *Eyes Wide Shut*-ass party where everyone's in a mask, and the albinos in white serve people in leotards. Everyone at this party is really horny. Roscoe and Jason make their escape and are hauled off but have to make it to a ship where they can bolt with the princess, and the dude who cut off wieners is all, "no big deal, this is a part of my plan." With zero context.

The princess wants to be taken to The Pirate Moon, and this is where her father was last seen. Jason and the Princess (they never really say her name. Google tells me it's Karina (Mary Crosby). They steal a motorcycle that looks like the grandad of Elon's weird-looking trucks. Of course, they make it onto the ship, but Roscoe is left to get a ride from a black pimp robot that talks jive. Again, not weird and racist.

They get onto the ship using computer controls that look more like a big Lite Brite than a computer. They make it to the pirate ship, and while looking in a closet, they find an egg, which erupts, and Jason is informed it's a "space herpe." So now that thing is just roaming the ship, looking like the Alien's cousin.

They make it to the Pirate Moon. Angelica Houston mangles a pirate and cuts another guy's head off in her first real scene. Despite the title and all, we're still not seeing a lot of ice or water.

The princess does some recon. They're looking for a pirate who last saw her dad. They talk to him, he lives in some outer rim outpost; out of nowhere, bounty hunters come. And they're driving this big-ass skull truck out of *Mad Max*—if it was an 80's cartoon. These bounty hunters are like the most non-excited killers I've ever seen. Like, no one is out for blood, instead, they laugh a lot.

They make it out alive and back to their ship. Now, we're on some new planet full of babes in bikinis where Bruce Vilanch is like a pimp lord? Out of nowhere, we find out that he's only a head on a robot body. Jason carries the head around for protection against the angry bikini babes. So, they find her dad, except he's a robot? The real dad is on some other planet. One they don't know. Every robot up until this point has looked like they were made from shit at a garage sale, and this king is a whole ass dude.

Looking at a wavelength on a screen back on the ship, the princess, out of fucking nowhere, gets it in her head that her ring and her father's ring might connect to tell a story. Ole' bodiless Bruce is now on the ship and just so happens to have her father's ring in his mouth. The princess takes it and does some weird spin with the two together, creating a Princess Leia-like video of her old man speaking in non-sequiturs about survival.

This plot is bonkers.

The weird sexual tension part comes to pass. Jason stops by the princess's room. His shirt is tied up in the middle like a Valley girl, complete with a sword. He knocks on the door and gives her a clear mixtape. The princess is rocking no bra with the high beams on blast. Immediately, the music to smash is called "passion storm," with scenes of waves and volcanoes erupting. Seriously. They're making out. It looks like a Fabio romance novel cover. But, somehow, it's fucking raining. Ok, the whole point of this movie is about water being the most precious thing in the galaxy and so scarce that it's worth more than gold, but somehow, it's cool to let it blast in some celestial fuck room?

The princess drops, "shouldn't you be at the controls?" Making a comment about Jason not steering the ship, he comes back with, "if you insist," and goes down on her, and guess what? The clouds part while making the storm rage harder with its precious commodity of rain.

WHAT?

And as predicted, post-smash, the original bad guy is back. SO, they're supposed to be looking for the 7th planet, and it's a place where there's a shit ton of water. The princess' dad is there, I guess. The original villain has found the ship but somehow made it to tail them into hyperspace, but this hyperspace is fucked because it makes time jump with every light year. (Don't look at me, blame them for these plot holes, ok?)

At this point, we're jumping into hyperspace. The bad guys are attacking, and pirates, robots, and dudes in chain mail are all duking it out, killing one another. The princess is like, "I don't feel good"—after Jason just creampied her. MID FIGHT, Jason runs to check on the princess who's now about to drop a kid. Within a minute of him checking, they went from post-bang to I'm having your kid, to hello, meet your son. Instead of being psyched, my guy is all, "he's not mine," After getting shot in the face with piss, he tells her "sorry about that"—in reaction to his kid.

Apparently, for every minute, it's like five years. Time keeps jumping; everyone is a geezer with comical gray hair and long beards. And as we're jumping deeper into time, Jason, the baby two minutes ago, is now a thirty-something swashbuckler who knows how to fight.

But now the new Jason looks exactly like the OG Jason. And he kills everyone at the last minute. Wait now, fuck, "they came through it," and now, everyone is back to normal. All of the bad guys are dead, and everything is hunky-dory. But they all know she will be a momma, and no one mentions it. And the seventh planet it's earth.

So, instead of Star Wars level of badassery, we get tufts of chest hair, terrible special effects, and weird rape jokes. If there's any proverbial "proof in the puddling" when it comes to the level of perfect Star Wars maintained, it's that by the time this massive cinematic turd landed in life's waters, the original trilogy was in the can. Like, Yoda had already said the iconic shit, Luke found out that Darth Vader was his dad, the light saber battles, all of that, were on celluloid, and we still got...this.

I'm not saying that all space operas are bad, but *I am* saying that when you see these Great Value versions of movies meant to grab a few Han Solo fans' greenbacks, you immediately realize just how special those three movies were and still remain. And yes, nerds, go argue about plot holes and all that other shit on Twitter. Luke Skywalker changed the world, and Ice Pirates is $3 on Amazon. I spent an hour and a half of my time on this. You're welcome, Internet. I hate you.

IN AN ALTERNATE UNITED STATES, WITCHES WAGE WAR: REVIEW OF MOTHERLAND: FORT SALEM

BY J.Z. WESTON

Motherland: Fort Salem (Freeform) has been quietly telling a story about young witches in an alternate United States for two seasons now, with a third and final season set to start on June 21. If you want to know if it's worth your time to catch up, read on!

The strength of *Motherland: Fort Salem* is in its world-building. The show takes place in an alternate United States, where witches saved themselves from the gallows in the seventeenth century by pledging to fight America's wars. For over three hundred years, every witch born in the US has been required to join the army and to serve for life. Naturally, present-day opinions on this system vary. Some witches are proud of their service, while others compare universal conscription to slavery. There are draft dodgers, terrorists, elite witch families, and witches just trying to survive. The plotting can be a bit uneven from episode to episode (more on that later), but the world-building more than makes up for it.

The three main characters—young witches who have just arrived at Fort Salem for basic training—demonstrate the community's varied opinions about conscription. Abigail Bellweather (Ashley Nicole Williams) comes from an elite witch family and believes in the current system without question. On the other hand, Raelle Collar's (Taylor Hickson) mother recently died in battle. She hates the army and thinks the universal draft is essentially slavery. And then there's Tally Craven (Jessica Sutton), who enlisted over her mother's objections. She secured a dispensation for Tally (too many women in her family have died, so their bloodline is in danger of dying out), but Tally wants to serve, and she arrives at Fort Salem with a dewy-eyed idealism. Conflict between these three witches is inevitable, so, of course, they are all assigned to the same unit. What works well here is that none of them are shown to be entirely right or entirely wrong, and the three of them balance each other out to become stronger together than they are separately.

The first season, in particular, comes across more like a boarding school drama than military fantasy, relying on bickering and in-fighting to keep the stakes high. It also struggles with pacing and continuity, sacrificing both to keep the plot moving towards its destination. This improves in the second season, which dives deeper into the world and larger conflicts. Tally struggles with the realization that the witch army is not always on the side of the angels, while Raelle tries to find hope and purpose within what she knows is a fundamentally unfair system. At the same time, Abigail confronts what it truly means to be a member of the elite and how that both privileges and limits her. Each of these young women is a force of nature, and when they work together, they are capable of moving mountains. By the end of the second season, the status quo has shifted in a profound way, with the promise of more disruption in the upcoming third season.

It's clear that the showrunners have given a lot of thought to how the presence of a witch army would change American history (and from that, world history). Rather than provide some sort of opening monologue to provide exposition, the show doles out explanations very gradually. Since this world is completely normal to the characters, nobody explains anything until the viewer absolutely needs the information. For instance, we learn early on that the General of the witch army is over 300 years old. Other witches seem to live normal life spans. How and why did this happen? You'll find out... eventually. In the meantime, enjoy the wondering. There are myriad similar examples, tantalizing hints of a broader world that exists beyond the scope of the story.

Thanks to the conflict between witches and "civilians" (aka, non-witches), most other prejudice seems to be missing from this world or at least muted. Since witches are matriarchal, the witch army is decidedly slanted towards women (there are men, but they are non-combatants). And when your country is defended by an elite band of warrior women, it's apparently easier to accept women in power in other contexts. In addition, some of the oldest and most respected witch families are Black, and there are not just one but three high-ranking, powerful Black women on this show: the President of the United States, the witch army's chief of intelligence, and the officer in charge of training the new recruits.

Witch culture is also refreshingly free of homophobia. A lesbian romance is front and center, and nobody on base bats an eyelash (though there is pressure to have procreative sex, as well, in order to replenish the supply of witches). Same-sex love is treated as refreshingly, blissfully normal. The second season may have even introduced a nonbinary character (the actor portraying M is nonbinary, but no pronouns were used on screen for the character)!

Motherland: Fort Salem gives a unique explanation for witches' abilities: they have extra vocal cords, allowing them to create sounds that are impossible for regular humans. Sounds that create storms, move the earth, reveal what is hidden, and blast enemies. All of the magic we see on the screen is cast through the voice, which is both interesting from a world-building perspective and also symbolically powerful for a cast of young women who must learn to use their voices.

Given the strength of the rest of the world-building, the operations of the witch army are disappointing. Even I know that the general should not spend much time with new recruits. Let's just say that the witch army does not come across as a highly disciplined fighting force. This makes sense from the perspective of entertainment, but it's still frustrating that the show couldn't find a better way to make the plot happen.

Fortunately, the witch army works better from a philosophical point of view than a practical one. I expected the show to be fairly jingoistic, but the depiction of the military is nuanced. We see characters whose views of the witch army range from starry-eyed idealism, to pragmatism, to all-out hatred. The plot seems to take a critical eye on military policy without demonizing anybody. We see people with good intentions making bad choices, either due to personal loyalty, arrogance, or simple fear. This makes for interesting storytelling, whatever your personal feelings about the real-world military.

At its heart, *Motherland: Fort Salem* is a young adult drama. That means relationships, angst, and characters figuring out their places in the world. The plot can be a bit predictable at times, but it's hard not to enjoy watching these young women claim their power. And every new revelation about this world draws you further in. It's not a perfect show, but I thoroughly enjoyed it.

HAUNT AND THE HALLOWEEN HAUNTED HOUSE

BY HOLLY LYN WALRATH

THE SLASHER FROM THE WRITERS OF A QUIET PLACE EXPLORES WHAT MAKES A GOOD SCARE

When I was a kid growing up in the 90s, I was obsessed with Halloween. I trick-or-treated right up until age 14, which I remember vividly as my last Halloween—I finally realized I was too old for the practice.

I grew up in a small town in Texas. Halloween was a big deal in our town, mostly because, as a conservative religious community, Halloween was the one chance kids got to explore otherwise taboo subjects—horror movies, sexy dress-up, and the supernatural (including the forbidden topic of witchcraft.)

In our neighborhood, an older couple put up a backyard haunted house every year. I remember walking through their back gate, and they would have a short, gruesome show every fifteen minutes or so. The wife would pretend to rip out her husband's guts, or a spooky witch would brew body parts over a smoke-machine-fueled cauldron. Other neighbors set up haunted houses in their houses, complete with snacks, drinks, and games. On other Halloweens, there would be a haunted "maze" set up in the park across the street from my house. It was in line for this haunted maze that I met some of my best friends.

One year, my friends and I went out to a haunted trail in the woods. It was a full production. I've always been fascinated with how the haunted-house-as-show works. Inherently, it's about suspending your disbelief for long enough to get a good thrill. The fun is in knowing that while you may experience fear for a short time, in the end, you will get out safe.

Which is part of why I loved the movie *Haunt* (2019) so much. Streaming now on Shudder, *Haunt* follows a group of college students as they enter, and try to escape from, a haunted house on Halloween. This isn't your standard neighborhood haunted house, but more of a torture chamber. It shadows the recent phenomenon of "extreme" haunted attractions.

One such real-life haunt is McKamey Manor in Summertown, TN. It claims to be so extreme that no one has ever finished the experience, despite promises of a $20,000 prize. In order to enter, participants must sign a 40-page waiver, pass a drug test, have a completed sports physical and doctor's letter, present proof of medical insurance, pass a background test, and be screened via social media. Not to mention that to enter, you have to watch a two-hour film featuring people who went into the house telling everyone how much they regret the experience.

The haunted house is so controversial that a petition to close it on Change.org gathered hundreds of thousands of signatures. Petitioners argue that the haunted house is merely a torture chamber, and other rumors state even worse claims of the show-runners hiring felons or sexually assaulting guests.

Haunt takes this context and combines it with the horror tropes of Halloween to devastating effect.

The movie opens with Harper (Katie Stevens) and her roommate Bailey (Lauryn McClain) at home. Someone smashes a pumpkin on their doorstep, and Bailey immediately knows that it is Harper's boyfriend, who is abusive. We learn that Harper, who will be our final girl, is not only dating an abusive boyfriend but that her father was also abusive to her mother. This ultimately becomes the emotional thrust of the film that drives Harper to survive.

The friends gather after a night of partying to find a "haunt" (the filmmakers tried hard to slide the name of the movie in, but it was a bit heavy-handed). They stumble upon a haunt in the middle of nowhere after Harper is convinced they are being followed. After signing a waiver and handing over their cell phones, the group of friends follows a creepy clown-masked man into a labyrinthian haunted house in an abandoned warehouse.

The film slots characters into standard horror movie roles. Harper is the "different" final girl who is dating an abuser but finds herself falling for the jock, Nathan (Will Brittain). Andrew Caldwell does a fantastic job as comic relief in the character of Evan. The two other girls include Lauryn McClain as Bailey, who could be said to fall into a somewhat stereotypical "brown girl best friend" role but truly steals the final scenes of the film, and Schuyler Helford as Mallory.

Each character is given a plausible backstory for them to work through as they encounter more and more terrifying aspects of the haunt. None of the friends abandon each other, and all are depicted as fairly decent human beings, which is refreshing for a genre that usually devolves into characters leaving each other high and dry (or hung somewhere by their flesh).

The movie is very self-aware and meta, but this works given the premise and never feels overdone. Old Halloween chestnuts like the "stick your hand in a hole and guess the object" game and the "roomful of creepy mannequins" are expected but subverted.

As the friends navigate the haunted house, the delight in watching the film is the creativity put into the set design. Similar to most extreme haunted houses, each room is themed and has a different horrifying methodology. Reminiscent of other gorefest films like *Saw* (2004) and *Hellhouse LLC*(2015), the characters must solve an escape-room mystery to get out of each haunted house area.

What I enjoyed about the film is how it slowly unravels, letting us see behind the scenes as the characters break into the fourth wall of the haunted house, where the demented showrunners are pulling the puppet strings. Not only is the house not what it seems, but the masked "workers" of this hell house are also a surprise.

In my opinion, the villains here are the best kind because their motives are unclear and never explained in the film. The most terrifying of monsters is that which we don't understand. And so, I was pleased that the writers chose not to explain why the baddies do what they do here. Like other horror classics such as *Texas Chainsaw Massacre* (1974), we don't need a nuanced backstory of the villains to be scared as viewers. Leaving it unexplained adds tension to the film that is rarely explored in horror these days.

Haunt has some truly creepy and horrific moments. I went into watching it expecting a half-hearted Halloween flick and was surprised at how many twists and turns the film gives viewers. The setup does a fantastic job of laying out the story and then subverting viewers' expectations. There's gore here, but it's not unwatchable. (I only had to hide my eyes in a few scenes!)

Ultimately, the film also does a fantastic job of exploring the final girl trope. Harper is not just a good girl trying to survive—she is strong, capable, and enjoyable to watch figure out the mysteries of the haunt. The past abuse narrative and abuse-cycle tropes work well here to give Harper a deeper past and a satisfying ending. I enjoyed how the film depicted Harper as being able to survive because of her past history as a survivor, a connection most horror filmmakers don't put together.

In the end, Harper flips the script and makes the villains of the film go through what she went through. As one commenter said on a video for the real-life haunt McKamey manor, "I'd love to see him go through his own game." Part of the satisfaction of this is seeing the bad guy feel the same fear in retribution.

Haunt takes the haunted house and explores all the psychological trauma necessary to put yourself in danger and then find a way out of that danger. In the end, that's why we're so interested in haunted houses as humans. We all have some shadowy past that we need to escape from.

VAN HELSING RETROSPECTIVE

BY GRANT BUTLER

REVISITING THE PULPY MONSTER MOVIE BY THE DIRECTOR OF THE MUMMY

Like many people, I've always enjoyed the 2004 movie *Van Helsing* starring Hugh Jackman and was surprised at the negative reception at the time of its release. Directed by Stephen Sommers, it features the famous monster hunter as he takes on his nemesis Count Dracula (Richard Roxburgh) and encounters other classic Universal monsters along the way.

Sommers also made the 1999 film *The Mummy*, which was a huge box office success at the time of its release and has been a longtime favorite of movie fans, with retrospective reviews giving it high marks. I agree that *The Mummy* is an excellent example of a well-executed, fun summer blockbuster that you watch during a movie night with your friends after you've ordered some pizza. *Van Helsing* is very similar in that it's a movie built on being pure blockbuster entertainment. It's not trying to be complex and only wants to be a throwback to the fun, pulpy Universal monster movies of the past. And *Van Helsing* succeeds in this goal.

So if the two movies have a lot in common, why was *Van Helsing* so negatively received at the time of its release? Many movies, particularly those involving science fiction or horror, are often given a lukewarm reception before being appreciated later on. Stanley Kubrick's *The Shining* is one notable example, as, upon release, it was not exactly considered the classic it is today.

There are several factors that help account for a surprisingly negative reception for a film that, while is definitely not *The Shining*, is far from the worst movie you could watch. For starters, unlike *The Mummy*, which incorporated a certain *Indiana Jones* type of action movie flavor, Van Helsing was a throwback to the Universal Monsters movies. It's possible to view *The Mummy*, while sharing much in common with the classic monster movies, as being more of an action movie and doing what a good remake is supposed to do by making a significantly different movie than what came before it. By contrast, *Van Helsing's* gimmick is to bring all the classic movie monsters together for one story, which while new to modern audiences, had been done before in films like *Abbott and Costello Meet Frankenstein*.

It's also impossible to mention *Van Helsing's* reception without noting the lackluster reception of 2017's *The Mummy,* starring Tom Cruise. Not only was it received far worse both critically and financially than the 1999 version of *The Mummy*, the film's director openly called it the biggest failure of his life. After this, it's hard not to suspect people who may not have enjoyed *Van Helsing* at the time of its release may have a slightly different opinion now.

There's no doubt that, as it often does, the reception of the movie had much to do with timing. *The Mummy* was released in 1999, while *Van Helsing* came out five years later in 2004. Between the two films, the world as people knew it drastically changed with the September 11 terrorist attacks and the subsequent war on terror, and there is no doubt it significantly impacted the world and the type of entertainment it consumed.

Van Helsing was released when the big epic adventure of cinema was the *Lord of the Rings* franchise, with the final film in the trilogy having been released about six months before *Van Helsing*. It was incredibly well received by critics, earned 11 Academy Awards, including Best Picture, and grossed over a billion dollars at the box office.

Peter Jackson, the film's director, would also try his hand at bringing a classic movie monster to the 21st-century cinema when he made his own version of *King Kong*, which came out a year after *Van Helsing* in 2005. While it wasn't on par with the reception of the final *Lord of the Rings* film, Jackson's *King Kong* was well received. When considering *King Kong* was released in the post-9/11 era, it's not surprising that a movie about a giant ape causing mayhem and destruction in New York would register more with audiences than one about vampires and werewolves set in Transylvania in the late 1800s.

But there is one overwhelming cultural trend at the time that would explain the lackluster reception of *Van Helsing* more than anything else. The 2000s was the era where zombies were experiencing a period of massive cultural interest. After some well-received and popular zombie-themed video games in the late 1990s, zombies quickly became the dominant monster in entertainment once the new millennium arrived.

The first film that brought zombies to the modern era with a bang was 2002's *28 Days Later*, which was set in the UK and featured a new type of zombies: terrifyingly fast ones. One year later, Max Brooks published his bestselling *The*

Zombie Survival Guide and followed it up several years later with *World War Z*. 2004, the same year *Van Helsing* was released, would see the release of the cult classic zombie comedy *Shaun of the Dead* and Zack Snyder's directorial debut in the remake of George Romero's *Dawn of the Dead*. Romero's own film *Land of the Dead* would be released the following year, and he would return to the big screen with 2007's *Diary of the Dead* and 2009's *Survival of the Dead*. *28 Weeks Later*, the sequel to *28 Days Later*, was released in 2007, while 2009 also saw the release of *Zombieland*, which was a huge commercial and critical success.

The era also saw the release of the films *Resident Evil* (2002), *Resident Evil: Apocalypse* (2004), *Resident Evil: Extinction* (2007), and *Resident Evil: Afterlife* (2010), all of which were inspired by the *Resident Evil* video games. And of course, the capstone for the cultural interest in zombies was the television debut of *The Walking Dead* in 2010, which was a huge success.

But why were zombies received with more interest in the early 2000s than any other movie monster? For starters, the idea of zombies seemed much closer to home due to the unprecedented interest in the idea of biological agents and deadly diseases being weaponized, as did the idea of the complete destruction of the established order. Zombies would hit home in a different way for audiences in an era where the concept of the destruction of civilization is very much at the forefront of national debate because stories about vampires and werewolves typically don't involve civilization facing collapse and people needing to get creative to survive and fight back.

It's also important to note that the idea of you and your loved ones being bitten by a zombie is inherently far more terrifying than becoming a vampire or a werewolf. Going off the standard lore, becoming a vampire means that aside from being unable to set foot in daylight or having to drink blood, the person you are doesn't change that much. Being bitten by a werewolf can seem even less drastic, as aside from having to transform into a werewolf at the full moon, you are still, in many ways, the person you always were. Especially because in many vampire or werewolf movies, including *Van Helsing*, there exists some way to reverse things and return the person to their normal selves. But if you're bitten by a zombie, it is indisputable that someone bitten will turn into a mindless monster that'll attack anyone. This idea would have a unique resonance in an era where the idea is that anyone or anything could potentially be a danger to you and your loved ones due to unprecedented fears about biological or terrorist attacks.

With the context of the era in mind, the reception *Van Helsing* received at the time of release makes more sense. But enough time has passed that it's due for a fresh look.

DUSE IS WILD: REVIEW OF PROTECTRESS BY KENDRA PRESTON LEONARD

BY JAMILEH ALEXANDRA

> *"Athena was wise but had already had to deal with mansplaining*
>
> *gods that night"*

Protectress (*Unsolicited Press*, 2022) by Kendra Preston Leonard is a novel in verse. It is a necessary, healing 'Where Are They Now' episode, providing a meaningful epilogue to the Medusa myth. Leonard's celebration of literal and emotional sisterhood left me feeling satisfied, whole, and hopeful.

You probably recall the legend of Medusa from an indeterminate point in your youth: a school lesson on Greek mythology, Rick Riordan books, *The Clash of the Titans*. But since hearing that first hiss, you've likely noticed allusions to her story all over art and media from Picasso to *The Chilling Adventures of Sabrina* to UB40. She is a frequent symbol of feminine power (and failure) and blamed for her own downfall as often as Eve.

Medusa was one of three Gorgon sisters and a pledged priestess to Athena. Poseidon raped her. Athena set a huge precedent for victim-blaming, cursing Medusa with snakes for hair and a gaze that would turn onlookers to stone. Then Perseus murdered her, stole her head, and weaponized it. Because this myth has endured for millennia we now have a chance to unravel the story at its core: Athena's betrayal of Medusa. *Protectress* launches from questions about that event and spins a lyric tale of reparation.

> *a mortal woman made immortal because of her story ran*
>
> *from a temple, from a cave from Kisthene's dreadful plain*
>
> *seeking blindness, baldness, rebirth*
>
> *with her sisters*

Set in the present day, these immortal beings must make lives among mortals and wrestle with this ages-old trauma that partially heals only to fester again after a new insult. Medusa and her sisters feature equally in this drama, drawn together and apart as sisters do, walking their own paths but coming together when they need the support only a sister's arms can give.

This emotional tide and the waves on the sea of the Gorgon's homeland are a constant presence through this novel, lending it a rolling rhythm. The novel is in verse, but not a strict scannable form. Instead, the language is your setting and guide. In the context of poetry, you expect evocation, you draw meaning from the length of lines and stanzas and line breaks draw attention, forcing you to process a moment differently than in prose. All these expectations of the form serve this story well. Sometimes you are adrift in the music of a section, sometimes a line break heightens a comic note, sometimes it makes you feel the salt air. Primarily, the verse leaves space for the reader to walk beside these gods and goddesses and bear witness.

Up two concrete stairs, three;

a brindled cat waits,

impatient,

wanting the morning's

catch, leaning and shifting,

against Stheno's legs

like the palm trees in the yard.

Protectress does not skimp on the Greek language or the B-sides and deep cuts of Greek mythology. There are numerous beings and names dropped that are beyond average Greek myth knowledge. I took the 'look it up' approach because I like to know what the details mean. But you can definitely let it wash over you. The Greek language has a musicality to it that is put to good use here and context will get you most of the meanings. But if you don't know already know your nereids from your hamadryads, there's one small section that may not read as fluidly as the rest of the book.

I have somehow made it this far with only one quip about snakes. *Protectress* further distinguishes itself from the original myth and its many retellings, by not being obsessed with Medusa's physical transformation. Like the water in this tale, Duse's snakes are always in the consciousness of the text without being all over every page. They also feel very personal to Medusa and not about the fear they evoke. I loved this aspect of reimagining Medusa.

Medusa wakes and

wraps her hair, coiling the coils

under, blinding them

The last chapters of *Protectress* are a loving, cathartic exhale of the breath we hold for ourselves and our sister-friends every time we are blamed for violence that is done to us. It was a joy to have a book reach between my ribs and get into my lungs. These immortal gods are characterized by modern proclivities that provide humor, lightness, and new interpretations of the mythic. They also ground the story in a familiar human world, which is a stable foundation when the magic starts to fly. Yet, you never forget that you are reading an ancient story, honoring its original Bardic storytelling while resolving in a very satisfying and modern revelation of Medusa's true power. *Protectress* is available now from Unsolicited Press.

ABOUT THE AUTHOR

Kendra Preston Leonard is a poet, lyricist, and librettist whose work is inspired by the local, historical, and mythopoeic. She is especially interested in addressing issues of social justice, the environment, and disability through poetry. Her first chapbook, Making Mythology, was published in 2020 by Louisiana Literature Press, and her work appears in numerous publications including vox poetica, lunch, These Fragile Lilacs, and Upstart: Out of Sequence: The Sonnets Remixed. Leonard collaborates regularly with composers on works for voice including new operas and song cycles. Her lyrics and libretti have been set by composers including Jessica Rudman, Rosśa Crean, and Allyssa Jones. The author of numerous scholarly books and articles, Leonard is also a musicologist and music theorist, and her academic work focuses on women and music in the twentieth and twenty-first centuries; music and the early modern; and music and screen history. Follow her on Twitter at @K_Leonard_PhD or visit her site at: kendraprestonleonard.hcommons.org.

EVERYTHING IS NOT FINE: REVIEW OF COMFORT ME WITH APPLES BY CATHERYNNE M. VALENTE

BY CHRISTINA LADD

If you're not familiar with the phrase, "comfort me with apples" is a line from the Song of Solomon, and specifically from the King James translation. The fuller line goes "Stay me with flagons, comfort me with apples, for I am sick of love." I'd be sick of love, too, if I had to live in the nightmare that is Catherynne Valente's Arcadia Gardens, a heavenly place only so long as you don't ask questions.

Comfort Me with Apples (Tordotcom, November 2021) features an elaborately fabricated Eden, with as many HOA rules as it has beasts of the field and birds of the air. It's the first, only, and perpetual gated community, and like our modern ones, it's meant to keep people out. And in the largest house on the most exclusive street, we meet Sophia, who doesn't care that They Put Up A Parking Lot, because she's in love. With her husband, no less! And it doesn't matter to her that he's forbidden her from ever going in the basement of their too-large house, or that he's gone most of the time, or that when he *is* home, he patronizes and belittles her.

I should rewind a bit, though. "I am sick of love," is an archaic translation, and therefore may be misleading. The Hebrew can mean "I am sick *from* love," (most modern translations capture this), and I've no doubt that Valente is aware of the various ways the prepositions get used (or misused). Sophia may get sick *of* love, but she's also quite sick *from* it, from the disquietingly deep love she feels for a man she barely knows, and from the paltry love he shows her in return. She's sick as in *ill* and sick as in *tired of it.* It's a small detail, but this is a book like a mosaic, every small detail a shiny marvel that builds the glorious whole.

Valente is working with the Jewish myths that arose around the Genesis 1–3 creation and the Bluebeard fairy tale. If you're not familiar, Genesis involves the first male and female human being told not to eat from the Tree of Knowledge and then Eve, the woman, eating from specifically that tree; Bluebeard is about a woman who marries a man who tells her never to go into his basement and then her going into that basement to find it's full of his dead previous wives. Centrally, both stories are about *knowledge*: who has it, who doesn't, and what the consequences are for learning. You know you're vulnerable, wearing flimsy garments that only serve to give you away. The knowledge stains you indelibly, and it doesn't give you very much more power than you had before. So why, asks Valente (and most of the rest of humanity), do we want to *know* so bad?

Because of the first wife.

Bluebeard may have killed all his other wives for peeking, but why did he kill his *first* wife? What could she have possibly seen that he would have had to kill her for? Nothing—and that's the point. Bluebeard was always going to have killed his wives, including the protagonist. Her *lack* of knowledge would never have kept her safe. And it's the same with Sophia. Even if she were perfect, Adam would still have killed her. In fact, she *is* perfect. Adam says so. God himself says so. Every new wife is perfect. So maybe perfection includes curiosity and an instinct toward self-preservation, and maybe it's not about the perfection of the wife but the failure of the husband. Or the husband's father.

It all points back to the father and son: God and Adam eternally in cahoots, the patriarchy a united front. God gives Adam everything he wants, and everything Adam wants is a McMansion with a basement kill room. It's like he listened to too many true crime podcasts while cruising Zillow. Adam isn't just evil, he's *lame.* He's the most banal kind of evil even when elevated over all else, the father of all failsons. Except not really, because he's forbidden from having children.

This thwarted virility—or straight-up impotence—is important here because so many of our ancient myths are about inheritance. The Greek gods feared their children with good reason: usurpation and castration was not just common but *foundational*. And in Genesis, God banishes the human pair because they become "like gods," possibly a little too powerful for comfort. Family can be a male anxiety—and a female advantage.

In "Bluebeard," the protagonist-wife's family saves her. But Adam and Sophia have no other family...or do they? Because, as Valente cleverly observes, all of Adam's wives are of his flesh, and therefore related. They're sisters, and even if they've never met, even if all they hear of one another is terrible rumors, there is a bond between them. There's a bond, too, between Sophia and the other neighborhood wives, women she can talk to—only she can never quite bring herself to be honest, not because they won't understand, but because Sophia doesn't.

The understated strangeness of Sophia's gifts to Mrs. Fische and Mrs. Lyon is quietly shocking, an incredible moment of dissonance that worked brilliantly at setting up the pervasive unease. Even worse is the way that the animals must exist in a world not made for them. Valente never addresses it directly, but it's plenty damning (puns always intended) anyway: the best that God has to offer is shades of off-white and ecru and eggshell, all laid out in a detailed HOA, lest anything *look* out of place. Paradise isn't a location, it's a performance.

Speaking of, there's a play-within-the play here, which I always love. The animals—all of them subtle enough to give the serpent a run for his money—try to bend the beartrap rules apart enough for Sophia to get free, but of course, she can't. You can't speak in parables to someone who doesn't understand the underlying structures you're pointing to.

What they're pointing to is what Valente is pointing to: it's still about the first wife. There's a first wife in the larger Genesis mythos, not just the Bluebeard story: her name is Lilith, and most of what we know from the ancient sources is that she didn't want to do what Adam told her. Whether she's a demon or a feminist ahead of her time (and everyone else's time, too), she was most certainly banished outside the gates of Eden.

Valente clearly loves the ancient sources, and mixing them all together and plopping them down in suburbia works surprisingly well. There's mention of the Platonic myth of the divided self, and even the nameless wife whose creation grosses Adam out is actually part of the larger Jewish mythos. In Greek, Sophia means *wisdom*, and in many of the gnostic strains of Antique Judaism and early Christianity Sophia made the material world possible by her understanding, but others failed to understand *her* and so despised her. So yes, of course, all of these myths have to do with that most compelling trinity: power, gender, and knowledge.

Semengelof is a Jewish myth too, including his avian attributes. I *love* what Valente has done with him, made a creature of such perfect menace and yet such exquisite beauty. He's one of those minor characters who clearly could become a main character, or at least a recurring one. More of Semengelof! Oh, and about that name: I did not miss the slight but doubtless deliberate choice in the transliteration here, starting his name with *semen*. Valente is relentlessly clever with wordplay (see also her Fairyland series), and she's using all her powers to make sure we don't miss the nuances of gender at work here.

It *is* how feminists sometimes have to read the bible and fairy tales both: we are looking for all the little scraps out of place, the bones and hairbrushes, the little crescent-moon scars that were all our foremothers could send forward of themselves to warn us. *All is not as it seems. We are not as weak or foolish as the tales would have you believe, and some of us survived. And you can too. You can too, but you have to know what you're up against and what you can do. You have to* know.

ABOUT THE AUTHOR

Catherynne M. Valente is the *New York Times* bestselling author of over two dozen works of fiction and poetry, including *Palimpsest*, the Orphan's Tales series, *Deathless*, *Radiance*, and the crowdfunded phenomenon *The Girl Who Circumnavigated Fairyland in a Ship of Her Own Making* (and the four books that followed it). She is the winner of the Andre Norton, Tiptree, Sturgeon, Eugie Foster Memorial, Mythopoeic, Rhysling, Lambda, Locus, and Hugo awards, as well as the Prix Imaginales. Valente has also been a finalist for the Nebula and World Fantasy Awards. She lives on an island off the coast of Maine with a small but growing menagerie of beasts, some of which are human.

HOW FOUNDATION MISSED AN OPPORTUNITY: APPLE TV+ REBOOTS ISAAC ASIMOV'S FOUNDATION FOR A NEW GENERATION OF FANS

BY AARON EMMELL

Apple TV+'s *Foundation* series is hiding the seeds of a good show, but it has nothing to do with the novels it's ostensibly based on. Had the showrunners focused their story on the trio of cloned galactic emperors they invented, as it often seems they wanted to, the results would have been more interesting and coherent.

The series has a lot going for it—starting, of course, with those Isaac Asimov novels (Foundation series, 1942–1993, first published in *Astounding Science Fiction*) . They have their problems (infamously, almost all the major characters are men, and there's surprisingly little action for a story about the collapse of a galactic empire), but they've also profoundly influenced the science fiction genre and inspired generations of fans. The show's actors are phenomenal, and the series has a generous budget (generous enough that it repeatedly makes it into the headlines of reviews). Unfortunately, what the series *doesn't* demonstrate is an appreciation of what gave the books their longevity despite those glaring problems.

The show is not really about psychohistory, the books' major premise. Most of the characters seem to view psychohistory as a kind of mystical prophecy. By the end of the season, it's clear the showrunners feel the same way. The show isn't even interested in the more general idea of math's (and science's) problem-solving potential, since it's eventually revealed that even the mathematician Gaal Dornick's most important talent isn't actually math.

Screen adaptations don't have to mirror books precisely to be faithful to the source material, or, more importantly, to be compelling. The fidelity that matters is to the core ideas or themes, not individual scenes. In fact, getting to the heart of the story may mean taking different routes when you use different media. *The Lord of the Rings* films are widely acclaimed movies based on beloved books, but they tell the same story differently, each in a way suited to its medium. The books invite you to get lost in the world and its poetry; the films highlight and often streamline the action. But the action all drives toward the books' themes, and Peter Jackson, Fran Walsh, and Philippa Boyens wove that poetry and worldbuilding into the sets, the props, and the language the characters use and pass through. The fidelity is to the idea.

Some of the most obvious changes in the *Foundation* show are in fact aligned with the novels' central ideas, and enhance them by correcting some of the problems in the text. Dornick, the math prodigy enlisted to help fulfill Seldon's vision, is now a woman played by an actor of African and European descent (Lou Llobell), and it's a lot easier to believe that we're watching the events of a galactic empire when they include people who happen not to be white men. There's more action, which helps us get to the rest of the story. The problem, unfortunately, is the story itself.

This problem is evident immediately, with the first looks we get of Trantor. Much has been written about the grandiosity of the sets, and that's accurate. I also loved the shots of Dornick's home world, Synnax. It's true, as well, that the empire is in a state of decline when the story opens—that's part of the point, after all. But in the books, one of the reasons for the pushback against Hari Seldon, the creator of psychohistory, is that the empire doesn't *look* like it's in decline. This is crucial, because Seldon's unwavering goal is to use his knowledge of psychohistory to shorten the dark ages from civilization's impending fall from 30,000 to a mere 1,000 years. Yet the visual shots of the empire are all gloomy, and the empire itself is brazenly pseudo-fascist. In short, there's nothing here to fear falling from. Who will mourn this empire when it dies? What could be worse? The emperors justify their rule by claiming to enforce the peace, and superficially that's true, but they do so through acts of extraordinary violence on par with the worst actions of the Empire in Star Wars.

The books, in contrast, spend pages discussing how impressive the empire is. In fact, its capital, Trantor, is a literary precursor to Star Wars' Coruscant, a world so fantastically wealthy that it's been covered with a single, giant city—a connection I'm not sure would have occurred to me just from the show. This reduces the tension right off the bat, because the viewer wants the empire to fall, and we're immediately told it will. What's the downside? There's a cool space elevator, but not much else worth saving.

This aesthetic decision reflects the show's fundamental problem, which is that its creators seem more interested in space opera in general than the core theme of the book.

This core theme, of course, is psychohistory: the fictional mathematics that can predict human behavior in aggregate, turning social science into hard science. When a show is committed to its central theme, the conflicts are believable and intrinsic. But in the *Foundation* series, psychohistory is treated almost like a MacGuffin: a device that sets the plot in motion but could be replaced by another device to tell the same story. Because of this, the show must keep contriving various and variously convincing conflicts to keep the plot moving. There are many examples—the show itself is an example—but I'll focus on one: in the show, the empire is run by clones of an earlier emperor.

At this point, clones are a sci-fi trope. If you're looking for something to watch about clones, you don't have to go far afield. The poorly received Arnold Schwarzenegger movie The 6th Day came out way back in 2000. Tatiana Maslany already blew our minds in Orphan Black. Clones aren't some cutting-edge idea that speaks to our moment. For some reason, however, the series' creators seemed at least as interested in the angst of being an emperor's clone as they were in psychohistory. Ironically, because the relationships between the clones and the ideas behind them were carefully laid out in a way the other plot threads weren't, they ended up being the most compelling part of the show.

As a storytelling device, clones might appear at first to make sense. They're a way to keep the same antagonist even though the story covers a long period of time. Unfortunately, a cloned leader seems almost uniquely unsuited to telling the story of *Foundation*, which was partly inspired by Edward Gibbon's 1776 *The History of the Decline and Fall of the Roman Empire*. The books force us to consider whether any particular reformer, in a position of leadership, is capable of bucking historical trends. They raise questions of how societies shape people, and vice versa. If the leaders don't change, these questions never get fully addressed, even if the characters occasionally make reference to them.

Almost all the other narrative choices display the same disregard for the source material. For example, it's a nice touch that Eto Demerzel is presented as a robot, which is something Asimov only retconned in the sequels to the original trilogy—except that Demerzel blatantly violates Asimov's First Law of Robotics ("A robot may not injure a human being or, through inaction, allow a human being to come to harm"), indicating the show's eagerness to dispose of all Asimov's core ideas, not just the ones from *Foundation*.

The irony is that the questions suggested by psychohistory are more urgent now than ever. At a time when so many political theories have collapsed in the real world, is there a scientific way to chart a new approach? Is the onslaught of history inexorable, or can the right individual, the right innovation, the right grouping of people, change it? In essence, with so much going wrong around us, can we shape our own destiny?

In the books, after the Foundation's first "crisis," a message from Hari Seldon reveals that psychohistory had predicted the situation far in advance, due to the historical forces already in motion. In the show, Seldon's message at the end of the season is different. He had made some accurate predictions, but his primary role is to use his unique charisma, the type of charisma associated with politicians and prophets, to exhort the people watching him to make the right strategic choices. It's meant to be inspiring, but for me it was the opposite. After all the characters have gone through, and all the knowledge they thought they'd gained, they still need to wait for the right man, or perhaps the right woman with the right superhuman powers, to tell them what to do.

Which brings us back to the unexpectedly best part of the show. If you're going to stick with charismatic leaders, you might as well have some fun and make them clones.

RETURNING TO SKYWALKER IS BAD, ACTUALLY: ON LUKE, LORE, AND THE BOOK OF BOBA FETT

BY ANNIKA BARRANTI KLEIN

When Luke Skywalker peaced out on Ahch-To under the twin suns of his distant home planet Tatooine in *The Last Jedi* (2017), I sobbed alone in the Arclight Cineramadome, for that moment the only person in the world who understood that the great hero's journey was ending as it began. (Of course, I was not the only person; Rian Johnson clearly understood.)

The scene in the original *Star Wars* (1977) when Luke stands on a ridge and looks out at the sunset longing for a different life, when we first fully hear the Force Theme that for me embodies Star Wars more than even the Imperial March, is a defining moment. It tells us that we are about to go on a hero's journey. I believe that Leia is the main character of Star Wars, but there is also room for Luke to be the hero. Both can be true.

A contingent of Star Wars fans hated *The Last Jedi* (TLJ) because—as far as I can tell—they couldn't stand seeing Luke as not-the-hero. In TLJ, Luke is worn down and angry. He has made a choice to no longer be a hero. He has abandoned his own journey. He has good reasons! His attempts at doing what he believed to be the right thing (re-forming the Jedi order) backfired spectacularly and aided the rise of the first order. But some fans don't like those reasons.

Rey and, I think more crucially, Chewbacca and R2D2 convince him to finish his journey, and he does—on his own terms. It is his final act, his swan song before the aforementioned peacing out. It is a good and glorious end.

But these fans? Were not satisfied. And among them were, apparently, Jon Favreau and one Dave Filoni. Now, I love Filoni's work on Star Wars. LOVE. I am obsessed with Anakin Skywalker, who was an annoying little jerk in the prequel trilogy, because of *The Clone Wars* (2008—more on that later). I adore *The Mandalorian* (2019), which they both worked on.

In the finale of Season 2 of *The Mandalorian*, Luke Skywalker (voiced by a computer simulation of Mark Hamill and embodied by Max Lloyd-Jones and a lot of CGI) arrives from who-knows-where to collect Yodito (I mean Grogu) from Din Djarin (Pedro Pascal), who had, on Ahsoka Tano's (Rosario Dawson) advice, taken Yodito to a sacred Jedi stone where he called through the force to any Jedi who might wish to train him. While Yodito was communing with the force, Din had tried, unsuccessfully, to fight off a garrison of dark troopers who came to steal Yodito from Din and deliver him to Moff Gideon (Giancarlo Esposito). Din was aided in this fight by his former adversary Fennec Shand (Ming-Na Wen) and her new boss, Boba Fett (Temuera Morrison).

Boba. Fucking. Fett. Yeah, the one from *The Empire Strikes Back* (1980) and *Return of the Jedi* (1983). Yeah, the fan-favorite bounty hunter who allegedly died after falling into the Sarlacc pit in *Jedi*. Indeed, the very Boba Fett who had literally zero personality on screen, other than looking very cool, but who children of the 1980s were obsessed with because of a very clever and mostly accidental marketing campaign (see *Under the Helmet: The Legacy of Boba Fett*, streaming on Disney+).

Two episodes of *The Mandalorian*, two returning OG heroes (er, as much as one can call Fett a hero). Not to mention Ahsoka Tano and Bo-Katan, who are beloved by fans of *The Clone Wars*. The crowd, as they say, went wild.

So Luke showed up to aid Din in rescuing Yodito (I mean Grogu) and took him off to be the first student in his new Jedi school. The one that we know ends in flames later, when Ben Solo becomes Kylo Ren. Ooooooookay.

Flash forward to *The Book of Boba Fett*, a strange fever dream of a series that relies on neither plot nor character, but is simply a slow burn exploration of... lore? Which I guess is what the fans want. Some fans. Favreau and Filoni (and Robert Rodriguez), specifically, but based on reactions on Twitter and IMDb, plenty of others. For me, though? Going too deep into the existing lore makes the galaxy far, far closer and too small for me.

Episodes 4 and 5 of *The Book* did not feature Boba Fett at all, instead focusing on the ongoing adventures of Din Djarin after Grogu (ugh, fine) left with Luke. Din misses his little buddy, and when he finds the Mandalorian armorer, he has her melt down his beskar spear and make tiny armor for him. Then he travels to a forest planet where a Jedi school is being constructed, and Ahsoka Tano convinces him to stay away from Grogu, lest their strong bond distract him from his Jedi studies (this does not in any way make sense for the Ahsoka we know from *The Clone Wars*, who walked away from the Jedi order over their strict rules and bad decisions). Din gives her Grogu's armor and leaves.

And then we once again meet post-*Jedi* Luke Skywalker (this time embodied by Graham Hamilton), training Grogu. And it is a fan's fever dream, echoing Yoda training Luke on Degobah, complete with a training remote like Obi-Wan used to show Luke how to use a lightsaber. Luke's training is full of nonsense the old master himself might spout. Once again there is no character, no plot, only lore. I don't mind the show straying from Boba Fett, but I don't like where it strayed.

I would argue that this is fan fiction. It is an imagined bridge between the original trilogy and the sequel trilogy, with absolutely no new information whatsoever. Also, there is a cute homage to *Lone Wolf & Cub* in which Luke asks Grogu to choose between Yoda's lightsaber and Din's gift. This scene utterly betrays everything we know about Luke's character, but that's okay because it's cool. I guess. Maybe the problem is that it's fan fiction, but the fans have been given the keys to the multi-billion dollar kingdom.

When *The Clone Wars* explored what Anakin, Ahsoka, and the actual clone troopers were doing between *Attack of the Clones* and *Revenge of the Sith*, we were given more room to understand the nuances that should have been on-screen in the first place. Following the troopers and seeing the mistakes the Jedi made, getting to know Anakin Skywalker, knowing what was going to happen when Palpatine gave order 66—all made the series a tense tightrope walk between hope (I loved the characters and desperately wanted them to be okay) and dread (I knew that, with rare exception, they would not be). The show was a deep dive into both character and plot that made the galaxy that much bigger.

There is no need to explore what Luke was up to shortly after *Return of the Jedi*. Or rather, there is no reason to explore it in a show that is about a crime boss attempting to take down a crime syndicate, which is ostensibly what *The Book of Boba Fett* is about. There are books and comics that dive into how various characters passed the time between trilogies. If a live-action Luke is what fans really, truly want, there is the option to (gasp!) cast a new, age-appropriate actor. (Sebastian Stan is right there.) I can think of no reason to hijack a series that is not in any way about Luke Skywalker and turn it into the continuing adventures of Luke Skywalker. Especially not if he is going to look like a video game cutscene whenever he speaks.

I want the ongoing Star Wars universe to expand, not shrink, and in *The Book of Boba Fett*, the galaxy is shrinking. We spend all of this time with Boba Fett and the various people around him, but we don't actually get to know him at all. He begins the series as he ends it: an enigma in cool armor. I take it back: it isn't fan fiction, because fan fiction would give us *more*. I wouldn't call it fan *service* either, because I am not sure who it serves. In theory, it explores the crime factions we met in Solo (2018), but it doesn't tell us anything about them, either—it just kills a lot of them. Plus? It humanized the formerly one-dimensional Tuskens, who are a direct analog for Indigenous people, and then murdered them. Fan fiction would never.

HOW TO RETURN TO TATOOINE: DISNEY'S OBI-WAN KENOBI AND LETTING GO

BY ANNIKA BARRANTI KLEIN

Star Wars loves nothing more than to return to Tatooine. Over and over again, audiences find themselves on the lonely desert planet with dual suns. We return to Tatooine in the prequel trilogy, in *The Mandalorian (2019)*, in *Book of Boba Fett (2021)*, even in *Rise of Skywalker (2019)*. Most of these returns serve the opposite purpose than is intended: They make the galaxy feel smaller, feel like it is not made up of tens of thousands of star systems but is, in fact, merely made up of tens of thousands of moments in Anakin and Luke Skywalker's saga.

In *Obi-Wan Kenobi* (*Disney+*, 2022), the return to Tatooine feels earned, for perhaps the first time since *Revenge of the Sith* when Obi-Wan handed infant Luke to Beru and she brought him to meet Owen on the very ridge where we would pick up again with Luke in *A New Hope*.

Ten years after the events of *Revenge of the Sith*, Obi-Wan Kenobi (Ewan McGregor), going by Ben, is a haunted and broken man. He saw the clone troopers turn on the Jedi; killed his best friend, or so he believes; watched Padme die; and escaped to functional exile without anything resembling closure. All he has is Luke, who he watches from a distance because Owen (Joel Edgerton) and Beru (Bonnie Piesse) don't want him there.

Ben has a job, he has an eopie, he has a cave and a sentry droid, and a Jawa pal he buys things from. And he has a singular focus on Luke, watching him from a distance to keep him safe, much in the way a person who is afraid of flying grips their armrest to single-handedly keep the airplane in the sky. (Ben is also, as we know from *Attack of the Clones*, not a fan of flying.)

And then an old friend—Bail Organa (Jimmy Smits), the man who got Yoda and Obi-Wan himself out of danger during Order 66, the man raising Luke's twin sister—asks him for help. He refuses the call, like any good man on the Campbellian hero's journey. Bail asks again. And Ben sighs, digs up his lightsaber (which he buried with Anakin's), and goes to rescue the princess.

So here's how you return to Tatooine: you leave. You say, we've spent so much time already with Luke; what is Leia's story? And then, if you're (writer/director/showrunner) Debra Chow, you give us a story that, despite being very small, expands the galaxy. She also deftly closes some weird plot holes created by the prequels, bridging those stories to the original trilogy flawlessly.

The beautiful mess that is *Rogue One* (2016) showed us pockets of rebellion that *A New Hope* only hinted at. Like that movie, *Obi-Wan Kenobi* tells a small story within the framework of the Skywalker saga that enlarges the galaxy, that shows us hints of what viewers have always wanted: a vast galaxy where anyone's story could be important, not just the men of the Skywalker line. And it does it with a legacy character at the center, which is impressive.

I love the prequels, but I can't fully respect them. We don't need every character from the original trilogy to already be connected. We don't need Anakin to have built C-3PO as a precocious enslaved child, or Chewbacca to have fought alongside Yoda. But we have it, and *Obi-Wan Kenobi* honors that while allowing that there was more going on than just those connections. It gives us a rebellion in its early stages, a network of helpers already doing the work that Bail and Mon Mothma are quietly enabling from the senate; the work that Leia would take on as she grows up. It gives us a glimpse at the inquisitors who were previously only seen in *Star Wars: Rebels*, terrifying Sith-adjacent specters hunting down the remaining Jedi in the galaxy. And it does something else, something vital: it honors the women of Star Wars, in particular Leia, Padme, and Beru.

When Ben rescues Leia (Vivien Lyra Blair) from her kidnappers, he is thrust into the same Cranky Space Uncle role as Din Djarin on *The Mandalorian*—arguably also the role Owen is in—and he doesn't take to it very well at first. He seems to like Leia instantly (it would be very difficult not to) but he simply does not know what to do with her boundless energy, her intellectual curiosity, or the fact that she demands he prove that he is a Jedi, which would require that he use skills he hasn't touched in ten years—skills he is terrified to use. When he finally uses those skills, it is because she has fallen to her certain death, and he draws on his dormant connection with the force to stop her before she hits the ground. It's a beautiful moment, and it seals their trust in each other.

Female characters have existed to inspire men to greatness since time immemorial. This time, a female character inspires a man to find peace. But she is not merely a tool for his story; this series is a stealth Leia origin story in which we see the spark of the rebel leader she would become. She knows instinctively when to trust people and when to lie, and she makes choices based on her moral and ethical center. She loves deeply and she trusts herself just as deeply.

She asks Ben about her "real" parents, pressing him for information that Bail and Breha have not given her. He pretends not to know, but she can tell that he is lying. At one point, she even asks if he is really her father. In a moment that will probably inspire countless pages of Obi-Wan/Padme fanfic, he says he wishes that he was, but he means that he wishes Anakin had not been her father, that it is too painful for him to think of his friend's turn to evil, of that being her parent. And it is too painful, too, for him to think of Padme, but he would rather think of her than of Anakin.

But we, the audience, know something Ben does not know: Anakin survived and became Darth Vader. And then a young, driven, angry inquisitor, Reva (Moses Ingram), tells him. Reva is singularly focused on finding and capturing Obi-Wan, and of course, she has a secret agenda—one driven by revenge—that is revealed over the course of the series. Reva's character mirrors Anakin's in many ways, which gives Ben an opportunity to respond differently to someone in pain, almost a do-over of his failed friendship with and mentorship of Anakin. And Reva also brings Ben and Vader (Hayden Christensen) together, allowing Obi-Wan to forgive himself for the burden he's been carrying all this time: his belief that he killed Anakin. I won't spoil their ultimate scene together, only say that it included the best lightsaber fight I've ever seen on screen, and warn that it may be difficult for some disabled viewers to watch.

The Obi-Wan that we meet in *A New Hope* has a history with Vader that we are not privy to; the much younger Obi-Wan that we meet in *The Phantom Menace* meets Anakin for the first time; and the Obi-Wan that we leave in *Revenge of the Sith* has a deep history with Anakin, explored even further in *The Clone Wars*. They are not just Master and Padawan; they are brothers, and in *Obi-Wan Kenobi* we see how Obi-Wan changes from the man who killed Anakin in *Revenge of the Sith* to the man who kills Darth Vader in *A New Hope*.

The Jedi are not supposed to form attachments. This is a very important rule that is hammered into the audience's skull over and over again as it is broken over and over again because the Jedi are, it turns out, people. Obi-Wan may not form any romantic attachments (except when he does, as referenced in *Clone Wars*), but he forms plenty of non-romantic attachments, and those attachments are part of what makes him who he is. It is when he comes to terms with this that he finds peace. And it is by allowing himself to be attached to Leia *and say goodbye to her* that he lets go of his vice grip on Luke and returns to solitude; maybe this time it is because he chooses to and not because he has to.

And now we know why he was her only hope ten years later. I'm not crying, you're crying.

WAITING FOR OUR BETTER ANGELS: A REVIEW OF BE HERE TO LOVE ME AT THE END OF THE WORLD BY SASHA FLETCHER

BY TAYLOR JONES

"This nation was built on stolen land with the blood of slaves ripped from their homes. What did you think would happen here? That all these bodies could stay buried? That ghosts wouldn't choke our dreams?"

Sasha Fletcher's debut novel *Be Here to Love Me at the End of the World* (*Melville House,* 2022) offers the reader a chaotic, dreamlike, stream-of-consciousness-adjacent narrative that almost, but never quite, makes linear sense.

There are no heroes, only a small cast of characters living their lives. Sam and Eleanor are the tethers of the story. They are somewhat unprepossessing people, shown mostly doing prosaic things like coming and going from work or cooking elaborate meals, but those mundanities are contrasted with the larger, more disorienting context in which they happen: a world disconcertingly close to our own in which nuclear missiles may or may not be headed for New York City, the sky occasionally opens up to rain disaster down on innocent summer camps, the police (and more surreptitiously, the secret police) run amuck, and angels make frequent appearances as either video-game characters or potential agents of change, but spend most of their time jammed into "an incredibly small closet" filled with the smell of burning feathers, largely impotent even with flaming swords in their hands. The titular end of the world is a constantly looming threat, but everyone still has to go to work and pay bills. It sounds familiar.

I know the state of mind evoked in this book all too well. It's that underemployed, Millennial, liminal space in which you are just comfortable enough to get complacent, but not comfortable enough not to feel bad all the time.

You have enough money to live, but not enough money to thrive. You heard about your parents paying for college and buying a house with minimum-wage jobs, but you will be saddled with crushing debt for the rest of your life for the same things or less and you feel like, somewhere along the line, someone pulled a fast one on you. You know enough to be angry at the world, but not enough to do anything about it.

Be Here to Love Me lays the blame for this malaise squarely on the history of America, which the country has failed to reckon with: "This nation was built on stolen land with the blood of slaves ripped from their homes. What did you think would happen here? That all these bodies could stay buried? That ghosts wouldn't choke our dreams?"

The villains in this story are the police (constantly shooting innocent people in the background), the secret police (constantly black bagging people in the background for undisclosed reasons), and the state. The book makes a claim: "If you have love in your heart the state is your enemy. If you have love in your heart, you're an enemy of the state." There's plenty of evidence presented for this claim. So much evidence, in fact, that the book sometimes feels more like an uncited history lesson than a novel, a Wiki-walk through the darkest parts of American history including, for starters, the Vietnam War, Saddam Hussein being on the CIA payroll, the assassination of Fred Hampton, and the invention of California.

Ultimately, the book asks: "What in the world are you, are any of us, going to do about it?" The narrator is justifiably angry, but sometimes that anger seems formless and undirected—just like real life. No answers are offered. At least the question is on the table, though.

This book feels written for people whose attention spans have been bludgeoned unconscious by the constant onslaught of social media, whose hearts are pummeled by the emotional whiplash of being shown a cute cat video, then footage of the bombing of Kyiv, and then a story about a 12-year-old girl selling lemonade to pay for her own heart transplant. Or a sequence of similar things, every day, every hour, until we put down our phones and go make dinner and try to love the people in our lives as best we can. As Fletcher writes, "...it's not that we forget, it's that there are just too many tragedies, every week, forever and ever, and to remember them all would kill you. Your heart would break and stop beating and you'd die. So we forget." This book asks us, bluntly, not to forget, even in the face of everyday mundanities. Even in the face of everyday apocalypse.

As for love: it's there, and the narrator offers it fiercely and freely to the reader but remains agnostic about its effectiveness. There's a dream-like sequence where "a great speckled bird" stands at the foot of Sam and Eleanor's bed and asks, "What's the plan? Love with an open heart? Keep paying off your student loans until the 1099 gets dropped on your fucking head? Keep going to work and coming home and cooking dinner and hoping the world gets better? You gonna tell me love can change the world?" No one can truly answer questions like these. Sam and Eleanor don't even try; they just want to get through the day and enjoy a nice dinner.

They *are* in love, though. That love is both beautiful and meaningless. As the narrator sardonically recounts: "'You are the light of my fucking life,' [Sam] said, 'and I love you with all my heart.' Meanwhile, people kept dying." Love doesn't change the world, or save it. It doesn't accomplish much of anything. It's just part of life, and maybe worth it, even if the world is ending.

ABOUT THE AUTHOR

Sasha Fletcher is the author of the novel *Be Here to Love Me at the End of the World*, a book of poems, several chapbooks of poetry, and a novella. His work can be found both online and in print.

THE GIFT OF HORROR: THE 1980S HORROR FLICK TERRORVISION INSPIRES A CAREER IN HORROR

BY TODD SULLIVAN

On lazy Saturday afternoons in the 1980s, monsters invaded homes. Their looks varied, but their murderous intentions were all the same. Some wore bladed gloves, wielded machetes, or carried chainsaws. They would stalk partying teens in isolated areas, cut through young flesh, hack through bone, and have the walls shaking with the screams of their victims. Others, less humanoid in shape, oozed over gates and seeped under doors to engulf unsuspecting victims sleeping in beds or sitting on toilets. Those ensnared would slowly dissolve into jelly before being digested by amorphous creatures. Finally, there were the reanimated corpses living beneath our feet. They rose up from graveyards, mindless and starving for brains, or calculating, cold, and hungering for blood.

The portal through which all of these Saturday afternoon nightmares flowed was the television. The key that opened the lock was the remote control. In my home in New Orleans, Louisiana, the gatekeeper was my older sister, who loved horror movies above all others. This would have surprised many who knew her, as she was highly intelligent, becoming valedictorian of her high school class in 1990. Horror is generally considered to be the bottom of the literary barrel, hovering in the dregs with erotica. Yet my sister saw something in it that intelligentsia miss, and since she controlled the TV remote, I, too, eventually discovered the secret through her afternoon gift of horror.

My sister didn't only diet on "highbrow" horror, like Stanley Kubrick's *The Shining* (1980) or Steven Spielberg's *Poltergeist (*1982). She liked it raw, bloody, and absurd, and one movie from the 1980s that best encapsulates those three adjectives, and also one of her favorites, was a little-known film titled *TerrorVision*.

On the surface, the plot of Ted Nicolaou's *TerrorVision* (1986) is as goofy as its title. A family in Small Town America buys a new satellite dish for their television, but the reception is poor. As they attempt to fix it with a TV controller so big that it actually has to be cradled in two hands (this *was* the 80s), an alien garbage disposal team on the planet Pluton converts a ravaging multi-eyed beast with a gaping maw of sharp teeth into a beam of energy. They then shoot the beam randomly into space, where it hits the family's satellite dish, resolving the poor reception of the TV while at the same time allowing the beast to enter into the home of the unsuspecting family through the television.

What follows next is carnage and chaos as the beast first attacks the grandfather, who never trusted satellite television and warned the family against using such new technology. He's dissolved into goo and slurped up by the monster.

Next to follow are the parents and another couple, all bored middle-aged adults who turn to swinging to generate excitement in their lives. The beast sneaks into the bedroom, or as the couples call it, *the Pleasure Dome*, while only one of the four swingers is in the bed. It consumes her body but keeps her head, which it uses like a puppet while it hides the rest of its appendages beneath the sheets. The beast lures the other three swingers into the strangely cavorting bed, where it devours them one at a time except for their heads.

Finally, we come to the two kids, who at first have success in taming the beast with heavy metal. Why would this work, you may ask? Again, it *was* the 80s.

However, when the kid's scheme to use the beast for profit, the monster becomes enraged and eats them, too.

Imagine me, at eight years old, watching this carnage on Saturday afternoon because, in the 80s, horror movies such as this played regularly on the weekend on the few channels that existed on basic cable. Beside me sat my older sister, poking fun at moronic character reactions to obviously dangerous situations and laughing at the boundless appetite of the multi-eyed, sharp-toothed beast. Many may wonder what redeeming quality a movie like this could possibly have.

An undeniable quality of horror is that it creates an impression. Horror in fiction, or horror in reality, is oftentimes very difficult to forget once heard or read. We remember the names Michael Myers and Freddy Kruger but not so much the names of the teen victims or even the final survivor of each installment. Serial killer Ted Bundy's name is easily recalled, but not one of his dozens of victims. I haven't seen *TerrorVision* in at least 34 years, yet the scene of the beast using the heads of the swingers to lure them into the bed one after the other is as clear today as it was three decades ago.

When you have a message that you truly want people to remember, sear it into them with a grotesque image. That has a greater chance of punching through mental objections to linger in the subconscious.

One such example of this is the first victim in *TerrorVision*, the grandfather. He is shown to have an exaggerated fear of the new technology of satellite TV. His fear is ultimately justified by the arrival of the beast, which originates from a great distance from the physical location of the family itself. Decades after this movie's release, we see how our technologically advanced devices, capable of beaming signals across the globe instantaneously, have fostered the cultural shift which is social media. One can perfectly personify the societal ills of Facebook, Instagram, TikTok, Twitter, etc., as the terrorizing beast from *TerrorVision*. With its many staring eyes and its wide maw of sharp teeth, the beast is always watching and always hungry, devouring one family member after another. Social media, too, keeps constant track of us with its algorithms and cookies monitoring every website we visit. Social media also has a boundless appetite, consuming ever greater quantities of time from users. Constant notifications, comments, memes, sharing of photos, flame wars, hot button issues, etc., keep users hooked and constantly checking their feeds for the slightest most trivial updates.

The monster in the movie eats the body but keeps the head, which it uses like a puppet to seduce and manipulate other humans. The constant flow of information on the internet does similarly, getting into people's minds and having them parrot strange and unhealthy ideas, if not dangerous ideologies, that flow from sources far away from their actual physical bodies.

The kids in *TerrerVision* believe they can make a profit from the monster if they can only control it. This results in them, too, eventually being consumed because of their greed. On the internet, people think they can make fortunes through taming the web and becoming social media stars. Yet look at the lives that have been damaged or destroyed in the process. Those who have engaged in risky behavior and stunts, or those who have made a job of ruining the reputations of others, all in the name of clicks. Videos that get the most amount of views are of disasters or of people doing dangerous activities that can lead to tragedy.

The makers of *TerrorVision* saw the future coming, and they dressed up their warning in the absurdity of bad acting, terrible hairdos, and a voracious multi-eyed monster with a gaping maw of sharp teeth that ripped apart the flesh of an unsuspecting family.

Three decades ago, while I watched this gore fest beside my older sister, I simply found the movie scary, and later on, memorable. *TerrorVision* was only one of many flicks I watched because of my sister. After we got a DVD player, yet another new technology, and were able to rent movies, the number of frightening creatures only multiplied in our home on the weekend. Yet despite the fact that horror is often considered to be the bottom of the literary barrel, hovering in the dregs with erotica, I don't regret the movies I watched in my childhood. Today, I write horror fiction, and can only hope my narratives show flickers of foresight into human behavior like *TerrorVision*, and sear appropriate warnings into the mind of my readers. I thank my older sister for the gift of horror she gave me all those years ago in introducing me to the genius of the genre.

JAPANESE FILM *MISSING* SURPRISES WITH ITS TAKE ON THE SERIAL KILLER GENRE: A THRILLING AND HORRIFIC EXPLORATION OF HUMAN GREED

BY HOLLY LYN WALRATH

TW: This review contains discussions of depression, suicide, and abuse of people with disabilities.

Missing (Fortissimo Films) is the directorial debut of Katayama Shinzo, a former assistant director of popular Korean filmmaker Bong Joon-ho of *Parasite* fame. It follows a father named Santoshi (Jiro Sato) who is trying to provide for his daughter Kaeda (Aoi Ito) after the death of her mother (Toko Narushima) from ALS. In the midst of this family drama comes the film's villain, a serial killer called "No Name" (Hiroya Shimizu), who draws the family into his web of horror.

Missing opens with a haunting bit of foreshadowing, in which depressed father Santoshi Hirada practices using a small sledgehammer in a courtyard. It is only at the end of the film when the audience learns the true horror of this image.

When Santoshi goes missing, his daughter sets out to find him in less-than-ideal circumstances. Everyone around her abandons her one by one, from a school boyfriend to a teacher. Society has branded her father as an outcast because he is unemployed and commits petty crimes (or so it seems.) Kaeda ultimately falls into the path of the serial killer No Name while searching for her father.

All of the actors in this movie are fantastic. Jiro Sato is a heart-warming father figure, and Aoi Ito is sharp and funny as his daughter. Hiroya Shimizu is satisfyingly equal parts evil and hot as the calm, detached serial killer, No Name.

No Name's modus operandi is to lure depressed women to him so that he can "help" them complete suicide. He targets his victims through social media. No Name believes he is doing the world a service by removing those with depression or disability from it, as he says, "There are some people in this world that want to die. They want to, but they can't express it."

The film draws heavily from the serial killer trope in horror, mixing quirks like No Name's obsession with classical music, a la Hannibal Lecter, and real-life stories of serial killers in Japan.

The character is likely based off of Japanese serial killer Takahiro Shiraishi, who in 2017 killed nine people, including three high school age girls. Shiraishi would lure women to his home after meeting them on Twitter, where he went by the username *hangingpro*. He would strangle his victims and then dismember them, keeping their bodies in freezers and storage boxes.

Alert: Spoilers ahead!

This thought-provoking film is full of twists and turns that challenge the serial killer genre in horror with a fascinating exploration of grief, disability, and the moral ambiguity of human desire.

We learn that Santoshi's wife and Kaeda's mother was disabled and that Santoshi's depression is related to the loss of his wife. As her sole caretaker, the burden of caring for her becomes too much for Santoshi to bear. The film flashes back in time several times, showing us the backstory and unraveling the audience's expectations.

Ultimately, the film struggles to add nuance to its representation of chronic illness and disability, choosing to equate disability with a complete loss of autonomy and joy. While it paints Kaeda's mother in an empathetic way, the complexity of the caregiver relationship is still represented as a "death is the only way out" deal.

For me, as a chronically ill person, every day is a struggle to put aside the failures of my body and choose joy. And yet, I can understand that not everyone is in a position to find hope. This is why we need better representation—to avoid the tragically disabled trope.

The final victim in *Missing* is portrayed as unique in that she chooses both death and, unable to commit suicide herself, becomes disabled in the process. So, the film both looks at long-term illness and disability as a result of injury as equally soul-crushing circumstances. And while this may be true for some people in these situations (or perceived as such), for others, disability is absolutely not, nor should it be, a death sentence.

Setting this problem aside, I still think the film is worth watching for its management of these complex issues and for a different cultural outlook on them. While it is true that many people who are disabled struggle with depression and suicide, I think the film takes an extreme view of the matter. It highlights how there is far more risk for those who are disabled and without economic support.

Missing is a fascinating film with a deeply complex subject matter and fantastic acting. The viewer walks away feeling a deep sense of dread and disappointment—that the characters couldn't do better for each other. Those struggling with depression should steer clear; they will find no hope here but plenty of retribution.

ENDS AND EDGES: REVIEW OF THE LAST HOUSE ON NEEDLESS STREET BY CATRIONA WARD

BY CHRISTINA LADD

It is impossible to write a meaningful analysis of *The Last House on Needless Street* by Catriona Ward (Viper, 2021) without spoilers, and so I'm not going to try. What follows is a spoiler-heavy, even spoiler-gleeful review. However, I would caution anyone who hasn't read the book to be very careful about spoiling yourself on this one. It is a multilayered, profoundly thoughtful, and wonderfully suspenseful book, one that any review cannot truly do proper justice. I will be discussing some of Catriona Ward's themes and insights, but mostly for those who have already read it. To the uninitiated, this is the sum total of my review:

The Last House on Needless Street is great. It is *great*. You should read it. Please come back and talk about it when you have, there are so, so many wonderful things to say.

***** Spoilers Follow *****

Those twists, eh?

I suppose it's not enough anymore for a book to have *a* twist. Audiences have grown jaded from years of surprises both earned and forced (ahem, *Star Wars*), so it's not terribly surprising that authors are trying to up the ante. Ward, though, doesn't seem to think it's a competition. *The Last House on Needless Street* may be in conversation with some genre conventions for horror and mystery, but she's not trying to respond to anyone or one-up them. Her books are helixes, the twists are literally part of the DNA. Not having them would mean that the book was not hers.

The Last House on Needless Street is a book that has twists not for their own sake but because what we think of as twists—unexpected events nonetheless grounded in established character and plot—are a natural extension of the characters and events Ward is tackling. These twists feel so necessary because Ward is dealing with twisted people. Ward allows us to think that *twisted* goes hand in hand with *evil*, but then she spends the rest of the book complicating that notion. Trauma twists people. So does guilt. So does greed, and so do the very best of good intentions sometimes, too. Ward's twists arise not from over-simplification (ahem, *GoT*), but from this complication.

Ward does a lot with *implication*, too, and says a lot of interesting things about it as she does. The narrative breaks off at significant moments, and relies on us to understand and fill in what is, sadly, now a fairly common story: a mentally unstable loner (Ted) is stalking, kidnapping, torturing, and killing women. We think Ward obeys horror conventions when she refuses to lift the curtain since what we *don't* see is always scarier. But Ward's understanding of horror goes even deeper, and she uses our expectations against us. What we don't see is so, so much more complicated than kidnapping and murder. So much so that she forces us to question why our minds filled in those particular blanks.

We put that story into the blanks, Ward knows, because we've seen it before. *Ad nauseum*, in fact. We expect women to be in danger, men to be the cause, and the police not to do much. We expect the mentally ill to be perpetrators, not victims. We even expect—the more despairing among us, but 2020 made us a majority—that the community is more willing to notice the use of environmentally unfriendly spray paint than it is girls going missing.

That's part of the horror, says Ward. We're so inured to it that we don't even look at it anymore. We think we know how the story goes. Ward, though, wants us to be attentive to particularity. She's not trying to take away from the larger conversations about violence against women, or children, or where community and police responsibility are lacking. She instead wants to point out that victims and victimizers both hide in the places we as a society do not look, the unpleasant places where we *could* ask questions, but that would be *uncomfortable.*

Why does that woman keep getting fired? Why does her child always seem to be hurt, why is he so nervous all the time?

Ward seems like a magician because we're always looking in the wrong direction, away from these simple questions. We want to see epic clashes of good and evil in their most acceptable (read: stereotypical) forms, a determined young woman fighting a crazy fat man. Ward creates twists by telling what we should already know, what we (hopefully) learned in kindergarten: we shouldn't judge people by how they look.

We also shouldn't judge people by the archetypes they seem to fill. Hollywood loves to tell us that vigilantes—underdogs if ever there were any—are the heroes. That they get *results*, and they do it *in spite* of the rules. Enough, says

Ward. That story is as tired as it is untrue. Dee may wrap her quest for vengeance in grand concepts like Justice and Truth, but in the end, it's all about herself. Her unwillingness to *see* compounds not just her own trauma and guilt, but also the trauma of others. Meanwhile, the longsuffering and overworked cop is ultimately absolved because she hasn't failed at all. She sees what's going on. She tries to get Dee to see it too, but it's not something that can be done by brazen vigilante work, brandishing a gun or stalking a suspect.

Likewise, serial killers aren't genius-level masterminds of manipulation and forensics Hollywood loves to show. They're just good at playing on people's natural aversion to getting involved. "Someone else will do something," say the people who exiled her, leaving her free to terrorize other communities. "It's someone else's problem," say the people who fire her but don't otherwise report her. Ted's mother gets away with abuse and murder for so long because people aren't willing to bear the scrutiny on themselves or their organizations.

I'm reminded of another book, *Pet* by Akwaeke Emezi. "We are each other's business," they say in the town of Lucille. People are happy enough to be in each other's business when it comes to who they love or what they say on the internet, but not so easy when they have to look at hard things, upsetting things, tragic things. Ted also knows this sad truth: it's easier to not see.

Ted, who witnessed everything, who could not *help* but see, was forced to become his own community. He had to offer himself the comfort he needed from others but never received. Those disparate parts need to learn to talk to one another before he could see his life as a whole, and he needed to speak with others in order to really begin his healing.

And who ends up being the hero? Aside from Ted (in all his aspects), the hero is just some *guy*. Some regular guy who really wants people to follow the rules, who wants to protect the environment where he lives. This ordinary community member is the one who rescues Ted physically, and then sticks around to support Ted saving himself mentally. If failures of bureaucracy kept Ted's mother from prosecution, then bureaucracy also triumphs in the simple citizenry, strangers taking an interest in what goes on in their community.

As we look back on the book, we see that a lot of people were ready to help. All the people we thought were such fools—the women in the shop who dismissed Lauren's plea for help written on leggings, the neighbors who never seemed to see Lauren playing in the house—were never actually ignoring abuse. They just didn't know what they were seeing. Everybody has incomplete pieces of the puzzle, including the perpetrators. Including the victims. Including *us*, the audience. We, too, failed to grasp what we were seeing.

We shouldn't let that happen, Ward says. We should look. And we shouldn't look away.

ABOUT THE AUTHOR

Catriona Ward was born in Washington, DC, and grew up in the United States, Kenya, Madagascar, Yemen, and Morocco. She studied English at the University of Oxford and later earned her master's degree in creative writing at the University of East Anglia. Ward is a three-time winner of the August Derleth Award for Best Horror Novel: for *The Girl from Rawblood*, her debut; *Little Eve*; and *The Last House on Needless Street*. *Little Eve* also won the Shirley Jackson Award for Best Novel. Ward is the international bestselling author of T*he Last House on Needless Street* and *Sundial.*

WHAT IT MEANS TO BE A WOMAN (AND A WITCH): A REVIEW OF JUNO DAWSON'S ADULT FICTION DEBUT, HER MAJESTY'S ROYAL COVEN

BY TAYLOR JONES

Juno Dawson's adult fiction debut and first foray into fantasy, *Her Majesty's Royal Coven (Penguin*, 2022), does two different things very well. First, it speaks to the present moment with candor. Dawson, according to press materials, "felt compelled by the persistent transphobia in British feminist circles to write something about what it means to be a woman," and the book delivers on that promise, offering glimpses into many different ways to navigate womanhood. Second, the book gives readers a wild fantasy romp full of magic, plot twists, and action that never lets up—right up to the last page, a hair-raising cliffhanger that will leave the reader in an agony of anticipation for the next installment.

In the world of the novel, five girls grew up together learning witchcraft under the auspices of Her Majesty's Royal Coven (HMRC), a covert government department founded by Queen Elizabeth I to protect the world from supernatural forces. As young adults, they were thrown into a war started by a Voldemort-style witch supremacist, and not all of them ended up on the same side. Now, the four of them who emerged from the chaos of the war whole are dealing with their trauma in vastly different ways. Niamh has become a country vet; Elle is a devoted wife and mother; Leonie is leading Diaspora, an inclusive coven for witches and warlocks of color; Helena is the High Priestess of traditional, bureaucratic HMRC and struggling to interpret dire prophecies from her oracles about a "Sullied Child" who will cause the apocalyptic rise of the demon Leviathan and the end of witchkind. Into this fraught situation falls Theo, a young warlock with extraordinary abilities, a troubled past, and a potential connection to the prophecy. When Theo is revealed to be trans, it goes some way toward explaining her powers, but Helena's unwillingness to accept a trans witch into HMRC starts a chain of events that tears the group of childhood friends apart.

Dawson gets inside the minds of four very different women who make up her cast of main characters. Gentle Elle desperately wants "normalcy" and hides her powers from her husband and children but can't quite escape the complications of the coven or her friendships. Niamh is happily ensconced in a quiet life that belies the strength of her powers. She's principled and kind, but she's done things in moments of extremis during the war that will come back to haunt her. Fiery Leonie, a Londoner to the core, is much more confident forming and leading her innovative new coven than she is making decisions about her personal life. And then there's stubborn, ambitious Helena, whose supreme confidence is both the source of her strength and the seed of her greatest weakness: her inflexibility. The ending hints at other perspectives to come in the second installment, and deeper secrets to be revealed about the womens' pasts.

Dawson gives each character a unique voice, in particular Leonie, the only BIPOC member of the main cast (she is Black) and the one with—understandably—the most mixed feelings about their shared childhood. She's usually the one who speaks most directly about the injustices of the world of the novel—so like our own—but Dawson gives her enough personality and spirit to keep her from feeling like a mouthpiece. Helena, a very different sort of narrator, is rigid and traditional, unused to questioning her own power as a witch or her own privilege as a white cis women. When Leonie splits off from staid HMRC to form Diaspora, Helena takes it as a personal slight and a betrayal rather than a well-earned critique of existing power structures.

"'Of *course* Leonie has trans witches in her *woke* coven,'" Helena exclaims bitterly at one point, encapsulating in a few words her unwillingness to change and her disdain for those who question the status quo. It's no surprise that she tries to make trans witches' existences political, while they just want to exist. Leonie points out that "'Helena's life is so fucking cushy that she has all the time in the world to muse on the potential theoretical, philosophical, academical ramifications of trans lives. Theo just wants to fuckin' *be.* Don't quite seem fair, does it?'"

The book is firmly character-driven and delves deep into the ways friendships forged in childhood can last long past grievances that would sever a weaker bond; how sometimes those friendships last past the point where the relationship makes any kind of healthy sense. It's an exciting and sometimes surprisingly brutal read, with cinematic action scenes that played out vividly in my mind's eye and social commentary that, while very pointed, avoids becoming preachy. *Her Majesty's Royal Coven* manages to thread the needle and is both a gripping summer read and a thoughtful examination of real-world issues. The book doesn't take a simplistic view of morality, but it also doesn't let the characters escape the fallout of their actions.

"Are you a good witch?" one character asks Niamh after finding out about her magical abilities.

No, she answers. "'There are no good witches or bad witches, there are just witches and the choices we make.'" Dawson doesn't shy away from showing us those choices in all their complexity—and all their consequences.

ABOUT THE AUTHOR

Juno Dawson is a #1 Sunday Times best-selling novelist, screenwriter, journalist, and a columnist for Attitude Magazine. Juno's books include the global bestsellers, THIS BOOK IS GAY and CLEAN. She won the 2020 YA Book Prize for MEAT MARKET. Her first adult fantasy trilogy HER MAJESTY'S ROYAL COVEN launched in 2022, becoming an instant best-seller.

She also writes for television and has multiple shows in development both in the UK and US. Her debut short film was THE BIRTH OF VENUS (BBC 2020) and she created the first official Doctor Who scripted podcast DOCTOR WHO: REDACTED (BBC Sounds 2022). An occasional actress and model, Juno had a cameo in the BBC's I MAY DESTROY YOU (2020), a recurring role in HOLBY CITY (BBC 2021) and was the face of Jecca Cosmetics Play Pots campaign.

Juno grew up in West Yorkshire, writing imaginary episodes of Doctor Who. She later turned her talent to journalism, interviewing luminaries such as Steps and Atomic Kitten, before writing a weekly serial in a Brighton newspaper. Her writing has appeared in Glamour, The Pool, Dazed and the Guardian. She has appeared on Pointless Celebrities, BBC Women's Hour, Front Row, ITV News, Channel 5 News, This Morning and Newsnight.

Juno lives in Brighton. She is a part of the queer cabaret collective known as CLUB SILENCIO. In 2014, Juno became a School Role Model for the charity STONEWALL.

SNARK, BULLIES, AND THE UNDEAD: REVIEW OF BLUMHOUSE AND EPIX'S UNHUMAN

BY EMILY WAGNER

A group of misfit high school kids, an inept P.E. Teacher, and a wacky bus driver all on a field trip to the wilderness: What could go wrong?

Turns out, a zombie apocalypse of sorts.

This is the premise of Blumhouse Television and EPIX latest movie, *Unhuman* (2022). Blumhouse typically produces horror, but it's purer genre like *Paranormal Activity* (2007-present) and *Get Out (2017). Unhuman* is different because it provides fun and horror in equal doses. It's filled with bonkers one-liners and non-stop action, zombie-smashing and blood.

On the bus are all the cliques known to high school; nerds, loners, jocks, and bullies who call each other names like randos, Jumpstreet, and meat-heads. Their goal is to earn some extra credit, but after the bus hits something, a red liquid covers the entire windshield, and the bus crashes. The radio plays a message about a chemical attack. Then, in the movie's ever-present snarky style, the dimwit P.E. teacher opens the bus door to a zombie—because, why not?—and proceeds to get his face half-eaten. Now it's up to the band of bickering classmates to save each other.

Their first test is when so-called 'Brace Face' gets dragged from behind on the bus by the zombie. Some wonder if they should save her, while others just want to help themselves. That's an overarching theme—how, or if, to work together. Another is bullying and standing up for yourself. Not even a zombie apocalypse can stop this crew from tormenting each other.

After the bus crash, the group finds an abandoned building to hide out in. Through a boarded-up window, Ever, played by Brianne Tju, spots Brace Face screaming and running for help towards the building. Ever begs the others to help, but they don't. Ever seems to be the only one who cares about saving people. Meanwhile, most of the others are too busy bullying each other to be bothered, which turns out to hurt them throughout their ordeal. A jock and a nerd argue about fat camp. Two BFFs argue about why one is hanging with the popular kids instead of helping out. They say to follow the "heroes, not the zeros." The film clearly wants to send an anti-bullying message because the more the kids do it, the worse their situations become. They are so busy bullying, they forget to look for weapons.

The rooms in the abandoned building, which looks the home of an underground rave, get creepier and creepier as the characters make their way through them. The attention to detail in set design makes it even more interesting. Vibrant colors and visual effects like screen wipes play up the vibe. The characters' slow-motion reactions to the first death were genuinely believable.

Ever has the clearest character arc. Towards the middle of the movie, she becomes increasingly frustrated with the self-appointed leader of the group and chooses to ignore his demands. When she leaves with Steven, one of the nerds, to go back to the bus, a discovery reveals a massive plot twist that flips the narrative upside down. She also opens up a lot to Steven about her feelings of being an outcast.

After the plot twist, the movie becomes not only horrific visually, but thematically. A few of the characters reveal their true, evil selves and push things to the ultimate limit, but don't worry there's lots of cool sword fighting and badass female action. Finally, the crew is working together.

Unhuman, for what it's worth, has lots of after-school special like themes: friendship, loneliness, anti-bullying, and teamwork. Friends Ever and Tamra have a nice reconciliation in the end that basically includes them all. The movie pushes the horror genre in some mind-bending ways, but don't expect Walking Dead level gore here, though. Oh, and keep watching past the end credits for a brief scene that will delight viewers who enjoyed the film.

We give it 3 out of 5 stars. *Unhuman* is currently streaming on VOD.

A PREDATOR RETROSPECTIVE: HOW 35 YEARS OF PREDATOR LEAD TO PREY (2022)

BY GRANT BUTLER

This year not only marks the 35th anniversary of the original *Predator* film, *Prey*, the latest film in the *Predator* franchise, was released on August 5. So what was it about the original film that led to a franchise that is still with us to this day?

For starters, it's one of the defining movies of the 1980's. *Predator* is big, bold, and filled with many quotable lines, including one of the most famous lines of Arnold Schwarzenegger's career. Nor was Schwarzenegger the only future governor on set, as Jesse Ventura, the future governor of Minnesota, famously said the phrase "I ain't got time to bleed."

At first glance, *Predator* is an incredibly simple story, but the movie takes that very simple concept and executes it very well. *Alien* was a great blend of science fiction and horror, *Aliens* was a great blend of science fiction and action, but *Predator* is a great blend of action, horror, and science fiction.

But there's far more to it than that because while *Predator* may start out like a typical high-octane action movie, it quickly becomes something far more. When faced with the realization they are dealing with a highly intelligent organism with superior technology, Dutch and his fellow military men get creative in order to outwit the Predator. They have no choice but to adapt and think on their feet in the hopes of surviving. When Dutch and his team encounter the Predator and have no idea what's going on, it's unnerving to them, and the fear they show is palpable. When Billy, who his comrade points out isn't afraid of any man, doesn't hesitate to admit he's afraid, it's a chilling moment. Especially because Billy quickly points out what they're dealing with is no man.

And much like the film, the monster is an excellent combination of horror, science fiction, action, and intelligence. The Predator is not some bloodthirsty brute that's after carnage for the sake of carnage. It methodically watches the military men in the jungle and assesses them, and it doesn't hesitate to spare Anna, a female insurgent Dutch and his men capture, when it can easily see she is no threat to it at all, and no thrill to hunt.

All of this is radically different from a generic action thriller, especially from the era it was made in. What makes both the Predator monster and *Predator* the film unique is both the monster and the elite military men that it hunts. There's plenty of action, but it's secondary to the real battle, which is psychological and strategic. Unlike the vast majority of movie monsters, the Predator isn't out for the kill or to feed. Not only does it want to hunt, it wants to hunt something worth hunting. Something that'sa worthy prize. Not only is Dutch and his crew a worthy challenge to the Predator, Dutch could also lay claim to being the Predator himself in the end.

This original and intelligent story unfolds in a movie that is also well shot and full of genuine suspense and tension. So when you have a simple and original story filled with genuine suspense, an intelligent and original monster, intelligent and real characters, high octane action, quotable dialogue, well done special effects in an era when special effects were good, but didn't define the film, and a claustrophobic jungle atmosphere, it makes for a film that is very difficult to recreate or top. *Predator* is a film that does a lot with what seems like very little, and the result is something that is just as compelling today as when it was first released in theatres.

Prey, the new film in the *Predator* franchise, is something quite different from what's been done before. Not only is it more of a prequel than a sequel, it takes place during the 1700s in the Comanche Nation as a young woman trained as a warrior tries to protect her people from something unlike anything they have ever encountered before. Now streaming on Hulu.

GHOSTBUSTERS: AFTERLIFE AND THE CONCEPT OF "FAN SERVICE"

BY HOLLY LYN WALRATH

DOES RETCONNING AN ENTIRE MOVIE IN A FRANCHISE TRULY SERVE THE FANS? AND IF SO, WHICH ONES?

Ghostbusters: Afterlife is a truly fantastic film. It takes the concept of the original *Ghostbusters I* and *II* movies, classics for their genre of contemporary ghost story/comedy mashup, and gives them new heart and a young, relatable cast. It's a film kids love, as I can attest, because I saw it with my 11-year-old niece who could not stop giggling for most of it.

I loved that she loved it because I grew up a huge fan of Ghostbusters. The original Ghostbusters film came out in 1984. I wasn't born yet, but as a late-80s kid, I grew up loving the franchise thanks to the animated series *The Real Ghostbusters* , which ran from 1986–1991. In 1997, they released Extreme Ghostbusters as a second animated series. Both were so popular they even made a 30-minute spinoff called *Slimer!* that focused just on the ooey-gooey green goblin. While the concept of slime was first started in 1979 with the show *You Can't Do That on Television*, 90s kids know the worth of a good sliming, and I attest the popularity of the Slimer character to the idea that slime is a perfect end to any good reality show.

Ghostbusters was ubiquitous in my childhood. I was a latchkey kid and grew up in daycare because my mom was a busy nurse and my dad worked long hours at an airline company designing flight software. Classic early Millenial. I went to daycare twice a day: in the morning before school from about 6 to 8, and in the afternoon from when school let out to when my Dad got off work. The morning daycare was my favorite (although I was often half-awake) because they had a coveted toy: A "dollhouse" replica of the Ghostbusters fire-house. I would stay awake while other kids napped just to play with this toy.

As a fan, I should have loved *Ghostbusters: Afterlife* right? But instead, I left my watching of it feeling off-key and resigned. The film franchise I grew up loving feels like it's been highjacked.

Ghostbusters: Afterlife follows the story of a single mom Callie and her two kids, Phoebe and Trevor, who travel to Summerville, Oklahoma after Callie's estranged father dies unexpectedly—which is convenient because the family has just been evicted from their NYC apartment. For fans of the series, it's immediately clear that Callie's father is Egon Spengler, former Ghostbuster. The film's story continues the story from Ghostbusters I, retooling the wickedly hot Hittite god, Gozer the Gozarian, and her two terror-dog minions, the keymaster and gatekeeper.

There are some expected leaps in logic as to why Gozer would settle down in rural Oklahoma, mostly explained away by the presence of Ivo Shandor, the architect of 550 Central Park West, who apparently moved to Oklahoma to start a Gozer-worshipping cult and bring about the destruction of the world.

In a lot of ways, the film is truly wonderful. It's flashy and sharp. The soundtrack (despite lacking the classic "Who you gonna call?" except in the end credits) is killer. It's got a hint of romance between mom Callie and the local summer school teacher, played by 90s heartthrob Paul Rudd (who can't love Paul Rudd?). It's got a whip-smart STEM-loving girl lead in the form of Phoebe, played fantastically by Mckenna Grace, who manages to capture that Egon vibe through a lot of sarcasm and nerdery, with the help of a pair of Harry Potter eyeglasses and perfectly managed frizz. It's got a mostly useless, girl-obsessed, vaguely rebellious older brother, played by Finn Wolfhard of *Stranger Things* fame. They even throw in two characters for diversity among the otherwise white cast: Podcast (Logan Kim) and Lucky (Celest O'Connor), who are arguably better actors than the somewhat flat Carrie Coon and deserved more screen time.

The film captures the joy of seeing things like the P.K.E. meter and proton pack get dusted off and used by a new generation. It brings back the delightfully disturbing Stay Puft marshmallow man in tiny form. It's both curious and heart-wrenching seeing Phoebe engage with the ghost of her grandfather Egon, who is brought back to life through a CGI rendering of Harold Ramis. While I'm not a fan of CGI-ing dead acters back onto the screen, this was a heartfelt tribute to a talented actor gone far too soon.

In an interview, director Jason Reitman says that he wrote the movie as a tribute to both his father and Harold Ramis, even saying that he gave it to Ramis' widow and daughter to read before the movie was made (Fatherly). Not to pull back the veil, but I was fascinated to learn that the on-set Egon was played by Bob Gunton and that the CGI version was later added in, with "a scan of Gunton, looking at the facial muscles, the wrinkles and folds, the 'tics and squints' that made his skin believable" (The Wrap).

While the film is somewhat lacking in comedy (it's funny, but not that funny), it's still very enjoyable to watch. It hits the right beats and pulls on the right heartstrings. It's family-friendly.

Like I said, I should love it.

No One's Talking About Why Films Get Retconned

At one point in the film, the writers attempt to explain the rules of this world. Kids don't know about ghostbusters because they haven't been around since before they were born. Ghosts exist but haven't been seen since the 1980s when the original Ghostbusters saved New York City and the world from Gozer. It slips past *Ghostbusters II* in a few ways (notably, the Ectomobile was repainted with a 2-finger peace sign that no longer exists, but we could argue there might have been multiple Ectomobiles) that are easily explained. But the film makes no mention of the 2016 Ghostbusters film or events in it, even as Phoebe pulls up videos on YouTube of the original ghostbuster team.

Ghostbusters 2016 was the victim of a targeted hate campaign led by, I would argue, both the media and "fans" who were particularly angry that the film was given an all-female cast. The discussion at the time by the media was particularly frustrating to me, a female fan because most headlines and articles argued that it was "fans" who were mad at the cast being female and the fact that they would dare reboot the film without the original cast. There was no voice given to the fans who loved Ghostbusters and wanted a female cast. Harassment campaigns are sexier than people being excited about the film.

Among the frustrating events surrounding the so-called "backlash," Bill Murray was one of the original cast who at first didn't want to appear in a cameo of the film. I grew up loving Bill Murry. But as I get older, I feel like more and more of his past roles feel super cringeworthy to me. Every single interview he gave on the subject of Ghostbusters 2016 feels deeply sexist to me:

"It was only 'cause I knew these girls were funny." (Jimmy Kimmel Live, 2016)

"I was in that movie just because they asked me, and I knew if I said no, I was saying I didn't support that movie. I felt like, OK, I'm going to support them because I support them as people. So I did that one, and I would do this next one." (Science Fiction)

"When you see the film, and you'll delight in the film, it sort of rumbles along in the beginning. You're going, 'Oh God, are they going to pull this thing off?' I felt like a stepfather to the whole thing. There is no quit in these girls. This is a tough

movie to pull off, because it's a big concept. There's a lot on the plate—there's a lot of expectation." (Movieweb)

There's a subtlety to these responses, but one can't help but wonder if the implication is, "I didn't think it would make because it was women." It's not lost on me that Murray repeatedly calls the female cast "girls". And his reference "I support them as people" seems to try to humanize the actors, as if to say, despite being women, they are still human. It wasn't lost on me that even in *Afterlife*, Bill Murray's character Peter Venkman immediately greets Gozer by reminding her that they broke up, *ha ha I'm still a womanizer.* In retrospect, a lot of Venkman's dialogue and actions in the original film are so cringeworthy that it's strange in a "family-friendly" reboot that they decided to reintroduce that into the new film.

Part of the "backlash" to the 2016 film was due to the cast being strong, powerful comedians who have remade the female comedy landscape, breaking down gender barriers. Kristen Wiig is partially responsible for a huge shift in the way our society views female comedians. In 2015, Kate McKinnon's portrayal of Hillary Clinton on SNL became iconic and is still referenced today. And Leslie Jones broke both race and gender barriers by showcasing a kind of comedy that's bombastic and, yes, representative of being a female comedian.

In 2019, Leslie Jones posted on Twitter in response to *Afterlife* under the trending hashtag #LadyGhostbusters:

"So insulting. Like fuck us. We dint count. It's like something Trump would do. (Trump voice) "Gonna redo ghostbusteeeeers, better with men, will be huge. Those women ain't ghostbusteeeeers" ugh so annoying. Such a dick move. And I don't give fuck I'm saying something!!"

One can't really blame Jones for the strength of her response to the film, given that her experience with *Ghostbusters* 2016 nearly made her quit social media due to the endless barrage of abuse and racist attacks she received. One thing that stands out to me in her response is the mention of Trump—the timing of the 2016 film feels very pertinent in retrospect.

Right now, *Afterlife* is trending on Twitter because of the Ultimate Collection shipping, a boxset that includes *Ghostbusters I, II,* and *Afterlife.* No 2016 lady edition allowed, thank you very much.

I enjoyed the heck out of *Ghostbusters* 2016. It was hilarious and weird and filled with the female gaze and flipped a lot of stereotypes on their head. It responded to a lot of the tropes of the original Ghostbusters films with a feminist viewpoint. The women in the film face the particular issues of women academics—instead of being given funding to perform "experiments" on female students just to get in their pants—they are fighting for professional recognition. It's true satire.

Another example is the Aldridge Mansion Museum story. The ghost of the haunted house is Gertrude Aldridge, who is said to have killed her entire family in their sleep and was subsequently locked up in the basement for the rest of her life, fed through a slot in the door, and never released. The story is highly reminiscent of the story of famous ax-murderess Lizzie Borden. It's also fundamentally about sexism—a woman accused of a crime, and instead of being imprisoned or tried for the crime, she is tortured by her father for the rest of her life.

When I told my friend what I thought *Afterlife*, I said, "It has a lot of fan service. There's a lot that's just there for the fans." But then I started thinking, wait, which fans are we serving here? If I, a fan, felt alienated by the film, then was it truly serving fans? This isn't to say all fans are going to enjoy a film reboot, but the question is **why are movie creators catering specifically to the most vocal and most toxic fans?**

If the majority of media agree that these "fans" who hated *Ghostbusters* 2016 were "trolls," then why are we retconning that film?

After all, *Ghostbusters* 2016 was just as chock-full of easter eggs as *Afterlife*, just as full of fun, fan-service tidbits. And it's not like one sold that much better than the other. According to Wikipedia, *Ghostbusters* 2016 grossed a worldwide total of $229.1 million, while *Afterlife* grossed $204 million worldwide (The Numbers). Sure, one was released during a pandemic, but as of the date of this publication, only one was also given a sequel.

There is little backlash to the reboot being purely that—a reboot that doesn't really tread new ground. The plot basically rehashes the same plot of Ghostbusters I—Gozer shows up, a group of Ghostbusters bust her, and nothing entirely new is created. It's a beautiful memorial, but not much more than that. And maybe that's okay. If this film had come before *Ghostbusters* 2016, I wouldn't have minded. There's nothing wrong with a film that just is there to make fans happy.

The trouble comes when it's the shittiest, most toxic fans who hold sway.

It's as if there's a group of fans living in an alternate dimension, where their understanding of what the Ghostbusters franchise means is entirely different than my own. And if anyone dares to have a different experience of the franchise, they can't handle that. Is this really what fans want? And endless retread of the same tired plot, the same hokey jokes? How many times do we need to watch Bill Murray's character harass a woman and call it comedy?

I would love to see more directors stand up to the trolls. I'd love to see more continuations of my favorite franchises from all points of view, told by the fans whose voices have been previously ignored, and if they do tell their stories, they're abused to the point of giving up and leaving the fandom. Surely, there is room to explore a lot of different fan interpretations. But the reality is, if the media continues to put forth these narratives and give voice to abusers who want their narrative to be the loudest, things aren't likely to change.

Retconning is a revision of history that's sometimes necessary, but we need to look at what is being retconned and why. The idea of retroactive continuity is meant to make up for inconsistencies—but inconsistencies are inherent to fandom and multi-billion dollar franchises. It's which histories get erased that we should be questioning.

Oh, and no one gets slimed. I will avenge you, Slimer.

RETURN OF THE KILLER KLOWNS (FROM OUTER SPACE): THE CULT CLASSIC HORROR FILM GETS A VIDEO GAME REBOOT

BY PROF. RYAN FAY

If you are a horror historian, you know that trends tend to happen in cycles that usually span twenty to thirty years each. Dracula, Frankenstein's creature, and the Wolfman dominated the 1930s and 40s as the Universal Classic Monsters and gave rise to the creature features of the '50s. In 1960, Alfred Hitchcock redefined the horror genre with his film adaptation of *Psycho*, as Norman Bates inserted himself as a human monster among the classic icons. Linda Blaire terrified the United States into a satanic panic with her 1973 depiction of a possessed teenage girl in *The Exorcist*, the first horror movie to win an Academy Award. Then the '80s happened.

The 1980s would forever change the horror landscape, as it saw the horror genre take a massive step forward in its evolution. Larger-than-life characters like Freddy Krueger and Elvira were at the height of their popularity, and the genre started to embrace comedic relief in the form of over-the-top kills. Horror-comedy *Ghostbusters* leaned into the lighter side of the hybrid genre to become a summer blockbuster, creating space for the film that capped off the decade: *Killer Klowns from Outer Space* (1988).

Commercially underwhelming on its initial release, studios were unwilling to provide sufficient funding for a sequel. Now the film has hit cult classic status, even getting its own maze at Universal Studios' Hollywood Horror Nights, and a video game is set to launch in 2023 (*Teravision Games*). When new viewers sit down to watch *Killer Klowns from Outer Space* for the first time, not only will they be treated to the bright colors, catchy soundtrack, and the tongue-in-cheek comedy of the time, but a small dose of social commentary as well.

In 1988, the Chiodo brothers produced a perfect parody of *The Blob*, which had premiered exactly thirty years earlier in 1958. Let me know if you have heard this one before: something crash lands in the woods, some young people go to check it out, find something strange and dangerous, they try to warn the police, and the police don't believe them, resulting in several preventable deaths. The Chiodos were able to capture the generational conflict and distrust between the police and young adults, both of which are exemplified in the character of police officer Curtis Mooney.

The first time we see Officer Mooney, he sneers at a young man openly drinking beer in a crosswalk. Our initial impression leads us to believe that Mooney may not be one to crack down on every infraction, but he certainly is not happy with the "kids these days."

This only lasts until Mooney arrests two college students—dressed in stereotypical "punk" attire—for drinking in the park and threatens them with inflated charges. When a younger officer, Dave Hanson, tries to ease tensions and reason with the college students. Hanson witnesses a klown use a shadow puppet dinosaur to eat a group of people and calls Mooney at the station for backup. Mooney assumes that Hanson is working with the town to drive him out of the force by making Mooney look foolish, shouting, "you won't make a dummy out of me," before cutting off Hanson's radio. Shortly thereafter, Mooney has one of the klowns, Jumbo, in a cell with the two college kids from earlier and threatens to go beyond the police brutality to the edge of torture. Ultimately, Jumbo turns Mooney into a literal dummy, using him as a mouthpiece to threaten Dave just before dumping Mooney's dead body on the floor.

It is important to note that the portrayal of the older police officer is all done in clear jest. Mooney, played by the late Jack Vernon, who was known for mostly playing villains, is clearly paranoid and of a generation that seems in the process of being phased out of society. In the early confrontation with the college students, Mooney teases Hanson for his training at the police academy, something that has since become standard practice. Unfortunately, the generational conflict and distrust of police the Chiodo brothers made fun of in the '80s has only gotten worse forty years later.

Police officers and young adults not liking each other is an old trope, but one that each generation seems to have a new take on it. Given today's political atmosphere, the tension between the police and the public is at an all-time high. On any given day, a social media feed could be full of videos showing police in full riot gear pushing otherwise peaceful protestors away from buildings. While a film like Nia DaCosta's *Candyman* (2021)—a direct sequel to the original 1992 film of the same name—makes a poignant commentary on the specific relationship between the police and Black Americans, it is unfortunately evergreen. We could use a film that satirizes oversupplied and under-trained police departments for an audience that might ignore DaCosta's take, and a film like *Killer Klowns* could fill that space.

Whether the klowns' video game—currently positioned as a competitor to the popular *Dead by Daylight*—will be successful enough to inspire a reboot of the franchise is yet to be seen, there does seem to be growing support for the project. The super Chiodo bros. wanted to make a trilogy and a television series that would have continued the stories of Dave Hanson and the teens of Crescent Cove after the initial invasion.

Maybe the klowns work best as a parody like they did with *The Blob* and could play off Jordan Peele's recent alien-based horror film *Nope* (2022). After all, who couldn't use a laugh these days?

INTERVIEWS

"UNKNOWN NUMBER": INTERVIEW WITH HUGO-NOMINATED AUTHOR BLUE NEUSTIFTER

BY MEGAN WEGENKE

HOW A TEXT MESSAGE STORY ON TWITTER GOT NOMINATED FOR THE HUGO AWARD

The short story "Unknown Number," by Blue Neustifter, was originally posted on Twitter in July 2021. Told in the form of a series of text message exchanges, it tells the story of Gaby, a trans woman who has a fateful encounter with a still-closeted version of herself from a parallel universe. The story has since been nominated for a 2022 Hugo Award for best short story. Interstellar Flight Press member Megan Wegenke talked to Neustifter about the story's trans themes, its nontraditional format, and the persistent allure of multiverse storytelling.

INTERSTELLAR FLIGHT PRESS: The idea of meeting one's pretransition self via time travel has been something of a trope in trans fiction for a while. However, "Unknown Number" makes a point of avoiding the easy answers, and many of my trans friends and I felt that it works a lot better as a result than many other narratives that play with similar themes. What was your approach to telling a story with this kind of premise? Were there any points where you decided to swerve away from what the more "expected" thing would have been?

BLUE NEUSTIFTER: Absolutely, I think many trans people (including me, obviously) have thought a lot about the idea of "if I could go back in time and tell myself". One of my favorite works about this is "Énouement", by Samantha Richardson, found here. I read it a couple of years ago, and it really shaped my own thoughts and feelings about what I'd tell myself if I could, and its DNA of kind sympathy for one's past self is definitely intertwined in "Unknown Number."

Honestly, my main approach to writing this was to make sure I actually put myself in the headspace of both the protagonist (Gaby) and the other character (who I'll just call U for the sake of clarity, as she shows up on the text message screens). It's been about six years or so since I was in the place that U was, and it was frankly a pretty awful time for me, mental health-wise.

The idea of not just being trans (I already identified as nonbinary) but actually *changing a bunch of my life to be trans* was terrifying and required a leap of faith I simply couldn't seem to make. I was scared and desperate and wished I could reach forward into the two futures I saw ahead of me—one where I took the leap and one where I didn't—and ask them both how they were doing. For U to be the character she was, I knew she had to be even more desperate.

So a lot of the writing was digging into the back of my brain, tapping into that time and what it felt like to have that aching void inside of me, and going, "What would I have said if someone had given me this opportunity?"

Regarding swerving away from the "expected," I think maybe the primary pitfall I wanted to avoid was... I didn't want it to be easy. I didn't want Gaby to immediately buy the premise of what was happening, and I didn't want U to just go, "Oh, great, you're a girl, question answered, thanks." The former would ring far too hollow to me, a person who has been doxxed and has had close loved ones be doxxed as well. If someone showed up out of nowhere with detailed knowledge about my life, my reaction would be, "Ah, that one website did more digging on me."

I wanted that very real tension to be present on Gaby's side. And for the latter point... listen, that dark period for me lasted a couple of years. The idea of physically transitioning occurred to me a few times during it, but the thought was like a hot stove burner; I could never get too close to it without jerking away in pain. There were times during those two years when a scroll could drop from the sky saying, "You, Blue, are trans, here's some estrogen," and I'd still have looked up at the deities and gone, "Yeah, but... I'm not *really* trans, right? You meant this for someone else?"

Similarly, I've sat with some very dear people for months as they examine the idea of their gender and still can't make out the shape of it, even if I feel like I could make a pretty good guess as to where they'll end up. Everyone has their own timing on this journey, and a lot of us aren't open to the answer until we're damn ready for it. For some of us, having someone grab us by the shoulders and tell us the answer would push us further *back* into the internalized closet. So, for me, it was really important that U reacted similarly to how I did and some others have, with fear and uncertainty ever well past the point that the dam is clearly breaking.

"For some of us, having someone grab us by the shoulders and tell us the answer would push us further *back* into the internalized closet."

Finally, I think the other major subversion (if you want to call it that) that was important to me was having U be the one to take the initiative. I *love* a good "I'm going back to tell myself the truth" story; they're cathartic and lovely. But for this, for what I wanted to make, I wanted it to be the choice of the person who was wondering. I didn't want a *deus ex genus* to show up and hand her the answer. Because, again, getting handed the answer might have made things worse for a lot of us. We have to find it ourselves. Not that we shouldn't be given the *tools* to figure it out—representation in media, education about transness and the ways we can modify our bodies and lives if we wish, all this vital information that is often withheld from us—but the final step of the journey is ours and ours alone. Not even our future/alternate-universe self can make that leap for us.

That's why I wanted U to be the one to reach out rather than, say, Gaby inventing this communication to tell all her other selves. That's why I wanted the story to end the way it did, with hope but also with uncertainty, because the answer, the future, is U's and hers alone.

IFP: It's really cool seeing a story with such a nontraditional format get nominated for a Hugo! The idea of such a deeply personal revelation coming from an SMS exchange with a stranger feels woven into this story's nature. Was this formatting approach the plan from the beginning, or was it something you came to later in the process? Were there any particular challenges to writing a story entirely in text messages—or any new opportunities it opened up?

BN: My writing process, for better or worse, involves a lot of quietly chewing on a partially-formed idea, exploring it until I feel like I understand it well enough to write it. "Unknown Number," unsurprisingly, started as a "going back in time to tell yourself" idea, but during the year or so of "chewing on it," I realized it just would fall apart under any scrutiny.

Even setting aside messy questions about whether figuring this out earlier would make you someone entirely different, there's also the sticking point of "Isn't there a bunch of other stuff Gaby should warn her past self about?" I like to write my speculative fiction as emotionally realistic as I can; I'm okay with handwaving the speculative "hook" (parallel dimensions, ghosts, vampires, etc.), but I want people to act and react in grounded, honest ways. I couldn't imagine a trans woman in Gaby's position not warning herself about, say, Donald Trump, or Doug Ford, or COVID-19. I wanted Gaby to be U's counterpart, someone who knew U better than anyone else ever could, but I didn't want her to be an oracle. I realized that for that dynamic, alternate timelines were a more honed version of that relationship.

Once I knew I was doing an alternate-timelines story, I just... knew the format. I'm not even sure how I knew, exactly, I just knew it would be essentially a script-based conversation, and the moment I knew that, I knew it was text messages. I have always been captivated by epistolary stories; my mom gave me a copy of *Z for Zachariah* (Robert C. O'Brien) when I was young, which is a book written entirely in the form of diary entries from a young girl in a post-apocalypse. I was *obsessed* with that format, with its pseudo-realism and the ways that it artificially limited the reader's viewpoint.

That fascination has never gone away for me. I'd done some writing in the epistolary format before (a Twitter-based short story I wrote called "Patches from the Universe" took the form of "patch notes" from the creators of the universe as they fixed it), but never in a way that was viscerally visual in the way of my favorite epistolary stories like *House of Leaves* (Mark Z. Danielewski). So when the idea occurred to me that this could (*should*) be text-based, the jump to realizing I could use one of those "fake SMS message" websites to give it that extra bit of realism was natural.

I think the main opportunity this format gave was that the story had immediate emotional resonance. Thanks to social media, a lot of us are very used to parsing stories from images; we're constantly sharing screenshots of tweets, of DMs, of Tumblr and Reddit posts as tiny little flash-fictions of each other's lives. So that gave the story an "in" to a lot of people and allowed the story to begin *in medias res* with little exposition; we're used to looking at screenshots and collecting the context as we go.

The texts also gave it an immediate *beat* to move to, a pace. Writing in these text screenshots used a skill that I'd been honing from using Twitter as a writing platform for a few years; the trick to a story that is chopped up into little bits is that each bit needs to have a wholeness to it, a tiny bit of closure, but not so much closure that you aren't compelled to read the next one. There's a rhythm to it, and this format enhanced that rhythm.

"Thanks to social media, a lot of us are very used to parsing stories from images; we're constantly sharing screenshots of tweets, of DMs, of Tumblr and Reddit posts as tiny little flash-fictions of each other's lives."

Finally, in terms of marketing, if you want to call it that, I think the format lent itself to a type of virality that is hard to hit with written fiction. Social media *loves* images; Twitter and Facebook's algorithms clearly prioritize pictures over pure text, and posting the story in a single image per tweet meant that there were these tiny bite-sized nuggets, each of which could be shared. It's hard to get word-of-mouth going for self-published writing. While I didn't write "Unknown Number" in this format specifically for it to go viral, I can't argue that its success didn't, at least to some extent, depend on how social-media-friendly the format was.

The main challenge with the text format was simply time and energy. The script for "Unknown Number" took less than a third of the writing process; most of the other two-thirds was painstakingly creating each "screenshot," including estimating how much time had passed for each screen (to update the clock in the top-right) and keeping the battery indicator moving steadily downward in a realistic manner. I frequently found a mistake and had to go back and redo a screenshot, or sometimes several, if I messed up the time stamps. And I also had to make edits to the script on the fly to keep each screenshot ending on a "beat"; the space was limited, and the script had to get nudged around so that the closing line of each screenshot had just a bit of oomph to it. (There are a few places where I cheated; some of the screenshots are actually a *little* bit larger than the rest as I pushed the text program to slightly-bigger-than-a-real-screen for the sake of fitting the dialogue I wanted.)

I was posting the screenshots to Twitter before I was fully done making them all, which led to me scrambling under time pressure as I realized I had no idea how to convincingly Photoshop the "Message not received" indication in the final image, but people were waiting for the end of the story. Finally, this format has made it *hard* to put into any sort of more permanent sharing solution than social media; for the Hugo packet, it needed to be in PDF and ePub formats, and I eventually needed to beg for help and have someone more tech-savvy than I help get them into these formats in a way that didn't look terrible and had alt-text for accessibility. (My eternal gratitude to @SciFantasy on Twitter for saving me when I was at my breaking point on this.)

IFP: The two Gabys first find common ground with the question, "When we were a teen we were interested in multiverse stuff right," and this shared curiosity about roads not taken being what finally gets them to start talking for real. Multiverses and alternate timelines are having a cultural Moment right now (between the MCU, Everything Everywhere All at Once, and several other examples), but this is an especially grounded and personal take on the concept. What's different about the resonance of these tropes when you're using them to tell a specifically trans story?

BN: Unsurprisingly, I share Gaby/U's fascination with alternate universes; that one episode of *Sliders* stuck with me for two decades, and I watched *Sliding Doors* more times than I can say. I think multiverse stories speak to a lot of us because we all, trans or not, have major decisions in our lives that we look back and go "what if" about. (I'd argue that for things like the MCU, multiverses are less appealing on this front and more because it provides a way to tap into lots of various nostalgias quickly, but that may be somewhat cynical of me.) I think it also provides us a way to conceptualize how much *who we are* is based on *what we do*. Through multiverses, we can not only explore the ways that our lives could be different but also the ways that *we* could be different. What if I was a kinder, more generous person? Or had better boundaries? Or stopped caring about what others think? In a way, it can be a way of almost trying on different selves, seeing if there are others we'd want to be.

I don't know if I can say if these stories have a different resonance just because of transness, honestly. I mean, they speak to *me* differently because of how they hit me in the gender, but I have no idea what it's like to be cis and don't want to claim that cis people just can't experience them the same way I do. I think the question is more about whether the multiverse is being used to tell a *personal* story or not.

The MCU use of multiverses is generally more of a means than an end; it's a great way to bring lots of people together for a big conflict. For *Sliders*, it's used as a great way to jump between genres and setpieces with very little legwork on the travel. But take, say, *Spider-Man: Into the Spider-Verse*: yes, there's also a giant superhero conflict there, but it's also using multiverses as a tool to examine the character of Miles Morales and his growth into his better self. While *Spider-Verse* isn't a trans narrative (at least explicitly: I've got head-canons about Liv Octavius), I think it still hits a similar resonance for me as "Unknown Number" in that it uses multiverses to explore who a character is, who he could be. I tend to think of my process through transition as a small, individual version of the literary Hero's Journey, where you receive the call to be something bigger, end up hitting rock bottom and come back someone totally different.

For me, for "Unknown Number," the multiverse was a tool to help make that journey explicit and in a way that wasn't totally internal; it let me take the frantic monologue of my anxious past self and turn it into a dialogue instead.

IFP: A lot of the experiences of growing up with gender dysphoria that Gaby shares with herself were incredibly familiar to me as a trans woman reader (that thing about not feeling like you're "allowed" to play as female characters, in particular, gave me some real deja vu). Of course, not every reader of this story is going to have such a direct familiarity with these kinds of experiences. Were there some parts of this story that you expected to resonate differently with a cis audience, or specifically added with that outside perspective in mind? Conversely, which things did you expect would be pretty universal?

BN: I'm both glad they felt so familiar and sorry you went through that too. I definitely remember the weird, sick feeling of guilt I felt when idly fantasizing about what being a girl character in a comic I had would be like when I was six or seven. When writing "Unknown Number" (and another earlier story in a similar vein, "Ghosts", about a closeted trans person and a ghost in their home who writes on their fridge), my main goal was writing for a trans audience. If only trans people read it and liked it, that would be enough for me. But, I also wanted to... kind of highlight aspects of our lives, our experiences, that spoke to something more universal. I think most of us as people have a lot in common in terms of the struggles and fears we have in our lives. The contexts of those struggles can be very different, but the emotional core of them is often the same.

There are a couple of points in the story I tried to gently highlight that. Particularly Gaby's response to U saying, "I've wasted so much time," when she says, "everyone does in one way or another." All or mostly all of us have had some big thing in our life that we waited on out of fear. Trans or not, a lot of us know that sunk-cost feeling of "I missed my shot, if I wanted to do this I should've started years ago," and I wanted to point that out, draw a connective line of empathy there for cis people in the audience.

And then there was Gaby's speech about what it means to "be happy." That was a difficult but important lesson that I was lucky taught in some cognitive behavioral therapy workshops I took to help with my depression during the pre-hormone difficult years. Regardless of whether a reader fully connected with the whole trans thing, I wanted to share that important insight I'd thankfully been given, that little nugget of life wisdom. In American capitalism, we're really sold the dream that if we work hard enough, if we hustle and grind enough, we'll eventually "make it," we'll reach success, we'll finally be stable, be comfortable, be happy. And life just isn't that simple. Happy as a permanent goal is great when you want to *sell* something, but for actually living your life, it's setting up a goal you'll never fully reach. Every bad day will feel like a failure, like backsliding, like more proof that you aren't doing it right, aren't doing it hard enough. So I tried, through Gaby, to help a reader let go a bit of that impossible perfectionism in a way that fit the story and her and U's character arcs.

IFP: How difficult was it to differentiate the narrative voices of the two Gabys, given that it's a large part of the point of the story that their respective life paths are only a short "distance" away from each other?

BN: That was actually one of the least difficult parts of the story for me. I remember quite strongly what it was like to be in U's position, to be exhausted and depressed and terrified that there's something missing in your life and even more terrified that maybe nothing is missing and this is just how life *is*. And I know Gaby very well; I know what it's like to be a trans woman in a world that's scary for trans people, how the hypervigilance and fear of being singled out or attacked can make you tired and jaded and prickly.

While I certainly have writing faults, dialogue has always been one of the parts of fiction that has come easier to me. I am used to having fake conversations with other people in my head all the time (probably partially an anxiety thing, "feeling out" conversations before they happen), so when I write dialogue, my brain is pretty good at just putting fictional people in a room together and going "Okay, how would she react to them saying that" and then "How would *they* react to *her* saying that." U and Gaby, in particular, were both such clear facets of myself, of my life, that it wasn't hard to immediately hear the ways they'd interact, how they'd bounce off each other. Even if their dimensions weren't that far apart (at "minimum girl distance"), the two of them were in such vastly different places in their emotional growth that they were incredibly different people, so their voices came pretty naturally.

What was harder than giving them distinct voices was a reason to keep talking; I struggled a lot with how to make Gaby realistically stick with a conversation that felt so much like being doxxed and harassed. But that, too, worked out in that it gave both characters arcs. The story wasn't just U figuring out some stuff about her gender, it was also Gaby softening her edges to let U in, to reach out and help someone else who was hurting the way she had once hurt.

IFP: I feel like the most pivotal moment of the story is when Gaby tells her alternate self, "Stop hiding in my life. What is YOUR answer?" It's very much part and parcel of how this story avoids easy answers. Did you know from the beginning that that was what this story was leading to, or was it something you discovered in the writing?

BN: I knew the story was, of course, about U figuring out her own gender, or at least getting a kickstart on that journey. I didn't, however, plan Gaby's pivotal speech at that moment. I knew the beginning of the story, I knew the emotional catharsis for U it would reach, I had a couple of specific beats in mind, but the rest was written on the fly as the two characters bounced off each other. In some ways, that speech was partially a product of my own frustration with my past self, with how much she hesitated and spent two years asking "what if"s.

Again, I've been U, I remember how much evidence I had that pointed to the clear answer and how much I still hesitated and doubted. And looking back, I don't want to tell her the answer, but I do kind of wish I could say to her, "Okay, time's up, pencils down, just submit the answer you know is right." Throughout the story, U is seeking information, but that information-seeking is also a form of deflection, of living in a fantasy. Something needed to break her out of that for her to have any growth. Gaby's like me; she hit that breaking point by slowly sinking deeper and deeper into depression until the only thing left to break was her denial. She wouldn't want to see someone else have to go through that, especially another version of her. So, she tried to move that process along in her loving but firm and somewhat abrasive way.

IFP: This story covers plenty of heavy topics, but it's also frequently very funny, and I loved the sort of rueful dark humor the two Gabys share over the absurdity of their situation. What was your favorite line to write?

BN: I'm really glad to hear that people find the humor in it, too. I liked writing Gaby's quick, if acerbic, wit. I had someone comment on the story that it has a very "trans sense of humor" and I take that as a compliment; honestly, trans people are some of the funniest people I know.

You asked my favorite line to write in the context of humor, so I'll answer that first: I have several, but I think Gaby's early comment of "If you're asking if I named myself after Xena's girlfriend, I think you probably already know the answer" was my favorite, because the humor feels so specific to these two characters, to the fact that they *are* the same person, that they both grew up with the same heroines and wanting the same things. (Also, it serves extra purposes of quickly establishing Gaby's queerness and the ties between their two selves over shared childhood media.)

My truly favorite line to write wasn't a funny one, though. It was "I love you, Gaby." This wasn't something I'd planned going into the story; it wasn't something I'd even planned more than a dozen or so lines of dialogue in advance. But when I pushed the story to an ending (by closing the wormhole, as it were), I knew that the characters would feel a sense of loss, of a kind of desperation for some kind of closure and something to commemorate that they were here, that this did happen, that it mattered. And for many trans people, names can be so important. Choosing a name for yourself is a form of reclaiming power, reclaiming your identity, of taking the script that was written for you, and beginning to make whatever edits you want. In this very particular circumstance of alternate selves, Gaby could almost make a gift of her name to her other self, a legacy she could pass on. Regardless of whether U ultimately would choose the name Gaby for herself (I have thoughts on that but prefer to not weld extra canon on post hoc), the *gesture* there was important. It was a crystalline-clear moment of Gaby saying, "I see you, I believe you, and I know you can do this." It was an act of trust to share this precious identity she'd created for herself with another her that needed it.

"And for many trans people, names can be so important. Choosing a name for yourself is a form of reclaiming power, reclaiming your identity, of taking the script that was written for you, and beginning to make whatever edits you want."

The fact that she says "I love you" was important to me, personally. Loving myself has been a very difficult journey. Like many people, I learned to love *others* very strongly but had no idea how to show that same care and compassion for myself. I had certainly never said "I love you" to myself or my reflection until well into my transition. Now I try to show myself, show that woman in the mirror, the same sort of deep caring I try to give others. I wanted Gaby and U to share that, if only for a moment. So while it isn't on the topic of humor, that was my favorite line to write. I actually had to stop for a few minutes after writing that line because it hit me harder than I expected, and I needed to recompose myself. I'm glad I've seen others connect with that moment, too, because it was really important to me.

ABOUT THE AUTHOR

Blue Neustifter (she/her) is a white, queer trans woman and 2022 finalist for a Hugo Award in the "Best Short Story" category for her epistolary story "Unknown Number". In addition to writing genderful speculative fiction, she is a statistician and avid board gamer (as well as published board game designer). She lives in Ontario and deeply loves her partners and many pets, and is trying to help make the world a little better for trans people how she can.

BRIDGING WORLDS IN AFRICAN SPECULATIVE FICTION: INTERVIEW WITH NEBULA-WINNER OGHENECHOVWE DONALD EKPEKI

BY MAR VINCENT

Interstellar Flight Press is delighted to chat with Oghenechovwe Donald Ekpeki, guest editor for our short story collection call and a talented writer and editor celebrating African speculative fiction.

INTERSTELLAR FLIGHT PRESS: First and foremost, congratulations on the Nebula win for your novelette, "O2 Arena!" How does it feel to be the first African-born Black author to win the Nebula Award and the first African winner in the novelette category?

OGHENECHOVWE DONALD EKPEKI: I still find myself reeling every time I think about it consciously, remember that it's something that happened to me in particular. It's not really something you expect, plan for, really hope for. It's not happened before to someone like me, it's not something I think can happen to someone where I am. But it did. And that's something I struggle to process daily, and I dare to hope that the little things that have prevented this before, access, visibility, and marginalization, are changing for the better.

IFP: "O2 Arena" is a story set in a dystopian future that doesn't feel so far removed from our current time. What inspired this piece, or what was the 'story seed' that the story built from?

ODE: Well, it was inspired by real events. I did attend the Nigerian Law school, Lagos campus. We live at the cusp of climate disaster, if not in it. I'm disabled with many respiratory issues, and breathing is a daily struggle for me. So in a way, I live in that world. It's my own arena, and I have to engage in those fights daily. I and people like me here. Our lives are the story seed. I also had a friend who passed from cancer. The hashtag #SaveVoke on social media documents the reality of that story.

IFP: I would love to know more about your work as an editor. When you're reading submissions, is there something specific you look for in a piece? What was your process for gathering essays in the non-fiction anthology *Bridging Worlds*? How is editing a nonfiction project different from editing fiction?

ODE: For me, it's about how stories touch me. How they make me feel. I look for what sets a spark off inside me. The ones that make me feel something, those are the ones I want.

The *Bridging Worlds* anthology was about people, their personal stories. So in that way, it was different from the fiction anthologies I edited where the stories were the focal points of it. This one had the people at the heart, and their own stories were what we needed to tell and hear. So I started by reaching out to the people I know, whose lives and experiences would undoubtedly give us the insight we need. So the fundamental difference between the fiction and nonfiction story for me would be that fiction is a story by the writer, while the non-fiction is the story of the writer.

IFP: What are the greatest influences on your work? Which authors do you consider your greatest inspirations?

ODE: Well, everybody I read, I learn something from them and am moved to try something out from what I learnt.

But some of the authors who have influenced me positively are Ben Okri, African speculative fiction writers like Suyi Davies Okungbowa, Wole Talabi, Tendai Huchu, Tlotlo Tsamaase, Makena Onjerika, Tade Thompson, and more. Writers I see and interact with everyday.

IFP: What is one thing about Nigerian culture that you think Western readers probably don't know but that would help them better appreciate your work (or Nigerian speculative fiction on the whole)?

ODE: Well, it's not so much Nigerian culture but how language works. Your culture and identity is in your language. Language is a vehicle that carries those things scattered about in it, little flavorings that are conveyed in your expressions.

Sometimes Western readers see this and think it's bad or wonky writing if the dialogue doesn't work. But I'll like them to remember that just because something doesn't sound good to them doesn't mean it isn't good. We must keep interrogating our biases everyday that are possibly imperialist, and how we other things—a decolonization of the mind.

IFP: Where would you suggest interested readers start if they want to get acquainted with African speculative fiction?

ODE: I'd recommend a number of speculative fiction anthologies as the work of African writers is most plentiful in short form. Longer work requires stability and resources many on the continent lack.

Anthologies like *AfroSF* volume 1 to 3 (storytime, 2013), the *Dominion* anthology (Aurelia Leo, 2020); the *Year's Best African Speculative Fiction anthology (Caezik SF & Fantasy*, 2023) and *Bridging Worlds* (2022) Pan-African pandemic non-fiction anthology are both free to download online.

Folks can look at *Omenana Magazine*, can preorder the incoming *Africa Risen* anthology (Tordotcom, 2022), and then check out the works of authors like Suyi Davies Okungbowa, Wole Talabi, Dare Segun Falowo, Tlotlo Tsamaase, Mame Bougama Diene, Rafeeat Aliyu, Nuzo Onoh, and more.

IFP: What are you working on next? Where can readers find you?

ODE: Everything. I'll just say everything and leave it at that. Cuz I fear if I tried to elaborate, we'd go on forever. So stay tuned and watch as things unfold. Thanks!

ABOUT THE AUTHOR/EDITOR

Oghenechovwe Donald Ekpeki is a Nigerian writer and editor of speculative fiction whose work can be found in publications including Apex, Asimov's, and Strange Horizons, and who has edited anthologies including the first *Year's Best African Speculative Fiction*, *Dominion*, and *Africa Risen* (forthcoming on Tordotcom in 2022). He has also guest-edited for Interstellar Flight Press and won awards for his contributions to SFF including the Nommo, British Fantasy, and Otherwise awards—and, with his 2021 novelette, "O2 Arena," he has become the first African-born Black author to win the Nebula Award.

MINTY FRESH: A VAMPIRE PULP NOVELLA: INTERVIEW WITH DEBUT AUTHOR J. CORVINE

BY B. RAE GROSZ

"GOTH BITES VAMPIRE, GETS BAD CASE OF THE VAMPS"

Araminta "Minty" Chase is in a bad mood even before she falls out of the window and lands on a vampire. And it goes from bad to worse when a second run-in with the vampire results in Minty starting to become one herself. But the thing that really sets Minty off is when her werewolf kid brother, Sid, is abducted and taken to a mysterious research institute, and she's determined to get him back, no matter what. B. Rae Grosz talked with author J. Corvine about how hir novella, *Minty Fresh (Self-Published,* 2022*)*, came to be.

INTERSTELLAR FLIGHT PRESS: When and how did you first come up with the idea for *Minty Fresh*?

J. CORVINE: In 2015-16, I was frustrated. I wanted to write horror, to write about monsters, but everything I wrote persisted in turning out ordinary. I usually start stories by thinking of a first line. Given the way that first draft starts, I probably meant for the name to be unusual from the start. The problem was the story itself kept veering to ordinary. I was getting increasingly frustrated with this weird goth girl on an impromptu coffee shop date with a cute goth guy she'd just met, even though she was quickly becoming very fun to write. I sat there one day, staring at this story I wanted to be good, but that was turning into everything I was trying to branch away from, and then I wrote, "That was when the vampire walked in."

IFP: So, we've got the vampire. How did the pulp in the Vampire Pulp develop?

JC: I tried to write at least another draft of *Minty Fresh* but eventually dropped it to concentrate on short stories. I'd finally reached a point where I was better at 1) writing and 2) combining my strengths, like snappy dialogue and distinct characters, with the weird horror I wanted to write. Monsters and the grotesque depicted in colorful writing became my Thing. And then, in 2018, I came up with the concept for what is now my next Vampire Pulp novel. It took me a couple of years to finish, but I really hit my stride with it. That first draft was meandering with a lot of filler, but after that dreaded halfway point, it started getting so good. I had fun playing around with magic and more fluidity of the self and transformation, and there was a lot of banter and friction between the main characters, which always leads to a good time. After it was done, I took another break to write more short stories and continue submitting them. Trying to become a professional writer meant I needed a website. While putting it together, I had trouble figuring out how to get across what I write. My best friend said, "What about 'vampire pulp'?" and I latched onto it. I write pulpy stuff, I write about vampires and other monsters, and I love the way it's silly and tongue-in-cheek, memorable in its oddness, and even kind of punk, all at once. It's very Me.

IFP: There's a lot of great silly and tongue-in-cheek and memorably odd humor in *Minty Fresh*. Was there a scene that was especially fun to write?

JC: I love writing Minty; everything she says is incredibly funny to me. She looks at the world through this lens of "Who is out to get me today?" and "How can I show I don't give two shits?" The scene in the alley behind the goth club, when the vampire she meets confronts her, was a lot of fun. Minty acting cocky, drunk off booze, and the afterglow of her restroom hook-up, then realizing "I am, in fact, in a great deal of trouble" was a highlight for me.

IFP: When there are people out to get Minty in a very real way, the only thing she cares about is her kid brother, Sid, who's already been got.

JC: Minty and Sid's bond has always been her strongest since her earliest iteration. As I started paring off more and more of the story to get to the heart of it —to *Minty Fresh*—Sid was rehauled to be much younger than originally, so the dynamic shifted drastically. They didn't just love and trust each other. Sid *depended* on her. He was helpless. With that change, the whole thing suddenly, finally, had a heart: Sid. It's Sid's love for and trust in Minty that is the catalyst for everything. No one has ever needed Minty before Sid. She thinks of herself as a crummy person because he's the best thing in her life, yet she continually lets him down in little ways. When he's taken, she does whatever it takes to get him back. Not because she thinks she can but because she can't let him down again. And because she knows wherever he is, he *trusts* her to.

IFP: Minty gets some help from Lou, who is definitely a different love interest than the "cute goth guy" you mentioned from the early version. How did she become part of the story?

JC: It was one of the last things I figured out as I pulled *Minty Fresh* out of the rubble of those early drafts. Minty has always been a serial dater, antsy about commitment and unable to decide why, and she had an unfortunate habit of hooking up briefly with people she works with. One person mentioned in passing was a butch security guard named Lou, short for Louise. She was entirely a background character. Once I started finally getting somewhere, I thought, okay, someone connected to this conspiracy could *already be working at the agency*! I'll just repurpose this one character I've already got—ooh, she could be a werewolf! And I thought Minty's characterization would benefit from another important relationship, so I decided to explore them as a couple. Lou developed the rest of the way as I wrote it.

IFP: Part of Minty's character development over the course of the story includes her starting to realize that she's non-binary. The vampire she meets at the beginning is also non-binary. And at one point, it's stated that "Vampires aren't really male or female." What inspired that particular worldbuilding detail?

JC: The worldbuilding I've done establishing what I'd guess you'd call my canon has been this mess of developing details between stories and updating them with each draft. Things I decided are true in *Minty Fresh* will change things in my next book. Details I worked out in that book's first draft informed things in *Minty Fresh*. I think the first time I specifically wrote that vampires aren't male or female was in Minty's first iteration. And I decided I liked that and have run with it ever since. I was working out some gender feelings with Minty back then, so she's always been non-binary. Connecting that with her monstrousness, with the way she feels detached from humanity, in *Minty Fresh* came naturally, given where I've ended up. And I love that 90s goth vampire aesthetic: dead complexion, spidery veins, blue lips, creepy eyes, sharp fangs. Something between a Romantic image and a fucking monster. In the end, I'm guilty of self-indulgence: I'm an androgyne, I'm goth, and I wanna be a vampire!

IFP: So, there's going to be a next Vampire Pulp novella?

JC: There are going to be many next Vampire Pulp novellas! My next book's working title is *Dead Ends*, which will be about a vampire without a name and an arrogant gay witch who shows up to ruin their life, at least as they see it. I'm having a lot of fun with it, right down to indulging in cameos, of all things. Right after that, I'm writing a novella about Sid to dig into his backstory. There are *very* tentative plans to write novellas centered on Lou and a couple of characters from *Dead Ends*, respectively. I've also got a couple of smaller side projects planned to explore Minty and Sid's relationship. Just lil' werewolf guy shenanigans with some horrifying undertones.

ABOUT THE AUTHOR

J. Corvine is an androgynous tea-swilling fiend and one of those fucking goths. Ze is also a writer of Vampire Pulp novels and short dark fiction about monsters, ghosts, and/or sad sack queers. You can find hir on Twitter @J_Corvine or contact hir via hir website, jcorvine.wordpress.com.

THE FANTASTIC MS YURIKO SMITH

BY CHRISTINA SNG

Christina Sng chats with the multi-talented Angela Yuriko Smith about the importance of heritage and preserving our stories.

INTERSTELLAR FLIGHT PRESS: Tell us about yourself and your Asian influences through your parents, your environment, and your heritage and history.

ANGELA YURIKO SMITH: I'm a third-generation American-Uchinanchu, more commonly called Okinawan. My great-grandparents came to Hawaii just prior to World War II. My mother and grandmother lived in Honolulu until my mother was about twelve. My grandmother married a man in the Navy and he relocated the family to Alaska. Growing up in Cheyenne, Wyoming I felt like an outsider, but I'm sure it was nothing compared to what my mom and her brother felt. They went from tropical to cold, had to learn a new language and customs, all while adapting to a new father figure. I think my family have been outsiders for so many generations it's become programmed in our DNA.

There is often a thread of defiant authenticity in my work—-accepting otherness even when it's considered horrific or "less than." In Japan, Okinawans are denied rights as an indigenous people, meaning Japan can decide what happens in the Ryūkyūan Arc even against the wishes of the people who live there. Okinawa is repeatedly sold by the Japanese government to the US military.

Despite repeated protests by the Okinawan people, the US military holds thirty-two installations on a combined 877 square miles. The US military occupies fifteen percent of all land. Plans are in place at this moment to build another base despite protests it is destroying the ecosystem and violating burial grounds.

On top of that, sex crimes committed by US military typically go unpunished by the US and Japanese government, including sexual crimes against children. "Between January 2015 and December 2020, sixty-nine Marines were convicted in Okinawa for sexual offenses involving minors, including possession and distribution of child sexual abuse images and actual or attempted sexual assault of a child. All of those found guilty received military prison sentences and bad conduct or dishonorable discharges." (NCIS CASE FILES REVEAL UNDISCLOSED U.S. MILITARY SEX CRIMES IN OKINAWA, by Jon Mitchell October 3, 2021)

To protect their children from discrimination, many Okinawans were told they were Japanese when growing up. As an example, I was named after my grandmother, but she made me promise I wouldn't carry her name on to any of my children. Her wish was for her descendants to "be better" by being more Caucasian. As a result, the languages and culture of the Okinawan people are considered extremely endangered. I myself didn't know there was a difference between Japanese and Okinawan until I was in my thirties.

This is criminal. Culture is what distinguishes us. To take cultural identity away from a people is an attempt to take away their power and worth. Sadly, this is a global crisis not reserved for Okinawans. Representation is vital for all people. Growing up, otherness was a burden to me. Now, it's a process of illumination.

The more I learn about my hidden heritage, the more determined I am to share it, as you can tell by my impassioned and overly political answer.

IFP: Are there stories your parents told you that differ so much from the typical horror in our genres?

AYS: The stories my parents told me were always based on real events. My childhood was full of demons and demi-gods that haunted family members, exorcisms and the idea that the spirits were always among us. The supernatural was so ingrained in my mind as a child I think I was probably in my twenties when I realized there was a difference between fictional horror and family stories. It was a shock to me when I realized Peter Straub wasn't relating personal events, though I sometimes wonder. Writers are a strange bunch.

IFP: What is one such story that stands out in your mind? (For me it is the pontianak and the ghost nuns sitting on fans in our Catholic schools here in Singapore!)

AYS: I would love to hear that story—-ghost nuns sound so interesting! One of the stories I remember hearing as a child (and as a child I may have some details wrong) was that one day an ancestor would come and ask me to be the medium in our family as he did to all the firstborn daughters. It was presented as a terrifying prospect and I would have to resist him at all costs. Family members had lost their lives in the struggle.

After I learned about Yuta (Okinawan mediums) I realized there is a lot of fear of being culturally different woven through this story. A few generations ago Japanese (and other Asian races) were heavily discriminated against in the US. Okinawans were discriminated against by the Japanese. My particular family were mediums, a subculture that receives discrimination worldwide based on fear. I can imagine the cautionary tales that grew from being the underdog of the underdogs that saw ghosts on top of it all. There was no social redemption for us. No wonder we have been told to ignore the call!

IFP: Have you translated these stories into fiction? Tell us about these stories.

AYS: Up until the recent *Tortured Willows*, a poetry collection which I am proud to share with you, Geneve Flynn and Lee Murray, I have been reluctant to bring these private parts of myself up. Part of it was a lack of knowledge. No one in my family wants to discuss these things because they "will be called back." When I dared to ask my cosmopolitan diplomat Uncle Shigaru about our history, his response was, "Don't ask about the past or the past will come back to you."

Another part of my reluctance to bring these true stories out is personal fear of ridicule and persecution. I think some of that was inherited, and some was mine from past personal experience. I cautiously explored the subject with *Escape Claws* (Self-published, 2017), a memoir-poetry hybrid collection I put out a few years ago, but that was a terrifying admission for me, and I rarely mention that book. I wound up going to a hypnotherapist to be able to write it, but a lot has changed in my mind recently. Anger has a wonderful way of evaporating fear, and the more I've learned about Okinawa, the more angry I've gotten.

IFP: Do you feel like there is a central thread connecting all our stories? A universal horror, so to speak?

AYS: I think the universal horror is a lack of knowledge. In all cultures, once we know how to defeat a monster, we have power over it. We can add the tools to our shopping list: remember to pick up the garlic, silver bullets, and smudge sticks, honey! It's *not* knowing what we face that is terrifying. Once we have our demons named, we find ourselves empowered.

IFP: How would you frame your story so that a universal audience could understand and identify with it?

AYS: I think much of my recent work has been more geared toward finding a connection between horror and ourselves. Too often the monster is the scapegoat for evil when it's the nice neighbor next door that is the real horror. I think the actual monsters have built up this concept that devils always have horns. Much of my recent work has a message more aligned with "by their works ye shall know them." To perpetuate the myth that evil can't be beautiful is to continue a dangerous lie.

IFP: What are good sources you would personally recommend for readers to learn more about horror in Asia given how diverse cultures in Asia are?

AYS: One thing I find fascinating about Asian literature, especially the old texts, is how entwined the spiritual and physical worlds are. There is no real distinction between the two worlds—they are different aspects of one world. I came across this recently when I was researching the nukekubi, a ghost that detaches its head and travels away from its body. I was reading old accounts of this being considered not supernatural but a common physical ailment mortals suffered from. In one story, a man was shocked to wake up from sleep to find a disembodied head on his chest watching him. This head stayed there until dawn when it finally left. The man rose and left his room. Outside, he met one of his neighbors, and he mentioned the head. The neighbor apologized and admitted he was afflicted with the "nukekubi ailment" and he thought he had it under control. He said he would move so the incident wouldn't be repeated.

Growing up influenced by both Eastern and Western culture I wonder if perhaps a lot of the modern problems we suffer from are because in the west the spirit world is reduced to sentiments suitable to hang on the wall but not bring up in polite conversation. Spirituality is for Sunday and only until noon. Perhaps in the Western world we are suffering from an alienation of part of ourselves. We have spent so long stamping out otherness that we are killing off a part of ourselves. Representation is vital to all of us, regardless of where our roots attach.

ABOUT THE AUTHOR

Angela Yuriko Smith is a third-generation Uchinanchu-American and an award-winning poet, author, and publisher with over 20 years of experience in newspaper journalism. Publisher of *Space & Time magazine* (est. 1966), a three-time Bram Stoker Awards® Finalist and HWA Mentor of the Year for 2020, she offers free classes for writers at angelaysmith.com.

A MYTHIC SOAP OPERA: INTERVIEW WITH RANDEE DAWN, AUTHOR OF TUNE IN TOMORROW

BY J.Z. WESTON

In *Tune in Tomorrow* (*Solaris*, 2022), Randee Dawn draws on her years of experience as an entertainment journalist to create a hilarious, insightful romp of a novel. Aspiring actress Starr Weatherby finally gets her big break, but instead of a Hollywood movie or a show on network television, she's cast on a soap opera for mythical beings. Once Starr travels to the other side of the Veil, she has to navigate fans of the show, her diva co-stars, and the demands of the network.

Interstellar Flight Press: You were able to draw on your years of experience with the entertainment industry while writing this book, but was there anything you found yourself having to specifically research?

Randee Dawn: A lot of the book is lived experience, amped up or twisted like a Slinky. You can take some of what happens perfectly literally, but only if you add a giant pinch of salt. But just having a lot of years covering the biz doesn't mean I know all about it. For one thing, I took an improv class—in part because when I've had a chance before, I've really adored improv—to get a sense of what it's like to open yourself to the "yes, and" of acting. Which then becomes a terrific metaphor for life. Instead of "no, but," what if we tried more often to "yes, and" with each other?

IFP: One of the perks of working on mythic TV is that the human actors stop aging. Much of the behind-the-scenes drama stems from the side effects of their greatly extended lifespans. What would you do differently if you knew that you would live effectively forever?

RD: First try and find a loophole or a way to exit—at a time of my choosing. I think the idea that you'll live forever is actually more terrifying than knowing you're going to die at some indeterminate hour on some day in the future. It's one of those unresolvable concepts that sounds awesome when you're young and loses its appeal the longer you're around: After a certain amount of rotations around the sun, you've seen enough to have a pretty good picture of what humans are good at, and what they're terrible at; the patterns start to look like ruts, and if you're paying attention, you can even develop a bit of prescience about what's to come, based on what you've lived through. Trust me: I voted for Ralph Nader in the 2000 presidential elections, thinking blithely that no way would Al Gore lose, never suspecting there might be questions on how the election was run, never believing that it would come down to a Supreme Court decision and dangling chads. Seeing how people reacted to Bernie Sanders in the past couple of elections brought it all back. There was no convincing them that, "Hey, I've been there. I like the nutty old guy with some wild ideas, but you're going to be shooting yourself in the foot to vote for him." Nobody wants to hear that. People have to make their own mistakes. So you get to a place where you've seen enough to have some wisdom, and the hilarious part is that right around then—nobody wants to listen to you!

That's a digression: My point is, what we all really want is not forever life, or too-short life, but the option to choose our own date and method of exit. The very religious may argue with this, but I'm talking on a practical level—it's the not knowing that makes us live a certain way, with fear and trepidation, but also recklessness and an inability to really plan our lives. "Live every day like it's your last" is a terrible assertion. What does it even *mean*? Today's my last day, which means I better spend all my money or give it away and go hog wild and live without consequences? What about when I wake up the next day—do I get to live *that* day like it's my last? But I've spent all my money/broken all my relationships/drank myself into a stupor/quit my job!

What I tried to do with the book is give the characters a taste of immortality. It's theirs until they choose for it not to be, after which they don't immediately drop over dead—but there are consequences because they are then people out of time. What would I do? After trying to find the way out so I could use it when I wanted, I'd start investing. I'd build up a lot of money, and then I'd use it to make people's lives better. Feed the hungry. Cure the sick. Fund alternative energies. Ameliorate climate change. Kick the oligarchs in the butt. I would not build a rocket to outer space.

IFP: This story is rife with puns, from the world-building to the chapter titles. In fact, every chapter is titled with a different pun on the main character's name, Starr. What inspired you to use that naming scheme?

RD: "Starr" is both a fun name and a personal statement for the woman named Samantha: She thinks it's a great name to have if she wants to be a famous actor. It's a name I'd seen used on a TV show that helped inspire some of my situations in the book, and it just fit the minute my brain suggested it to me. Then when I wanted to name the chapters to keep them separate in my mind as I wrote the book, I thought it would be fun to name them after her. Then it became a game: Can I do a different "star" pun for every chapter? Answer: Heck, yeah!

Also, I just want to say: The pun is a beautiful instrument. It's just important to know when to deploy it, and when to put it away.

IFP: You include a huge variety of mythical creatures in this book. You've got dragons, centaurs, a faun, brownies, cameradryads, a werepanther, and more. Which of them was the most fun to write, and why?

RD: Aw, I can't help but love Jason Valentine. His fauninness was just delightful and he spoke so loudly to me whatever situation I put him in. He reminds me of a friend of mine, who maybe isn't quite such a flashy dresser but always has a turn of phrase or way of looking at the world that makes me sure he's from a different universe. I'm also deeply fond of Kyle: We've all been Kyles for the fandoms and other things we love. Letting that love out at full-capital-letter levels. We should all embrace our inner Kyles.

IFP: In the world of *Tune in Tomorrow*, it's important for the mythic viewers to believe that the events in the show are real. This feels reminiscent of the way that fans of shows in our world often think of their favorite characters as if they are real people. For the mythics, the suspension of disbelief is what keeps a show alive. What are your thoughts on how the blurring of the real/unreal plays into our very human appreciation for fiction?

RD: I could probably write an essay here on the ways in which "truth" has become an elastic concept in our modern society. We live with people joking about "truthiness" and other people being quite serious about "fake news." We watch reality TV shows even when we know they're at least partially fictionalized. But on the other side of things, I go to fan conventions and people cosplay their favorite characters; they live action role-play (LARP) stories. We've gone beyond only wanting to read about adventures; we want to have our own, to be part of the bigger story. Virtual reality is growing. People love video games. The more we can be immersed in another world, the happier we are.

Does that mean we're unhappy with our own, slightly less vibrant reality? For some, that may be true. But the idea that people would watch a show and actively decide that the actors on it are really their characters is torn from reality—soap stars have many stories about being approached by fans (or anti-fans) who address them as if they're their character. And as long as they're safe about it and not harming anyone, I'm all for it: Lack of imagination is one of the saddest deficiencies I think most people can have. Anything that fires up our "what if" centers and gets us thinking about other worlds, other people, other ways of thinking—that's worth exploring.

IFP: What are you working on right now?

RD: Getting the book out! But between that, I'm starting a possible sequel—not directly on the set of *Tune in Tomorrow,* but in the universe. As is noted at one point in the book, *Tune* isn't the only show being made, and it's not the only kind of entertainment that exists for the fey. What are those other places like?

I have a premise and some characters. Do I have a novel yet? Well, dare I say it? Tune in tomorrow.

ABOUT THE AUTHOR

Randee Dawn writes about entertainment glam by day and fantastical fiction worlds by night. A former *Soap Opera Digest* editor, she now scribbles about the wacky universe of showbiz for *Variety, The Los Angeles Times* and *Today.com*. The co-author of *The Law & Order: SVU Unofficial Companion,* Randee appeared on L&O once! In the courtroom! Her short fiction has been published in multiple anthologies, and in her spare time she's a trivia writer for BigBrain Games. Based in Brooklyn, New York she lives with a brilliant spouse, a fluffy Westie, many books and never enough mangoes. More at: RandeeDawn.com / @RandeeDawn.

DIFFICULT WOMEN, CATHARSIS, AND TALKING SKELETONS: INTERVIEW WITH TIFFANY MEURET, AUTHOR OF LITTLE BIRD

BY J.Z. WESTON

Tiffany Meuret writes thrillers and dark fantasies about strong, stubborn women. Her second novel, *Little Bird* (June 2022, Black Spot Books), is odd and evocative in all of the best ways. In it, Josie's meticulously controlled and isolated life is disrupted by a new neighbor, a mysterious plant, and a talking skeleton (in that order). I was thrilled to get to ask Meuret a few questions about this new book!

Interstellar Flight Press: Josie is a misanthropic hermit whose anger and bitterness fairly leap off the page. This is a common enough character archetype for men, but is often considered unacceptable in a woman. Such characters run the risk of being deemed "unlikeable" by some people. Others of us enjoy seeing women depicted with the full range of human experience. What would you say is the best part of writing a potentially "unlikeable" woman?

Tiffany Meuret: The best part would be that she is a reflection of me. I'm sure many that know me have at one time thought of me as unlikeable, even if they like me now. Josie is my alter ego, someone I could see myself becoming under the wrong set of circumstances, so to create her all I had to do was lean hard into my own impulses. It was a relief in a way, as Josie was able to say some of the things I wish I had the courage or tenacity to say. All my sadness, all my rage at the time, all of it just funneled through her and exploded into the story that became Little Bird. And while I do understand she is unlikeable, I find that infinitely more fun to write. Sloppy, obstinate, mouthy little weirdos are interesting, especially in fiction. I have yet to write a character that people would consider pleasant, and I don't expect to start any time soon.

IFP: Your depiction of Po, Josie's chihuahua, does a lot to humanize Josie. At times, he seems to be her only anchor to the world outside of her house. Can you tell us about a special dog in your life, either your current pups or one from your past?

TM: Po is based entirely on one of my dogs now, Zeus (Po is short for Poseidon, in my mind, because I wanted to give him the name of Greek God, like my Zeus). Zeus is part Chihuahua, part Dachshund, and is the sassiest little asshole you will ever meet. He is also my heart, my boy, my best little friend. He is the one who loves me no matter how bitchy I am, how angry, or how sad. He is also featured heavily on my social media.

Po to Josie is Zeus to me, and how I imagine myself had I never had kids—just a spinster and her ridiculous dog, hating visitors and watching trash TV until they fall asleep together on the couch.

IFP: Skelly the skeleton is a delightful example of the kind of enigmatic figure that often appears in speculative fiction to disrupt the status quo. Her purpose, origins, and motivations are opaque to Josie. What influences did you draw on when crafting Skelly?

TM: Terry Pratchett's Death character was a huge influence, both in design and in attitude. I even fashioned earlier drafts to have Skelly speak in all caps, just like Death, however that looked a bit too cumbersome on the page once she gets into her longer stories and so it was changed. Other than that, I basically created Skelly to be the exact sort of personality I would need to pull me out of that headspace, and considering how hard-headed I can be, it would take something miraculous to make me change my attitude against my will. And Josie is even worse.

Another similarity to note, though not an inspiration, is the Yew Tree Monster from A Monster Calls. I did not read that book until after I finished Little Bird, which seems amazing considering the resemblance, but it always struck me how different people, at different times, from different parts of the world, crafted such similar otherworldly creatures for the purposes of coping with grief and loss. We must have been tapping the same well.

IFP: I noticed that every character in this book (other than the dog) is a woman: Josie, her new neighbor, her mother, and even Skelly the skeleton. The only men mentioned are gone from Josie's life, whether through death or distance. Was this a deliberate choice, or did it just evolve naturally?

TM: Deliberate. I tend to always center women in my work. Only now, after decades of writing and 6(ish) books do I have a main protagonist who is a man (in my newest WIP). It's not like I have a visceral negative reaction to men protagonists, but I have never had a man populate thoroughly enough as a character and person to feel confident to write about him. I am sure there are some biases involved in that decision-making, however subconscious, so this new book will be an interesting adventure for me.

IFP: This book deals with some intense feelings and events in Josie's backstory. Was it ever difficult to stay in that head space, and if so, what did you do to help yourself through it?

TM: It wasn't difficult, but cathartic. I was in that headspace. I was so angry when I wrote Little Bird, and so sad. It was a very tumultuous time of my life, and writing this book helped me sort through all those big feelings that I otherwise loathe to speak aloud. If anything, writing about Josie and Skelly helped me dig myself out of a hole instead of dragging me down into one.

ABOUT THE AUTHOR

Tiffany Meuret is a writer of monsters and twisted fairy tales. Her publications include Shoreline of Infinity, Luna Station Quarterly, Ellipsis Zine, and others. When not reading or writing, she is usually binge-watching comfortable sitcoms from her childhood or telling her kids to put on their shoes for the tenth time. She lives in sunny Arizona with her husband, two kids, two chihuahuas, gecko, and tortoise.

UNDER FORTUNATE STARS: INTERVIEW WITH DEBUT NOVELIST REN HUTCHINGS

BY MAR VINCENT

In a strange rift in space, two ships meet. The *Gallion* is a corporate research vessel bringing an alien ambassador to an important summit. The *Jonah* is a ragtag junker carrying a crew who believe they are still at war with that same alien race, the Felen. Uma, the *Gallion's* Director of Engineering, suspects the crew may be something else—the Fortunate Five, the first humans to broker peace with the Felen. Except, the Fortunate Five lived over 100 years ago, and the *Jonah's* crew have no interest in making peace with the Felen.

Ren Hutchings' debut novel, *Under Fortunate Stars*, is a space opera that blends heart and humor, action and adventure, in a tale that explores what happens when we meet our heroes, and they aren't quite what we'd expected.

INTERSTELLAR FLIGHT PRESS: What inspired *Under Fortunate Stars*? Where did the idea for this story begin, and how did it develop?

REN HUTCHINGS: *Under Fortunate Stars* is a love letter to so many themes and tropes that I love in sci-fi. It's got a first contact story, a scrappy found family, interstellar diplomacy, a mysterious space anomaly, a futuristic corporation... I've been a reader and fan of SF (and time travel stories) ever since I was a kid, and so the ingredients for this book have been percolating in my head for a very long time.

The spark that led to me actually starting the manuscript came from a conversation I had with my best friend, where we talked about urban legends and time-traveling ships. My original concept for the novel had a pretty different premise: it was going to be about a ship of historical re-enactors who accidentally traveled back in time to the event that they were re-creating.

The premise has since evolved into something different, but a lot of the characters and their arcs are unchanged since that early concepting phase. Some things have remained consistent since the very beginning—like Uma's deep and detailed historical knowledge. She's always been a huge history nerd!

IFP: One of the themes of *Under Fortunate Stars* is meeting your heroes—has this ever happened to you? Was your experience as unexpected as Uma's?

RH: Alas, I have never traveled in time to meet any historical figures who intrigue me (yet!), but I have certainly had various experiences meeting contemporary people whose work I admire and finding them a bit different than how I imagined. I do think that the human, multi-faceted, and fallible side of any "heroes"—whether they are currently living or in the distant past—is important to keep in mind whenever you look up to someone.

As far as historical figures go, reading about somebody's life—even if it's a reading of intimate documents like preserved journals or biographic material in their own words—can still never come close to giving you the full picture of who they were as a person. And that's the shock that Uma goes through when she meets Eldric Leesongronski, a famous hero whose life story she thought she knew inside and out. But then she's confronted with a complex, real person, one who's able to respond to her and push back on her assumptions in a way that the history texts could not.

IFP: I really enjoyed the relationship between Jereth and Leeg (as Leesongronski is called for short), as it felt like a core which the story built out from. Were they inspired by any friendships or relationships in your own life?

RH: I love their friendship! The banter, conflict, and connection between them were all so much fun to write. The way I wrote them isn't based on any one specific relationship from my life, but they do have a type of interpersonal dynamic that I find deeply compelling both in fiction and in my real-life friendships. I think it's fascinating when two friends who are very unlike each other in personality are brought together by circumstance or by chance, and end up having these shared experiences.

(This question did make me ask myself if I'm more of the Jereth in my friendships or more of the Leeg... hmm. It really depends on the situation. I am sometimes the smartass instigator of goofy shenanigans, but in some friendships, I'm definitely the more pragmatic one, so I guess I'm a little of each!)

IFP: You have worked in game development in the past—I'd love to know if this experience has helped your writing in any way?

RH: In game dev I worked mostly on the production side, coordinating project logistics, live ops and QA. I've never worked as a dedicated game writer outside of children's games. My overall writing experience has mainly been focused on long-form prose and novels. However, I do think that any experiences you have in a creative environment can't help but shape how you think about art and stories, and how you approach making immersive, enjoyable entertainment, no matter what format it takes.

I certainly feel like my experiences as a producer have influenced the way I approach things like revision deadlines—balancing that big artistic vision and desire to do as many awesome things as possible with clear plans for actually getting it finished on time.

IFP: What was your favorite part of writing *Under Fortunate Stars*?

RH: I feel like I could give ten different answers for this question, because the whole process of writing this book was some of the most fun I've ever had as a writer and as a storyteller! I deeply enjoy the hectic, chaotic phases of early drafting, when I'm following every idea and writing every scene that I have inspiration for until I see what sticks. But some of the best and most satisfying parts of the writing journey came during revisions, when I started to see how all these pieces would fit together, and the details of the character arcs became really clear to me.

IFP: What was the most challenging part?

RH: The cutting-and-rearranging revision pass that I did after my first draft was finished was extremely challenging, and it took several intense months. My original draft was nearly 200,000 words long, and I had to cut that by almost a third before the book was ready to query. Because my story structure is non-linear, I also spent a lot of time figuring out what order the chapters and flashbacks should go in, to best serve the unfolding of the plot as well as the emotional arcs that resonate between timelines.

IFP: Where can readers find you? What are you working on next (if you can share)?

RH: You can find me on social media as @voidcricket (Twitter/Instagram) and on my website at renhutchings.com. Right now, I'm working on redrafting a space heist book that has been on the backburner for a while, to see what new ideas have percolated while I was away from it. I tend to work on large story ideas over a long time, letting them rest and then returning to them a while later with fresh energy.

ABOUT THE AUTHOR

Ren Hutchings is a speculative fiction writer, writing mentor, and history grad. She spent most of the past decade working in game dev while also plotting twisty space novels. She loves pop science, unexplained mysteries, 90s music, collecting outdated electronics, and pondering about alternate universes. Her debut novel, UNDER FORTUNATE STARS, was published by Solaris in 2022. You can find Ren online at renhutchings.com, and on social media as @voidcricket.

HOT MESS VAMPIRES, STRANGE NAMES, AND B-MOVIE PLOTS: AN INTERVIEW WITH SFF AUTHOR BONNIE JO STUFFLEBEAM, AUTHOR OF WHERE YOU LINGER

BY MAR VINCENT

INTERSTELLAR FLIGHT PRESS: I'm sure one of the first questions people wonder about you is: Is that your real last name? Where does such a perfect SFF writer surname come from?

BONNIE JO STUFFLEBEAM: It's the name I was born with! My parents tell me it's German, and some guy I dated who spoke German told me it might have meant, "stump leg" or "one who hides behind stumps," and I honestly don't know which I like better.

If anyone wants to write reviews of my work and make a funny remark about my name, I do collect those on the bio page of my website.

IFP: Your stories are often noted for their deft balance of the familiar and fantastic. How do you go about blending these elements, or finding the common thread between them?

BJS: I'm drawn to the fantastic, so it's natural for me to wonder as I cook breakfast, for example, what it would be like if the pancakes imbued the eater with the power to talk to bread or some other nonsense. So, balance isn't something I consider when writing; it either happens or doesn't happen. But focusing on emotion is important: taking the emotions I've dealt with in my domestic life and transferring it onto the characters in their world that's gone a bit wonky.

IFP: What influences and inspires your work currently? Have these influences and inspirations changed over time?

BJS: Right now, horror films are a huge influence, but that's only been the case for about four years now—because I couldn't watch them before! When I first started writing, I was influenced a lot by other people's words: stories I read, song lyrics I heard. These days, I'm influenced more by thought experiments brought on by conversations with my partner or in the presence of friends. At some point, I got tired of writing more serious stories—and of writing at all—and decided to follow the fun, so humor and outrageous scenarios, like B-movie plots, have started to form a larger percentage of my influences.

IFP: Can you tell us a bit about your upcoming short story collection, *Where You Linger* , and novella, *Glorious Fiends*?

BJS: The theme for this collection—my first!—arose simply: it's all my stories that are set in the fictional town of Riddle, Texas. Many of the characters reappear, and the fantastic in the world of Riddle is floaty and strange. But most of these stories are actually older, and as I started to collect them, I realized that the theme of hanging on the past, and the literal and figurative ghosts of our old lives, is a strong presence. The order of the stories was easy to pin down, too: it starts with stories that involve humanity's distant past—dinosaur skeletons walking the earth with us—and moved through time, until the final three stories, which use sci-fi tropes over fantasy ones. The final two stories, which take place in the future, are the newest, written over the last two years.

The novella is pure fun. I wanted to tell another story about the characters I created for a novelette that appeared in the anthology *Evil in Technicolor*: a girl gang of classic monsters. Roxanne is a hot mess vampire whose love of women, both sexual and gastronomical, causes a lot of trouble within her trio of BFFs: Mx. Hyde and Medusa. In the novelette, Mx. Hyde and Medusa died, while Roxanne selfishly ran off, and in the novella, I explore her resurrection of her friends and how her selfishness plays out when a devil-type character demands that they give him additional souls to replace the souls of Mx. Hyde and Medusa.

I actually don't find working on novellas much different than shorts: they're longer, but it didn't feel that way, because the content was fun and needed a larger space in which to be told. But novels? That's a whole other story, and those are such a different beast than shorts.

IFP: When not writing speculative fiction, you work as a Narrative Designer of romance games. What similarities and differences do you find between these media and genres? Is your creative process different between fiction and narrative design?

BJS: The games I work on are interactive fiction, so I write scripts that include narration and dialogue, and there are a lot of similarities. With narrative design, though, I have to describe less because art will do a lot of that work, so the prose is super lean. As for differences in genre, the main one is that romance involves the Happily-Ever-After or Happy-For-Now, and then the horror I work on usually ends with one survivor whose life is forevermore fucked up. So, the tones are different—but the spicy sex is the same!

IFP: What do you do in your free time when not writing?

BJS: I'm a fierce protector of my free time, so I take weekends off and don't usually stay late to write, not even if I didn't get to work on my own stuff that day. My mental health is precarious, so I have to prioritize that over all else. But the answer to what I do with that free time? Is somewhat boring. I work out; right now, I'm lifting weights for my fitness. I have a weekly board game night with my friends. I have a lot of family functions, as my sister and her kids live in the same town, as do my in-laws. And, of course, I read and buy way too many books. Right now, I also stay up too late playing Wingspan on the Switch—and I take a lot of walks while playing Pokémon Go.

IFP: If you can share, what are you working on next?

BJS: I'm writing a horror novel, which is in the final stages of revision before being sent to publishers. It's got a fun infusion of humor and romance, so it's been a delight to work on!

I'm also in the process of editing several short stories, but with time being limited, all my processes are slow as hell.

ABOUT THE AUTHOR

Bonnie Jo Stufflebeam is the author of over 90 short stories, with work in *Popular Science*, *LeVar Burton Reads*, *Lightspeed*, and many more publications. Her work has been nominated for the Nebula Award and translated into six languages. This year will see the release of her first novella, *Glorious Fiends* (September 13th), and first short story collection, *Where You Linger* (out now from *Vernacular Books*). Learn more about her and her work at bonniejostufflebeam.com.

REALITY, TRUTH, AND MEMORY: AN INTERVIEW WITH DEBORAH L. DAVITT, AUTHOR OF *BOUNDED BY ETERNITY*

BY T.D. WALKER

The poems in Deborah L. Davitt's *Bounded by Eternity* lead us to ask: what might we lose if we chose to give up memories of what we've lost? Linking human and fey, reality and myth, the bridges between worlds bring the woman at the center of the poems back to her memories and, ultimately, back to herself. T.D. Walker spoke with Davitt about her novella in verse.

Interstellar Flight Press: *Bounded by Eternity* tells us the story of Eliza and her realities in the human and fey worlds, so I was fascinated by the ways in which you chose to allude to how reality manifests itself. Eliza is taken from one time in the human world and returned to another, as if our concept of the way in which we inhabit time is an illusion. The fey are "the Real" and humans "are but shadows on a cave wall," referencing Plato and his ideas of the nature of reality. Later, the king goes back in time and faces the possibility of unmaking himself and his relationship with Eliza. And Eliza's own reality as she experiences it shifts with the memories she loses and regains.

What do you want readers to question about their ideas of reality, particularly since you bring in human experience, enduring lore, and ancient philosophy? Did anything about your exploration of reality through your characters surprise you?

Deborah L. Davitt: That's a great question, Tammy. I particularly want readers to question their assumptions of their own identities, their reactions to the world around them, as based on their memories. Memories are malleable. Changeable. More so than we like to admit. The fey are unchangeable perfection, the "real." Objective truth, after a fashion. But human subjectivity, while it means that we're flawed, also means that we can change and grow, which is something that the fey cannot do.

This brought me close to some of the themes explored in my Edda-Earth novels, but I was pleased that I didn't repeat myself, focusing more on perception and reality this time.

IFP: Many of the individual poems use rhyme, though not all. Some, like "12. Uncertain Memory," use repetition of lines, and "13. His True Face" more so in its form. Others, like "6. The Anodyne" resist form.

What lay behind your decision to include poems that call on form and those that are strictly free verse? And how did that tension between form and resistance to strict form play in your telling of the story?

DLD: I love both free verse and formal poetry. Sometimes, a poem demands to be written as free verse; sometimes, form becomes your copilot, changing meaning as you go. Some of the form poems were written at the very inception of the project, and thus the meaning became what the form suggested. Some of the free verse poems were written when I knew where the story was going, and I needed a specific meaning *here*, as opposed to letting form assist me to find meaning, if that makes any sense at all.

IFP: You write short stories and novels as well as lyrical and narrative poetry. What parallels are there in your fiction writing process to your process writing *Bounded by Eternity*? And how did the process differ?

DLD: There's a distinction often spoken of between writers as "plotters" or "pantsers." A plotter has an outline and has nailed down every detail before they even begin writing. A pantser writes by the seat of their pants, never knowing where the words are going to take them till they get there. In prose, I'm somewhere between the two—I have a loose outline, and write towards what I call signpost scenes, but the characters can tell me at any time that something in the outline is ridiculous, they'd never do that, and thus things can change.

In writing a novella in verse, I found myself plotting less, and pantsing more; I didn't know that the story was going to have a happy ending till I arrived at it. It felt more organic, and some of that had to do with allowing form to shape meaning along the way, as I discussed earlier.

IFP: There is such poignancy in the poems that built the relationship between Eliza and Owen, the soldier. (I wondered whether you had in mind WWI poet Wilfred Owen, who was killed in battle, or Sir Owain of Arthurian legend.)

In particular, "37. A Frail Bridge" gave me pause, as the poem ended with Eliza's compassion: "as if simply treating him as if he were human / reconnected him with his humanity—/ a frail bridge, but a true one."

Eliza seems to be building on the bridge she built back to herself in "33. When You First Meet Yourself." Can you tell us a bit more about developing these two characters, in light of each others' experiences and their decisions at the end of the book?

DLD: I'm really glad you enjoyed the relationship between Eliza and Owen. It's definitely part of the experience that allows her to reintegrate her selves successfully. Owen wasn't named for anyone in particular; I wanted a simple name that would contrast with Oberon, yet remind the reader of him at the same time.

Coming from a military family, I have an abiding interest and concern for wounded and disabled veterans that certainly informed my portrayal of Owen. In my experience, most veterans have barriers to integrating back into society and reaching out to people around them, and I tried to portray some of those in Owen. But since he's able to reach out to Eliza and then to others, he does so in the spirit of *caritas*—disinterested love, not passionate. That's an important note about him, I think.

IFP: Last, I'd like to ask about *Bounded by Eternity* in the larger context of narrative speculative poetry. Are there other long-form narratives that you'd like to recommend to readers of *Interstellar Flight Magazine*?

It's a form that seems particularly well suited for speculative poetry—are there directions you'd like to see the form in general take?

Most of my experience with narrative poetry actually comes from older sources. I'm a huge fan of Edmund Spenser's *The Faerie Queen* and Boiardo's *Orlando Inamorato*, which Arisoto continued as *Orlando Furioso*. I'd highly recommend the recent translations of the *Inamorato,* as they're surprisingly accessible. Most modern readers will find Spenser pretty hard going, but that's what the footnotes are for. A lot of what I do is with an eye back on the classics, I'm afraid.

ABOUT THE AUTHOR

Deborah L. Davitt was raised in Reno, Nevada, where she graduated first in her class from UNR in 1997 (as Deborah McRann). While an undergraduate, she focused heavily on medieval and Renaissance literature from *Beowulf* to Shakespeare. She received her MA in English from Penn State, and later found work as a technical writer on projects ranging from nuclear ballistic missile submarines to NASA to computer manufacturing.

She currently lives in Houston, Texas, with her husband and son. Her poetry has received Pushcart, Rhysling, and Dwarf Star award nominations and has appeared in over fifty journals including *F&SF* and *Asimov's.* Her short fiction has appeared in *Analog* and *Galaxy's Edge*.

For more about her work, including her poetry collections, *The Gates of Never* and *Bounded by Eternity,* please see www.edda-earth.com. You may contact her on Facebook at www.facebook.com/deborah.davitt.3 or Twitter @davittDL.

MIDNIGHT SOCIAL DISTORTION: AN INTERVIEW WITH MARK O. ESTES, CREATOR OF A PODCAST FOR QUEER BLACK HORROR FANS

BY VANESSA MAKI

> "Horror, for me, is an escape. It was what I turned to in order to relax as a kid, whether it was books, movies, TV, or video games. Horror also is therapeutic. I used to say that movies in general were like medicine to my soul, but the more I looked at it the more I realized I was watching more horror/sci-fi/thrillers than comedies and dramas to cope with life."

The podcasting world is getting more diverse as time goes on. And Mark O' Estes' podcast, *Midnight Social Distortion* should be what you're listening to if you're looking to hear the perspective of a Black gay horror fan.

INTERSTELLAR FLIGHT PRESS: Your podcast, Midnight Social Distortion, captures the essence of queer Blerdom (especially horror blerdom). For the sake of folks who don't know—when did you decide you wanted to start this podcast? What sparked the idea?

MARK O'ESTES: I had always had an idea to do a podcast before they became a very popular medium. I just wanted to do one badly, but I didn't know where to begin. I didn't know if I would have the time, patience, skill, and support to enter into such a medium, especially when it wasn't the popular go-to source for entertainment at the time. Then a series of events happened (me coming out at a late age, the Get Out/Black Panther phenomenon, and the need to serve/have a niche to turn to when I wanted to discuss Black people in horror. So I started a blog that I admittedly poorly kept, which featured not only Black horror characters but Black Queer characters in horror too. This grew into the podcast that you know of today, which came to me late one night in bed while listening to white noise static.

IFP: What does horror as a genre mean to you and what do you hope listeners are getting from your podcast episodes?

ME: Horror, for me, is an escape. It was what I turned to in order to relax as a kid, whether it was books, movies, TV, or video games. Horror also is therapeutic. I used to say that movies, in general, were like medicine to my soul, but the more I looked at it, the more I realized I was watching more horror/sci-fi/thrillers than comedies and dramas to cope with life. I then began to wonder why that was and decided to explore this revelation. I pray that Midnight Social Distortion breaks that down for not only the audience but for myself as well.

IFP: Do you have a favorite episode you've done so far?

ME: I would say some of my early episodes where I opened with a creepy event that happened in my life. I had a lot of those go down when I was younger, but nothing of that kind as of late. I would also say that the Helen Shivers Memorial Episode was a big fave of mine as well.

IFP: Black queer representation in horror is still growing. Which is obviously fantastic and exciting. Who are some Black queer folks in the horror community that inspire or have inspired you?

ME: Ryan Kinney, aka Brother Ghoulish, is just an impeccably talented individual who inspires me to keep pushing no matter the obstacles. His genius execution of his creativity is awe-inspiring and infectious. Whenever I finish an episode of his podcast, I get a jolt of energy. Bobby Torrez and Michael Brown's People Under the Scares is also a great source for Black Queer Representation in Horror, and I must add Blerdy Massacre as well.

IFP: Do you have podcasts run by solely or mostly queer folks that you'd like to recommend?

ME: Along with Brother Ghoulish's Tomb, Brother Ghoulish's Dragula Breakdown, The People Under the Scares, and Blerdy Massacre I would have to add Horror Queers, Fear the Talking Queers, A Nightmare on Fierce Street, and so many more that I can't list them now. We are out there; just keep your ears ready.

IFP: What horror releases are you looking forward to for the remainder of this year?

ME: Well, most definitely Jordan Peele's *NOPE*; and *Halloween Ends*; *Bodies, Bodies, Bodies*; *The Black Phone*; *Evil Dead Rises*; the 'Salem's Lot remake, and the *Bring It On* horror movie, to name a few.

IFP: Any horror franchise(s) that you'd like to see make a comeback eventually?

ME: *A Nightmare on Elm Street* and *Friday the 13th*. It's long overdue. I would love to see requels of *I Know What You Did Last Summer* and *Urban Legend*, and wouldn't mind having a sequel to *The Faculty* as well.

IFP: Anything else you'd like to say related to the podcast or anything else you're working on in the background?

ME: Well, I'm approaching the one-year anniversary of Midnight Social Distortion as of this writing, and I may have something in store, but nothing grand and spectacular. Maybe a countdown episode. There aren't many episodes, so that particular episode will probably be short. And I have a few guest appearances on some podcasts coming soon. Other than that, I want to return to writing on the regular. I feel as if I'm getting a bit rusty in that department, and that scares me, lol.

ABOUT THE PODCASTER

Mark O. Estes is an aspiring writer who loves the written word. He is married to reading, writing, music, TV, movies, and most of pop culture, but his first and forever love is horror and all that comes with it. You can find him on Twitter (@theanticritic), Instagram (@markoestes/@midnightsocialdistortion), and his podcast Midnight Social Distortion.

THREE'S A CROWD(ED): INTERVIEW WITH CHRIS SEBELA, RO STEIN, TED BRANDT, AND TRÍONA FARRELL, THE TEAM BEHIND THE 3-VOLUME COMIC 'CROWDED'

BY JAMILEH ALEXANDRA

Once upon the before times, I made a new friend. We both loved tacos, queer stories, and seeing women dish sass and take names. Lucky for us, writer Chris Sebela, artists Ro Stein and Ted Brandt, and colorist Tríona Farrell published *Crowded Volume 1* (Image Comics, 2019) that year, whisking us to a Vegas-bright, roller-coaster paced, cackle-out-loud near future where you can crowd-fund, gig-work, and contactless payment a.n.y.t.h.i.n.g. Lucky for you, this team answered my questions about their book and how comics come together. *Crowded* is collected in three vivid volumes. One and two are out now, so you can catch up before volume three drops in February 2022.

These creators were generous with their time and insights. This interview has been lightly edited for length.

Interstellar Flight Press: Where do the ideas come from & how do you get the team together to develop a new book?

Christopher Sebela: Ideas come from about anywhere, really, or several somewheres. Some conversation I'm having with someone, a book I'm reading, a movie or show I'm watching, song lyrics—some throwaway thing in there gets stuck in my brain, and a metaphorical light goes off somewhere inside me where I feel like there's a story in this somewhere. And if that's true, the ideas begin to self-replicate and wander all over.

Assembling a team is a lot of trial and error and happy accidents and blind luck. I get to know people I want to work with, there are people I'm fans of, there are folks I've never heard of before but I see their work and it just feels right. Then it's a lot like asking people out, but trickier, because there's money and stuff involved and your relationship is going to last awhile, contractually.

Ted Brandt & Ro Stein: Any ideas we bring to the book are a direct result of what we've been given by the writers we work with. As far as getting the team together, we've at least been lucky to build up a great list of industry friends, so when we've been on creator-owned work it's always been easy to sort out a team.

IFP: The color in this book gives this universe its own personality. How did you arrive at this palette?

Tríona Farrell: I knew the book was going to be nonstop action so I immediately came to a bright, intense palette that emphasized light sources and the focus of action. What I wanted to get across was the sense of chaos in this world with these intense colors. Everything is falling apart in this world and everyone and everything is bombastic. Alongside this, each character had their own sort of unique palette, with Vita's being intense yellows and greys for example. These would show in the character's clothing and belongings so it was always clear where our main characters were. Palettes would change depending on the mood, but overall, there's always that focus on bright intensity to emphasize the fun action and dialogue.

IFP: This feels like a love letter and a sharply-observed long form comedy take on the current state of life these days? Is it intended to be either?

CS: Yeah, it's a bit of both. I didn't set out to do that. I just had this idea about crowdfunding assassinations for a long time and nothing else. That was back in 2013 or so, so I had a lot of time to let it linger in my head and in the world around me. The weirder life seemed to get in small ways, the more that stuff slipped into what felt right for the book. It's not meant to be a book that says, "This over here is Bad, and this over here is Fine," it's meant to be what living in this world is like, things get a little strange, but they're a part of this waterfall of "oh god what now" developments that hit us every week so that they begin to seem normal and commonplace. I could never write a book that condemns social media and the gig economy because it's stuff I use every day and rely on.

TB&RS: Yes, from the initial conversation with Chris, this was always intended to be a satire of the world as is. There have been a few close calls where it looked worryingly like several sections of CROWDED were in danger of becoming reality, so it's a good job we started when we did.

IFP: What's the most fun thing about creating these books? What's the most challenging?

CS: The most fun thing is also the most challenging, I get absolute freedom, which is completely terrifying when it's put in front of you. Sometimes I get overwhelmed with choices and having to decide how much is too much or not enough. But for 90% of the time, CROWDED has always been a book I've looked forward to writing. It feels like a break from everything else, because I know the characters and the world so well, the only challenge I tend to have anymore is not making each chapter 50 pages because I could just hang out with our cast forever and enjoy myself.

TB&RS: The most fun things are creating larger-than-life characters and rounding out the world with fictional brands. Both help us feel like the world and the people in it have a real identity. As for the most challenging, honestly, by the number of hours taken, it's planning all the environments. CROWDED, because it moves between scenes so quickly, needs a lot of different environments that the characters are interacting with, so there's not a lot of opportunity to just have characters in a panel. Everywhere needs to feel like somewhere.

IFP: Do you plan and work in six-issue arcs, or is that just the way they are collected? How long does it take from idea to hitting the shelves (for one issue, or six if that's the unit)?

CS: For CROWDED I planned them as six-issue arcs. I couldn't even tell you why, it just felt right when I was trying to outline things and like there was enough room to explore lots of things. We could look into the backstory of Trotter or Circe for a bit and then go back to Charlie and Vita in a library hotel, it gives the story breathing room so you can have the quiet, human moments impact as much as the big, flamboyant action scenes.

The time between idea and actuality varies a lot. For CROWDED, it was five years between coming up with the initial idea and putting out our first issue. A lot of that was me getting competent enough to write something like this and make it matter beyond just being a fun concept. It took me something like three to four years just to come up with Vita and Charlie. There's no standards for developing an idea into a book, sometimes it moves way too fast, and sometimes it takes forever. CROWDED took the right amount of time, I think.

TB&RS: The pacing of the arcs is entirely up to Chris, and he's always set it at six-issue arcs. Because of the enormous time and energy needed to plan CROWDED, it takes quite a while to assemble a single issue for us.

IFP: In my youth, I most often identified with the loner, assassin characters in books and movies. Vita is major wish fulfillment for me

(thanks!). Beyond her, there are abundant womxn and queer characters in the Crowded universe. Were there any specific inspirations for Charlie, Vita, and the way you populate this universe?

CS: No real specific inspirations for Charlie and Vita, except maybe friendships I've had in my life that are fun and madcap but also adversarial and frustrating. It's a dynamic I know well.

As for populating this world, I tend to write books with women as the main characters because I spent a lifetime absorbing dude stories in comics and TV and movies and novels and I didn't want to spend my life making more of those and adding to that wall. I wanted to make a book that looks like the world I live in, with the same variety of people I'm friends with and to treat it all as normally as I treat every day of my life. We have lots of queer characters and that's not a central point of their story, it's just who they are. I want to see more stories like that, so those are the stories I'm most interested in telling.

TB&RS: Not intentionally? Charlie and Vita weren't created with specific references in mind, they were designed in relation to each other and how Chris initially described their personalities to us. As far as the rest of the world of CROWDED goes, sometimes Chris will describe a specific additional character or background character, but otherwise, we just try to make sure there's as much variety as we can. One of the things we always try to do is make sure that everyone can see themselves somewhere in the book, however briefly.

IFP: We like to talk about craft at IFP and reality-check some of the romantic notions about writing. Is there anything about the process of creating comics you wish people understood better?

CS: The writing is maybe the easiest part of comics. It's everything that comes after that's hard. If you want to be a writer, you need to also figure out how to be a project manager, maybe you need to learn how to letter or color or do design work; you have to figure out how to become savvy at promoting your book and yourself. You need to bring more to the table than writing a script and calling it done. You need to be a part of the team and put in overtime if you really want it to happen.

TB&RS: We can't really comment on the writing side, but as far as art goes: it takes a lot longer than you think it will. Every panel you read in five seconds is the result of likely hours of labor. And it's hard! Trying to work all day every single day is a good recipe for burnout, and not a good recipe for good comics.

IFP: For people who love Crowded, where else can they support your work?

CS: I sell books of mine on my website at christophersebela.com , and I mostly social media on twitter, I'm @xtop on there. Otherwise, I'd recommend supporting small businesses and hitting up your local comics shop. Or the library, I'm in the library too.

TB&RS: Right now, CROWDED is our primary project, so that's the best way to support us. Or give us a follow on twitter, maybe?

APOCALYPSES, LIMINALITY, AND POCKET WATCHES: AN INTERVIEW WITH MERIDEL NEWTON, AUTHOR OF THE FUTURE SECOND BY SECOND

BY EMILY WAGNER

> "So many disaster movies and post-apocalyptic stories default to the idea that humanity is brutal and self-serving under the thin veneer of culture. I'd like people to think that maybe culture isn't just a veneer. Maybe culture is what's allowed us to survive and thrive in a way no other species on Earth has ever managed."

INTERSTELLAR FLIGHT PRESS: I just finished The Future Second by Second, and it was a great read. How did the idea for the novella come about?

MERIDEL NEWTON: Thank you! Honestly, the story for this novella developed pretty organically out of a number of ideas I'd been mulling over for a while. Partially, I really felt that the post-apocalypse had a lot more to offer as a setting than biker gangs and violence, and I wanted to delve into how real people might create an intentional community to survive in hard times.

IFP: The novella really flips the post-apocalyptic trope of everyone battling each other. The people of Osto truly work together. Do you think this could really happen in the aftermath of an apocalypse, and/or should it happen?

MD: If you're asking me if an apocalypse should happen, then no, definitely not! I am far too fond of chai lattes and the internet to fantasize about a world without them. But if you're asking if people can and should come together during such an event, then yes, absolutely. I think it's how we survived in agrarian societies for the majority of human existence. While many people have lost the everyday knowledge of how to farm a field by hand or raise sheep, I think the people who survive an apocalypse would absolutely be the ones who can band together to share such knowledge and recreate sustainable, human-scale living arrangements.

IFP: The title is *The Future Second by Second*. How does the element of time play a role in this novel?

MD: I use time as an almost liminal element in the story, and believe me, I know how pretentious that sounds! But one thing I have always found really fascinating is how self-contained societies and sub-cultures can almost redefine their notions of time to be slightly offset from the rest of the world. I've been to schools where classes or meetings are quietly understood to begin fifteen minutes after the schedule says, and offices where everything has five minutes of leeway. Some places would eschew the use of the clock altogether, if not for the need to interface with the rest of the world in some orderly manner.

In fact, time, and the use of the clock, was not nearly so widespread in the pre-industrial age even in Europe. The evolution of the workday is a creation of the capitalist need to regulate and regiment humanity; it's very much a modern construct. So when Vasha clings to her pocket watch, when she insists on setting a schedule for Drake's leadership and the election, it's an effort to cling to an old way of doing things, a past that she imagines to be more civilized. The fact that her present is a direct result of that past, of course, is a contradiction she prefers not to think about. At a certain point, we all need to choose the boundaries of our beliefs and fence them off from the wider world, or we wouldn't believe in anything.

IFP: How would you describe The Shelter, the place that the people of Osto live? How does it contrast with what is outside of its borders?

MD: The Shelter is not a pleasant place to live by any means, but it is better than almost any alternative in that world. It's meant to be the shell of a large warehouse store, like Ikea or Kroger, that's been hollowed out and turned into living quarters for hundreds of people. Quarters are close and the communal kitchens are serviceable, and there's enough work to be done that anyone can find a place. But on the upside, everything is shared fairly and everyone is taken care of, and there are so many people taking care of each responsibility that no one is overwhelmed or overworked.

IFP: *The Future Second by Second* features many strong female leads, especially Vasha. What inspiration(s) in real life or fiction did you draw from to create this character?

MD: Vasha will feel familiar to anyone who grew up in a large matriarchal family, I think. She's been in charge for so long that things run pretty automatically during calm times, but she expects unquestioning obedience during crises. She's not based on anyone in particular, but more an extrapolation of what a strong, long-time leader would need to be like in a time and place like Osto.

IFP: Speaking of characters, who was your favorite character to create for this book?

MD: Oddly enough, I'd have to say my favorite character to write was probably Devra. She's the character least like myself in the entire book: she's tough and confident and adventurous—and doesn't think too much before committing to a decision. I like to think that in a longer series, she'd have a whole subplot that's just camping out on her own in the woods, befriending wolves, and occasionally visiting town to see her boys.

IFP: The novel is set in the future, yet its characters seem to live in the past (i.e., electricity). Can you elaborate on that?

MD: Something I find myself haunted by is the concept that it would not be possible to rebuild our society if we lost it. This is true on two levels—the first is that we don't have the raw resources to rebuild—there's no new oil being made, no new rare earth metals or gold deposits to find. In the few thousand years, we've built civilization, we've depleted the planet's resources in more ways than most people realize.

The second level is the level of human knowledge. In pre-industrial days, it was possible for one person to hold all the knowledge to make the items used in daily life: candles, say, or houses, or violins. But if you think about the most prominent artifacts of modern life, no single person today knows how to make a computer or a cell phone. Not starting from raw materials on up. So an apocalypse—a complete collapse of civilization—doesn't have to be about a huge disaster collapsing infrastructure. It just has to be the loss of enough knowledge—enough people—that we no longer know how to run what we've got. That's what's happened in the future of Osto. Enough people died quickly enough that the knowledge of how to run power plants, network nodes, and manufacturing has been lost. Society has contracted in the 80 years or so since, to something that can survive without the massive artificial memory of the internet and computer systems. It's not that they're living in the past—it's that they're living without global support systems.

IFP: What do you hope the reader takes away from the novella?

MD: I'd just like the reader to come away with a more thoughtful take about the way people behave in disasters. So many disaster movies and post-apocalyptic stories default to the idea that humanity is brutal and self-serving under the thin veneer of culture. I'd like people to think that maybe culture isn't just a veneer. Maybe culture is what's allowed us to survive and thrive in a way no other species on Earth has ever managed.

IFP: This is the first book of a trilogy. Without spoilers, what can readers expect in the next installment (or two)?

MD: Readers can expect to see more of the world beyond Osto, and see what other ways people have found to survive. And they will, eventually, find out what happened 80 years ago—though I hope they remember that that isn't the point of the story.

ABOUT THE AUTHOR

Meridel Newton lives in Washington, DC and works as a research analyst by day. Her writing appeared in the 1001 Knights anthology, as well as disparate self-published releases. Her work spans many genres, but always reflects her interests in environmental science, social justice, folklore, and human geography. She can be found at www.thepuppetkingdom.com and on Twitter as @ridelee.

ESCAPING THE BODY: AN INTERVIEW WITH CHLOE N. CLARK

BY LESLIE ARCHIBALD

WHAT IT MEANS TO BE ALIVE AND THE CONCEPT OF TRANSFORMATION

> My body is always ready / to run, to catch, to save / but has a harder time / to settle, to want, to hold ("In Media Res" *Escaping the Body*)

Escaping the Body, the most recent collection by poet and storyteller, Chloe N. Clark (*Interstellar Flight Press*, 2022) is an evocative testament to transformation and wanting something different—more—better. Interstellar Flight Press caught up with the poet to discuss the curating of this collection and the issues and themes that are so important for today's women.

Interstellar Flight Press: Besides the physical and natural relationship to the body, the body has many religious or spiritual connotations. Why did you choose *Escaping the Body* as a title for this collection, and what do you hope your readers discern from the collection's title?

Chloe N. Clark: I think that we are tied to bodies in so many ways—our physical body, but also bodies of political power, cultural ones, etc. So, one of the things I was thinking about as I was forming these poems together was this idea of how bound we are and what that does to us.

Then there's the level that so many of the poems touch on illness, physical pain, (and positives too—taste, physical touch, etc), that I liked the idea of literally escaping the body as the overarching theme.

IFP: The theme of this collection is transformation. Can you talk a bit about why it is important to acknowledge transformations, especially our own?

CNC: I think it's important because transformation is THE defining characteristic of being alive—our bodies change their cells, we grow our hair and then cut it off, we grow into and out of love, we are shaped by everything around us. To not talk about transformation, to not dwell in it, is to disregard so much of life.

IFP: *Escaping the Body* is fiction yet the characters in the pieces are authentic and evocative. What is your process for creating authentic characters in fictional poems?

CNC: I have a hard time distinguishing poetry and fiction in my head, until once I have it out on the page, so a lot of that is my storytelling nature coming out. I think in characters and voice.

IFP: Maegan Poland says your poems "pivot on the hope of transformation." Can you talk a bit about that hope?

CNC: I think that many of us have that hope within us—we'll transform ourselves by taking this job or drinking more water or pursuing this person. But, then on a more hopeful level, we also all operate towards transformation that's more deeply within ourselves—being kinder, being more patient. I love that hope—it's my own.

IFP: *Escaping the Body* is your fifth published collection. Why choose Interstellar Flight Press for this particular collection?

CNC: This is easy—I love the books that IFP has put out and I think IFP really tries to create a community I want to be part of. Additionally, Holly Walrath is amazing. I've always loved her work, so having her as an editor is a huge plus.

> When you spent years rooted / to the ground, did it remind you of every time / you'd been rooted in place by fear? ("Questions We asked for the Girls who turned to Limbs," *Escaping the Body*)

IFP: Every day on the news, I see women abused, missing, or deceased and have experienced abuse in my own life. In "Questions We Asked for the Girls Turned to Limbs," was there a specific goal to shine a light on abuse and was there a story that inspired it or was it the collective stories resembling a war on women?

CNC: I think you can't address the body without also addressing the inherent scariness of being inside a body. Women face violence at horrific rates, so news stories about it are just part of our daily existence. I'm not sure I have a specific goal other than to say, "look at this world."

IFP: You have a talent for merging realistic details with fantastic elements as in "All Melusine's Daughters" and "Once They Sainted a

Mermaid." Can you talk a bit about the real world juxtaposed with the speculative or the fantastic?

CNC: To me, so much of our world is already tinged with the unreal—like the way that our emotions can change our perceptions of what is around us or experiences that toe the line of the uncanny, the spiritual, the outside of ourselves. But also, the world itself is so magical: there are underwater fish that make their own light, there's plants that can alter perceptions. Like woah. So, for me, it's easy to juxtapose them because we already live in a world so filled with strangeness.

> Pain has always hit me like a pillow / fort tumbling / onto my sleeping body ("Nociception", *Escaping the Body*)

IFP: In "Insert Bad Joke Here" you use humor as a catalyst to a painful separation. Can you talk about the contradiction of using humor to reflect pain and how that came about?

CNC: I think my family has always had a fairly dark sense of humor, and I appreciate that humor is a coping mechanism, I think laughter makes darkness a little less scary and that's an important thing.

IFP: I see you cook and post pictures of your creations on Twitter. How do you relate food to writing as a creative outlet? Does either help inform the other? If yes, how?

CNC: I constantly think about writing while cooking, it's a meditative act for me. So, I find food is directly part of my creative experience—if I'm stuck, I go knead out the story in a loaf of bread until it's sorted.

IFP: You have had a trying couple of years (more so than most of us). How has your writing helped you overcome adversity and/or taken back control of your narrative?

CNC: I am a fan of the idea that the best revenge is living a good life. I think the fact that I keep writing and telling stories is a great way to fight back against the awfulness of so much. So much of my writing centers on kindness and hope that I also think stands directly against the predominant narrative of hurtful people, so I think leaning into that is good.

ABOUT THE AUTHOR

Chloe N. Clark is the author of *Collective Gravities, Under My Tongue, Your Strange Fortune,* and *The Science of Unvanishing Objects.* Her forthcoming books include *Every Song a Vengeance* and *My Prayer is a Dagger, Yours is the Moon*. She is a founding co-EIC of literary journal *Cotton Xenomorph*. Her favorite basketball player will always be Rasheed Wallace and her favorite escape artist can only be Houdini.

SCIFAIKU, DARK FAIRYTALES, AND POETRY: INTERVIEW WITH CHRISTINA SNG, AUTHOR OF THE GRAVITY OF EXISTENCE

BY ARCHITA MITTRA

> "How we define monster is terribly subjective. I always get upset watching giant monster movies where humans feel compelled to destroy them even when the monsters have done no harm to us."—Christina Sng

Christina Sng's *The Gravity of Existence (Interstellar Flight Press,* 2022*)* is an exquisite collection of dark poems that meditates on monsters and myths, aliens, and apocalypses. In this interview with writer Archita Mittra, Christina sits down to talk about the subgenre of scifaiku, poetic influences, monsters, and retellings, along with some helpful advice for young speculative poets.

INTERSTELLAR FLIGHT PRESS: The poems in this collection fall under the genre of scifi-haiku (scifaiku). What drew you to scifaiku?

CHRISTINA SNG: I was drawn to the beauty and brevity of the form where so much can be said in a mere three lines.

IFP: As someone who has published several award-winning volumes of poetry alongside other creative work, was poetry always your preferred medium? What are your inspirations and influences?

CS: Poetry was always my favorite medium, even as a child. I think it's to do with how my mind finds a heartbeat in everything. The rhythm of words coming together to conjure a story.

I've been most influenced by the late Sylvia Plath, who was a master of the form.

IFP: While reading this collection, I was struck by how evocative your poems are, despite their brevity. With just a couple of phrases or sentences, you create such a vivid and emotional world for the reader to get lost in, such as in "Cinderella" (especially the bit about "glass slippers/stained with blood/from the stepsisters'/severed toes") or "Little Red in Haiku." It reminded me of another collection *The Smallest of Bones* by Holly Lyn Walrath that does something similar. So, tell us about your style. How did you hone your poetic voice? Is there a reason why you are drawn to brevity, as opposed to longer poetic forms or elaborate prose?

CS: My father was a man of few words, so few that when he spoke to me, I remembered, especially in his final years. There is great beauty in brevity. He taught me that. There is so much power in what's unsaid.

While editing, I would keep taking out words until the meaning completely changed. Then, I would backtrack to the last change, where the poem still retained its meaning and the edit was done.

IFP: In fact, my favorite section, "Childhood Tales," retells several popular fairytales with a dark twist. "Alice in Wonderland" particularly stood out to me in the charming way you evoke the Cheshire Cat's grin in the vision of an autumn moon. Retellings often focus on certain aspects of the original tale to offer a commentary on our times. So, what were your thoughts and aims when you penned these poems? As a reader or a writer, how do you approach retellings in general?

CS: With retellings, I like to add a modern-day touch. Many of these tales are borne from another age with different norms and ideals. Retelling the same story with our lens helps us relate better to it.

IFP: In other poems, such as "Magic," "Found Footage," or "Life on Kepler-452B," you manage to tell a complete story with such a few words. It has such a lovely flash fiction quality to it, recalling Ernest Hemingway's classic six-word story: "For sale: Baby shoes. Never worn." So, can you talk us through the process of writing a poem?

CS: Thank you for your kind words! As for the process, I sit down and get comfortable, pick up my favorite pen and notebook or else, my favorite note app, and think of a topic before writing.

It's strange to describe my writing like automatic writing. The story comes to me, and I'm just penning it down. The thinking part for me comes with the editing, which shapes the piece to how I want it to be.

IFP: I was also fascinated by the poems in the "Real Monsters" section of the book, especially "Blood" and "The Joy of Travelling". In those two, you write about vampires in a way that makes the reader curious

about the way they experience the world and also sympathize with their predicament. It brought to mind a quote by Vietnamese-American poet Ocean Vuong that goes, "What I really wanted to say was that a monster is not such a terrible thing to be." So, what is a "monster" to you? How do you feel about the way monsters have been depicted in media? What would you change about that if you could?

CS: To me, a monster is something that hurts others. We too can be monsters in retaliation or self-defense. It's all semantics.

How we define monster is terribly subjective. I always get upset watching giant monster movies where humans feel compelled to destroy them even when the monsters have done no harm to us.

In this way, the media portrays monsters as different from us and should be destroyed. I think that's wrong. That isn't teaching us inclusion, but division.

There's probably only one or two giant monster movies where the monster is led to a safe place to live in peace. But most, they are destroyed. I've watched many of them, and it's a demoralizing end to witness.

IFP: Poetry is often sidelined in literary markets, and speculative poetry seems to be an even niche genre. So, what are your thoughts on contemporary speculative poetry? Do you think speculative poets get enough visibility? Are there any upcoming poets that we should be reading or watching out for?

CS: Speculative poetry is a wonderful genre, with many poets doing incredible work. And no, we don't get enough visibility. There are too many poets to mention, but here's a guide: if you've not heard of them, give them a try. These days, most poets have samples online. If you like their samples, buy their book. They may become your next favorite poet.

IFP: What is your advice to young poets who are still struggling to find their voice?

CS: Write authentically. This doesn't mean send it out for publication when you're not comfortable with sharing this voice with the world yet. But write true to yourself. Your life. Your experiences. Your story.

IFP: What projects are you working on currently? When can we read more of your striking and evocative poetry?

CS: I'm compiling my next "A Collection of..." horror poetry tome for *Raw Dog Screaming Press*, and it's a monster of godlike proportions. It may take a while because it's not complete yet.

The goal is also to work on more fiction and finish this novel I've been pottering about with for over a decade.

In the meantime, you can find all my announcements on my Facebook page /christinasng.

Christina Sng's book of speculative haiku is out now from Interstellar Flight Press! Order your copy today.

ABOUT THE AUTHOR

Christina Sng is an award-winning poet, writer, essayist, and artist. Her work has appeared in numerous print and online venues worldwide and is translated into six languages. She is the author of A Constellation of Songs (Origami Poems Project), Catku (Allegra Press), 2017 Elgin Award nominee An Assortment of Sky Things (Allegra Press), 2018 Elgin Award runner-up Astropoetry (Alban Lake Publishing), 2017 Bram Stoker Award® winner A Collection of Nightmares (Raw Dog Screaming Press), 2020 Bram Stoker Award® winner and 2021 Elgin Award runner-up A Collection of Dreamscapes (Raw Dog Screaming Press), and the collaborative poetry collection Tortured Willows with Lee Murray, Gene Flynn, and Angela Yuriko Smith.

CONTRIBUTOR BIOGRAPHIES

Contributor Biographies

Leslie Archibald is a Houston based writer/reader bending genre and exploring multimedia literary projects. A graduate of the University of Houston, Leslie has remained active in Houston's writing community serving as board secretary/treasurer for Writespace, a literary arts center that supports Houston writers. When she is not writing, you may find her in the city with her camera documenting Houston's unique people and landscapes. Leslie is the winner of the 2017 *Spider Road Press* Spider's Web Flash fiction competition. Her winning piece "Sherry Baby" is included in the special section of *Companion of the Ash* released in December 2018. Her work may also be found in *Tales of Texas Vol 2* and T*he Best of Interstellar Flight Magazine: years 2 and 3*. Her poem "She Dances in indigo" was recently chosen for Color:Story2023.

Patrick Barb is an author of weird, dark, and horrifying tales, currently living (and trying not to freeze to death) in Saint Paul, Minnesota. He is the author of the dark fiction collection *Pre-Approved for Haunting* (Keylight Books/Turner Publishing), the novellas *Gargantuana's Ghost* (Grey Matter Press) and *Turn* (Alien Buddha Press), as well as the novelette *Helicopter Parenting in the Age of Drone Warfare* (Spooky House Press). His forthcoming projects include the novella *The Nut House* (Brigids Gate Press, late 2024), and the novel *Abducted* (Dark Matter INK, Fall 2024). He is an Active Member of the HWA and a Full Member of the SFWA. Visit him at patrickbarb.com.

Grant Butler is the author of the novel *The Heroin Heiress*. His short fiction has appeared in in *Sick Cruising, Mardi Gras Mysteries, Punk Noir Magazine, Close to the Bone,* and *The Siren's Call,* and his nonfiction has been appeared in

The Daily Drunk, Interstellar Flight Magazine, The Best New True Crime Stories, and *Hear Us Scream.*

Robert Dean is a journalist, raconteur, and enlightened dumbass. His work has been featured in places like MIC, Eater, Fatherly, Yahoo, Austin American-Statesman, Consequence of Sound, Ozy, USA Today, to name a few. He's appeared on CNN and NPR. He also serves as features writer for Hussy Magazine, Culture Clash, Pepper Magazine, and is editor in chief for Big Laugh Comedy, Texas' premier comedy production company. He lives in Austin and loves ice cream and koalas. His new collection of essays, Existential Thirst Trap is out now.

Mahmud El Sayed is a British-Egyptian writer based in London. He was the 2023 winner of the Future Worlds Prize and his stories have appeared in various places.

Aaron Emmel's stories have appeared in F*ireside Magazine, Daily Science Fiction, Apparition Lit* and many other excellent magazines and anthologies. He also writes essays, graphic novels and interactive fiction. Find him online at aaronemmel.com and on Threads at @aaronjemmel or Twitter at @justicioaje.

Ryan Fay is the editor at **Enfrightened Press**, which focuses on academic discussions of the horror genre. His expertise is in examining social justice issues in horror films and literature.

Grace Kameyo Griego graduated from Swarthmore College with a degree in Theater and English. Grace has written and starred in my own stand-up show called Mixed: A Solo/Stand Up Show, is the co-founder, producer, and lead voice actor of Strong Branch Productions, stars as Stella Thomas in Strong Branch Production's The Stench of Adventure, stars as Eshe in Aster Podcasting Network's SkillSet, and Grace's short story, My Favorite, was produced by the Wallis Studio Ensemble in the Ensemble Arts Exchange Podcast.

B. Rae Grosz (she/they) is a Pittsburgh-born writer with a morbid imagination. She is particularly fond of folklore, fairy tales, and ghost stories. Her first book, a self-published collection, *Half-Forgotten Ghosts*, is debuting in 2023, and she has a flash fiction pieces in the My Say in The Matter charity anthology and in Orchid's Lantern Volume 1: *Dreams*. She also shares free short fiction through her TweetFic account @anotherStorying and posts weekly writing prompts @vssGothic.

Taylor Jones writes fiction and poetry about the impossible present and the possible future, often inspired by her background in and love of biology. Her writing and art have appeared in *Reckoning, Spit Poet Zine, Smoky Quartz, South Broadway Ghost Society*, and *Barren Magazine.* She lives in Denver,

Colorado, in a house full of plants. Links to her work can be found at https://linktr.ee/trjonesartwork.

Annika Barranti Klein lives in Los Angeles in a tiny apartment full of books and people. Her poetry has been in *Fireside* and *Kaleidotrope*, and her short fiction has recently been in *Asimov's, Worlds of Possibility, The Future Fire, Weird Horror*, and *Fusion Fragment*. She is a member of SFWA, a former roller derby referee, and an erstwhile knitter. Find her online at AnnikaObscura.com.

Christina Ladd (she/her) is a writer, reviewer, and editor living in Minneapolis. She will eventually die crushed under a pile of books, but until then survives on a concerning amount of tea and pizza. Find more of her work at christinaladd.com.

Archita Mittra is a writer, editor, and artist, with a fondness for dark and fantastical things. She completed her B.A. (2018) and M.A. (2020) in English Literature from Jadavpur University and a Diploma in Multimedia and Animation from St. Xavier's College (2016). Her non-fiction has appeared in *Tor, Locus, Strange Horizons,* and elsewhere, while her fiction has been published or forthcoming in *Lightspeed, The Dread Machine, Anathema: Spec from the Margins*, and the Bram Stoker nominated "Human Monsters" anthology by *Dark Matter Magazine*, among others. Her work has been nominated for the Pushcart and best of the net prizes, and long-listed for Toto Award for Creative Writing in 2020. When she isn't writing speculative fiction or drawing fan art, she can be found playing indie games, making crafts, or deciding which new tarot deck to buy. She lives in Kolkata, India, with her family and rabbits, and may be found haunting Twitter and Instagram @architamittra.

Lee Murray is a writer, editor, poet, essayist, and screenwriter from Aotearoa-New Zealand. A *USA Today* bestselling author, her titles include the Taine McKenna Adventures, supernatural crime-noir series *The Path of Ra* (with Dan Rabarts), fiction collection *Grotesque: Monster Stories,* and several books for children. Her many anthologies include *Hellhole, Black Cranes* (with Geneve Flynn), *Unquiet Spirits* (with Angela Yuriko Smith), and *Under Her Eye* (with Lindy Ryan), and her short fiction appears in prestigious venues such as *Weird Tales, Space and Time,* and *Grimdark Magazine.* A five-time Bram Stoker Award®, and multiple Australian Shadows Award- and Sir Julius Vogel Award-winner, Lee is New Zealand's only recipient of the Shirley Jackson Award. She is an NZSA Honorary Literary Fellow, and a Grimshaw Sargeson Fellow and 2023 NZSA Laura Solomon Cuba Press Prize winner for her prose-poetry manuscript *Fox Spirit on a Distant Cloud.* Read more at leemurray.info

Brandon O'Brien is a writer, performance poet, and teaching artist from Trinidad and Tobago. His work has been shortlisted for the 2014 Alice Yard Prize for Art Writing, the 2014 and 2015 Small Axe Literary Competitions, and the 2020 Ignyte Award for Best in Speculative Poetry, and is published in Uncanny Magazine, Fireside Magazine, Strange Horizons, Reckoning, and *New Worlds, Old Ways: Speculative Tales from the Caribbean,* among others. He is the former Poetry editor of the Hugo Award-winning magazine *FIYAH: A Magazine of Black Speculative Fiction.* His debut poetry collection, *Can You Sign My Tentacle?*, available from Interstellar Flight Press, is the winner of the 2022 SFPA Elgin Award.

Gretchen Rockwell is a queer poet who can frequently be found writing about gender, science, space, and unusual connections. Xe is the author of the chapbooks *body in motion* (*perhappened press*) and *Lexicon of Future Selves* (*VA Press*) and two microchapbooks; xer work has appeared in *AGNI, Cotton Xenomorph, Whale Road Review, Palette Poetry*, and elsewhere. Gretchen's essays have also appeared in *Bright Wall/Dark Room* and *Drunk Monkeys.* Find xer at www.gretchenrockwell.com or on Twitter/Instagram at @daft_rockwell.

Chloe Smith is a physically disabled and autistic freelance writer from the UK. She typically writes about TV, film, books, and pop culture. Her opinion pieces and articles have appeared online in 'Digital Spy,' 'Little White Lies,' and more. To view more of her freelance work, check out her portfolio here: http://chloesmith.contently.com/. She's also on Twitter, @ch1oewrites.

Christina Sng is a poet, writer, essayist, and artist. Her work appears in numerous venues worldwide, including *Interstellar Flight Magazine, New Myths, Penumbric, Southwest Review*, and *The Washington Post.* She is the three-time Bram Stoker Award®-winning author of *A Collection of Nightmares, A Collection of Dreamscapes, Tortured Willows,* Elgin Award runner-up *Astropoetry*, and Stoker finalists *The Gravity of Existence* and "Final Girl: A Life In Horror". Christina currently serves as Vice President of the Science Fiction & Fantasy Poetry Association. Visit her at christinasng.com and connect at @christinasng.

Todd Sullivan currently lives in Seoul, South Korea, where he teaches English as a Second Language. He has had more than two dozen short stories, poems, essays, and novelettes published across five countries. He currently has two book series through indie publishers in America. He writes for a Taipei web and play series that focuses upon black and African narratives. He founded the online magazine, Samjoko, in 2021, and hosts a YouTube Channel that interviews writers across the publishing spectrum.

As a fine art professional, **Mar Vincent** has wielded katanas and handled Lady Gaga's shoes. As a veterinary assistant, she has cared for hairless cats, hedgehogs, and, one time, a coyote. As a writer (under Marissa James or Mar Vincent), her short fiction can be found in *Flash Fiction Online, Translunar Travelers Lounge, Zooscape,* and many other publications. She is a Pushcart Prize and Coyotl Award nominee, and a reader for I*nterstellar Flight Press*. She resides in the Pacific Northwest and can be found on Twitter or Mastodon @MaroftheBooks.

T.D. Walker is the author of the poetry collections *Small Waiting Objects (CW Books,* 2019), *Maps of a Hollowed World (Another New Calligraphy,* 2020), and *Doubt & Circuitry (Southern Arizona Press,* 2023). Her poems and stories have appeared in *Strange Horizons, Fireside, Jet Fuel Review, The Cascadia Subduction Zone, Luna Station Quarterly,* and elsewhere. Walker curates and hosts Line Break, a program created for broadcast on shortwave radio that features poets reading their work. Find out more at https://www.tdwalker.net

J.Z. Weston writes short stories and reviews. They have a soft spot for contemporary and urban fantasy and are particularly fascinated by how stories teach us to be human. You can find more of their work at jzwestonauthor.com

INTERSTELLAR FLIGHT PRESS

Interstellar Flight Press is an indie speculative publishing house. We feature innovative works from the best new writers in science fiction and fantasy. In the words of Ursula K. Le Guin, we need "writers who can see alternatives to how we live now, can see through our fear-stricken society and its obsessive technologies to other ways of being, and even imagine real grounds for hope."

Find us online at www.interstellarflightpress.com.

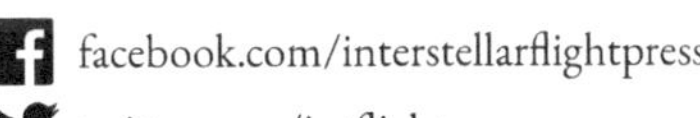
facebook.com/interstellarflightpress
twitter.com/intflightpress

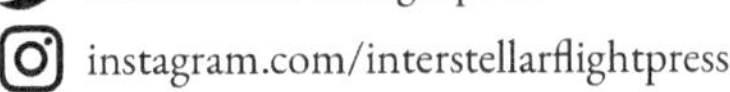
instagram.com/interstellarflightpress

patreon.com/interstellarflightpress

www.ingramcontent.com/pod-product-compliance
Lightning Source LLC
Chambersburg PA
CBHW061235210726
48293CB00003B/778

* 9 7 8 1 9 5 3 7 3 6 3 1 4 *